# The Death Gambit

by

# Michael Davies

# The Death Gambit



Cover design by Jen Trotter and Robin Shepherd

For information address
*michaelxdavies@gmail.com*

First Printing 2022

ISBN: 978-0-6454434-0-0

# Other Works by Michael Davies

The Nightmares of God
The Janus Conspiracy
Accounts of a Killing
A Friendly Killing
Dreamkill
Ready, Steady, KILL!
Helix Dreams
Helix – The Second Renaissance
Helix-Ascension
The Ninth of the Month Murders

### *For the Young Adults (12-18)*

The Many Worlds of Mickie Dalton
The Many Galaxies of Mickie Dalton
The Many Universes of Mickie Dalton
The Strange World of Mark and Anna

### *For the 8-12 age group*

The Julie Malloy Gang and the Smugglers
The Quest for the Locket
The Secret of Yuri Kirilenko
The United Nations and the Extra-Terrestrial
The Secret of Charlotte's Cello
The Star of the Yshan Kings
The War of the Yshan Empire
The Star of the New Yshan Empire
The Red Fog of Time
The Mysterious Recorder and The Door to Elsewhere
Prisoners of the Picture
A Step Back in Time
What Can't be Seen Can Exist
How I Spent My Evening

### *For the Little Ones (3-5)*

Mary's World

### *And in non-fiction*

The Business School Approach to Writing Your Novel

# Acknowledgements

This is the fourth book written in collaboration with my friend and colleague, Greg Dickson. As with the others, Greg would arrive at my place on a Sunday afternoon, we would spend two full days brainstorming the story, photographing the numerous white board contents we had created and then he would leave on Wednesday morning, both of us exhausted and exhilarated by the process. After two or three such sessions, we had the complete materials for the story. I could not have written these books without this joint effort.

To Penny le Couteur and "MJ" Spelliscy, sincere thanks for the many hours spent editing and reviewing the book and identifying the typos and the factual errors.

To Robin Sheppard and Jen Trotter for the cover design, the second they have done for me

# Foreword

*"The Death Gambit"* is a follow-on book to *"The Ninth of the Month Murders"* published in 2021. Key players from that book appear in this story.

Detective Inspector Melanie Carter, then a Detective-Sergeant, led the police group investigating the serial killings in the small town in southern New South Wales. She is a complex woman, blessed (or cursed) with extraordinary beauty and a brilliant mind that earned a first-class honours degree in Psychology and a position on the fast track with the State Police Criminal Investigations Branch. She has problems with men who are unable to recognise her professional skills and the only serious relationship she had was at University, but her fiancé was killed by a thug in Sydney. She has been unable to form a serious attachment since then.

Detective Senior Constable Alex Welland originally appeared as an exceptionally bright young patrol car officer who was recruited to help Melanie when the Covid pandemic caused severe staff shortages. He was later promoted and transferred to Criminal Investigation because of his highly intelligent and invaluable work.

Doctor Jack Savage, a psychiatrist and specialist in Criminal Psychology, had been regarded as the best police profiler in the State until he retired some years ago. He first appeared in *"Ready, Steady, Kill!"* an earlier book when the detective working on an outbreak of serial killings around the world asked him for help because of Jack's experience in such cases. Melanie asked for his help for the same reasons.

*"The Ninth of the Month Murders"* tells of a series of murders in a small country town. It slowly develops as a tale of how one extraordinarily "super-dominant" woman can drive a team of mostly damaged souls and submissive personalities into each committing one murder. This group is a writers' group and they each write the story of the murder as fiction, eventually collecting the stories into a book. As the police close in on that writers' group, Melanie finds that she also has a "super-dominant" personality, and several monumental battles are fought between her and the group leader.

One of that group is neither damaged nor submissive. In fact. Allan Miller is an American, arguably the world's best computer hacker who left the USA when the FBI began closing in on him, by creating a whole new persona with history, qualifications and assets, enough to fool Australian immigration authorities and becoming a permanent resident of Australia. Melanie's group discovers the reality through dogged, detailed investigative research. He then vanishes to create another persona for himself. Miller also appears in this book.

# Chapter 1

## *14ʰ September, 2025, Coastal NSW, Australia*

As the huge earth-mover shovel dumped the mix of soil and rocks at the side of the trench, a human arm rolled down to the bottom of the pile.

The operator stopped the engine, climbed down to the ground, stared at the limb and was sick on the grass.

The work supervisor walked up, irritation all over his florid face.

"What the hell, Phil?" he shouted and then saw the arm. He reached for his phone.

"About eight or nine years," said the Medical Examiner. He slowly unfolded his unusual length from his crouch over the arm, like a crane extending itself. "The soil quality has preserved the skin and muscle quite well, should be able to get DNA from it. Probably male, but we need to find the rest of the body."

Detective Inspector Melanie Carter turned to the work supervisor.

"This becomes a crime scene," she said. "We'll have to cordon off a good-sized part of this field."

The supervisor pulled a face. "We've got a timetable," he said. "The Council needs the pipe laid by a specific date to meet up with a pipe coming from the other direction."

"So you can't just shift sideways?"

"No way. The track for this is calculated to the centimetre. You can see the markers already laid out across the field. What if we start at the other end of the field and work backwards?"

"How long before you reach this part?"

"The schedule says three days."

"Okay," said the detective. "But whatever you do, don't get within ten metres of this patch until you've cleared it with us. I'll talk to the Council and clear it."

"Fine with me," said the supervisor. He cast another sour look at the detached arm lying on the grass and then whistled loudly at his crew standing around in various attitudes of interest.

"Other end," he shouted and began walking away, followed by the crew and the clanking of machinery.

Doctor Garry Rutherford, the Medical Examiner walked back to his car and started exchanging his shoes for rubber boots. "I'm going down there and start digging away with a trowel," he said. "You'll call for some experienced help?"

"Indeed," said Melanie. "And I'll join you. I'll need pictures of all this." She took out her phone and spoke briefly, then followed the doctor's example of exchanging her shoes for rubber boots that she always carried in the car for just such events, then descended the ladder into the trench.

The astonishments hadn't ended for the day.

"Bloody 'ell, doc, he's standing up!"

The four police officers working carefully with trowels rather than spades stopped. Doctor Garry Rutherford studied the large part of the body that had been uncovered. The officer was correct, the corpse was standing upright, the left arm had been torn away from the torso by the blades of the shovel, the left leg was fully visible and most of the upper half was now displayed.

"And it's wearing some sort of white costume," said one of the other officers.

"All a bit of a mystery," said the doctor. "It's definitely a male. Can you try and clear the head?"

Without answering, the officer began carefully scraping dirt away from the head of the corpse while the others stood and watched. After half an hour, the head was fully revealed, and a new mystery appeared.

"It's wearing a white hood, and some sort of metal headwear," said Rutherford.

"This is getting curiouser and curiouser," said Melanie. "How long before you can get him out of there?"

"Probably another hour."

"I look forward to seeing what you can get from it. What chances of DNA?"

"Pretty good, I'd say. We may know who this poor bastard was in a couple of days."

## Chapter 2

### *15ᵗʰ September, 2025, Coastal NSW, Australia*

"Hell of a way to start my first day here, Ma'am," said Detective Senior Constable Alex Welland.

Melanie Carter smiled. "I must admit, it's not every first day of a posting that begins with a murder. This one is definitely weird, too. The Medical Examiner will be here any moment to give us the post-mortem results."

As she spoke, the elongated body of the doctor appeared in the office doorway.

"Good morning, Inspector," he said and took the second chair across the desk from her. He looked left at Welland. "Who's this?"

"Doctor, this is Detective Senior Constable Alex Welland. He worked with me in that strange serial killing case in the south of the state a couple of years ago and he has just been transferred here. Constable, this is Doctor Garry Rutherford, the Medical Examiner."

The two men stood up, shook hands and resumed their seats.

"A strange case," said the doctor. "We haven't identified him yet, but we got good tissue from the body so we'll be able to extract viable DNA. The lab will be able to get it in a couple of days. He's a white male, about one sixty-seven centimetres, so shorter than average, estimated to be between thirty and forty, in good health and we estimate he's been in the ground for between seven and twelve years. Cause of death was a heavy blow with a blunt instrument just above his right ear that fractured the skull. Death would have been after some minutes, but he was unconscious immediately. We believe that because there was a good amount of blood inside that metal helmet he was wearing, so that was put on his head after the blow but before death.”

“Any thoughts on that helmet?” asked Melanie.

The doctor reached down to his briefcase and extracted an envelope and a photograph, sliding both across the desk. “That’s my report and a photo. I’ve got no idea about the helmet.”

Melanie studied the picture, shook her head and passed it to Alex.

“Nothing else to tell us, Doc?”

“Only what you saw, he was covered in a white gown, wearing only his underclothes and a white hood apart from that. The gown is a standard woman’s nightdress, made of plain cotton, sold at just about every clothing store and supermarket in the country. There was no label on it. It had been sliced from neck to near the bottom for it to fit over a man’s body, so just what the purpose was is beyond me.”

“Er..” said Alex.

“Something to tell us, Constable?” said Melanie.

“The helmet. It doesn’t look like anything specific. The band obviously goes round the head, then there’s another strip going from the front to the back. But there’s a small slot in that strip, looks like something should be in there. Doctor, did you find anything else in the site?”

"Well, now that you mention it, one of the officers found this…" Rutherford pulled a small object from his jacket pocket and handed it to Alex.

"A wooden horse?" said Alex. "Looks like some child's toy, not especially well made. Doesn't tell me anything."

"Sing out if anything comes to you," said Melanie. "But meanwhile, start going through the Missing Persons file. See if there's anyone matching this description."

"Will do, Ma'am," said Alex and left the office, just as Melanie's phone buzzed. She picked it up.

"Detective Inspector Carter," she said and listened for a few seconds before replacing it.

"They've found another one," she said. "Doc, you'd better follow me. I'll get Alex."


"Okay, this is becoming bloody weird," said the Council's work supervisor. "We did as you asked, moved to the far point of the field and started again and look what bloody happens."

The two police detectives, the doctor and the supervisor stood by the trench that was some fifteen metres from the edge of the field and ended abruptly. Standing out from the red earth was the head and right shoulder of a man. The rest of the body was still covered. A short distance away, the rest of the work crew stood silently, deeply shocked by the new discovery.

"The excavation crew is on its way?" asked the doctor.

"I called them as soon as I saw this sight," said Melanie. "They'll be here within the hour."

"Good, we need them," said the doctor. "We managed to get the last one out by careful digging, but I prefer to have the experts do that. I'll go down there and see what I can see." He walked back to his car, extracted his rubber boots and with them on, climbed down the ladder. After a few moments of study, he stood back and looked up.

"Standing up again," he said. "Traces of a cotton gown just visible, black this time. And guess what? It's fallen off his head, but I can just see a trace of something metal on his other shoulder."

"Looks like we've got a serial killer on our hands," murmured Melanie.

"Even weirder than our last one," said Alex. "Almost like they're following you, Ma'am."

"Don't make jokes like that, Alex. One serial killer in a career is too much." Melanie turned to the supervisor who had a resigned expression.

"Closing us down, I suppose?" he said.

"I'm sorry, but you do understand. This whole field is a crime scene. There could be more bodies here."

The supervisor pulled his phone from his pocket.


"Male, about fifty, been there more than ten years," said Doctor Rutherford. He stood with Melanie and Alex, looking down at the body on the table before them. There was still a large amount of mud on the corpse and the black gown which covered it, but enough of the gown had rotted away for the doctor to conduct a preliminary examination of the body.

"Any idea what killed him?" asked Melanie.

"Not yet, too much mud for me to see clearly."

"Can I see the metal bit?" asked Alex.

The doctor turned to a table by the wall and returned with a metallic object, handing it to Alex.

"It's been washed," he said. "There were no fingerprints. Looks like it's been bent a bit, maybe during the burial or perhaps by some shifting of the earth over the years."

Alex began studying the object, bending the metal a little. "Can I see the other one?" he asked.

The doctor nodded at a table alongside the other examination table a short distance away and Alex moved over. "No fingerprints on that, either," he said. While he looked at the two objects, the doctor began a careful examination of the body with a magnifying glass, moving away bits of the rotting cloth as he went. He stood up, handed the glass to Melanie and pointed at a spot on the body.

"Have a look at that," he said. "That's just under the heart."

Melanie took the glass and bent over to examine the spot he had indicated. She had seen marks like this before.

"Stab wound," she said. "One edge serrated, about three centimetres wide, angled upwards, straight into the heart, so a blade at least fifteen centimetres long. A hunting or fishing knife, perhaps?"

"Well done," said the doctor. "Exactly what my report will say."

Alex put down the metal objects. "I did some research at home last night," he said. "So far, nothing has come to me. This second one is a little easier, it's been bent around quite a bit, but the nearest thing I can think of is some sort of clerical headgear, maybe a bishop or archbishop."

"An antique?" said Melanie. "That would make it rather valuable, I imagine. Who would bury valuable items like that?"

Alex shook his head. "Not an antique, Ma'am. It's made of cheap metal sheeting, the sort of stuff you can get at any hardware store. You can see round the edges where it's been cut by shears. Somebody made this for some strange reason of their own."

"So somebody kills a person, dresses them in a white or black gown, makes some sort of imitation helmet for the body and then buries it standing up," said the doctor. "Inspector, there's a real sicko somewhere around."

"But we don't know how long ago these killings took place," said Melanie. "We need ground penetrating radar. It's a fair bet that there will be more of these."

* * *

"You really should be handing this over to the Homicide group in Parramatta," said Chief Superintendent Parker. His image on Melanie's monitor reflected concern, though she was not sure what was causing it.

"I know that's what the standard operating procedures suggest," she said. "But I dealt with them before on the previous case of a serial killer and they had no difficulties leaving that one with my team."

Parker smiled at some memory. "I know. And their

Chief Super has never quite forgiven you, but he couldn't work out just how you persuaded him. But I talked with him again yesterday and he seems reluctant to tackle the issue. I think he's frightened you might go up there and argue with him again. I gather you can have this effect on people."

"I think it was just staff shortages," said Melanie, feeling uncomfortable with this topic. "But I believe it's a fair argument that we have more experience in such cases as almost anyone else, and Jack Savage might be the most experienced person in serial killings and their perpetrators of anyone in Australia.

"Both still true," said Parker. "Okay, Inspector, you keep control of this one. I've authorised the ground penetrating radar and the temporary addition of Professor Jack Savage to your team. I hope to Christ this doesn't get as gruesome as your other serial killing case. Let me know if you need anything else and keep me informed."

"I will, Sir."

* * *

Little sound was heard. The hum of the occasional car on the road a kilometre away was the only thing that interrupted the low buzz of the ground-penetrating radar being operated by a young woman in a white overall. She had introduced herself as Pauline and she worked for a firm of building contractors who had done work for the police before. She was short, with a stocky build and traces of jet-black hair could be seen under the hood over her head. She had been tracking up and down the field, each line moving sideways by the width of the machine which resembled a medium-sized lawnmower. Neither Alex nor Melanie had anything to say as they watched the scene intently.

The purring stopped and the young woman waved at them.

"Something here," she said as they walked up to her. "Can't tell what, but something small is reflecting the wave back." She pointed at the screen mounted on the handles of the device. Melanie and Alex both moved over to look. The image was not easy to work out.

"There," said Pauline and pointed to a small blip in the middle of the screen. "That's what stands out."

Melanie pointed at the vague shapes of different shades. "What's all that?"

"Probably just variations in density of the soil," replied Pauline. "Could be outcroppings of clay, or just different density of soil after rain had soaked down over the years. But it could also be from having been dug before, possibly years ago."

Alex took a small device from his pocket and looked through the eyepiece at a metal pole at one corner of the field. He raised his clipboard and noted the distance, then repeated the exercise with a similar pole at the other corner. He drew the lines on a diagram of the field to intersect at the spot where they were standing.

"Always knew golf would come in useful, Ma'am," he said. "That tells me the distance to the flag on the putting green. And now it gives me the location of this thing."

"We'll mark it too," said Pauline and pushed a metal flag stick into the ground at the spot where she had detected the radar trace.

"Let's move on," said Melanie.

Two hours later, they found another one.

And twenty minutes later, a third. All of them showed a similar display on the screen of the radar device, as shades of different densities and a small blip indicating a metal object.

After another two hours, with no new discoveries, Melanie called it a day as the hour reached seven in the evening.

The next day, they found three more.

## Chapter 3

### *15<sup>th</sup> June, 1964, Percivale Hall, Surrey, UK*

"Congratulations, My Lord. A most splendid victory. The Grand Master title is well within your reach now."

The young man handing the winner of the championship his overcoat was himself dressed immaculately. His voice was well educated and low toned. Though tall, he was shorter than Baron William Percivale by a good three or four centimetres.

Percivale did not respond. He took the hand of a short, stout man a few years older than he was who moved up to him and shook it firmly.

"What do you think, Monty?" he asked.

"It's always a good thing when a true aristocrat beats up a Kraut at anything," said the short man. His voice was well-educated, trained to perfection, his appearance completed by the black blazer with a military badge on the breast pocket and neatly tied cravat in red silk that he was wearing. "All of us here want to congratulate you, William. It was a classic chess match, right up with Fisher-Petrosian a few years ago."

"Thank you, Monty, that's high praise indeed." Percivale waved behind him at the group of watchers of the match, all smiling with pleasure and admiration, standing a few metres behind him in the spacious room where the match had taken place.

Several massive paintings were hung around the walls, mostly of imperious men in the dress of different eras, staring down in contempt at the people on the floor. At the back, the television crew was dismantling the cameras and sound equipment that had been used to observe the match and broadcast it throughout the grounds of Percivale Hall, the home of the Percivales for nearly two centuries.

"Actually, you almost fucked up the whole thing," said a voice behind Percivale.

Slowly, Percivale turned, his face like stone. He stared down at the teenager wearing a school uniform blazer and tie.

"I beg your pardon," he said in tones that could have sliced through a stone wall.

"You were following the classic Speilmann – Rubinstein game," said the young man. "And you should have closed it three moves earlier than you did. But your mistake was to move the wrong pawn during the end game. Luckily, your opponent was just as careless as you were, and you were able to recover. But if he'd seen it, you wouldn't be standing here now, all covered in glory. Of course, the cameras recorded that howler and the whole world will soon know about it."

The silence in the area was profound, broken only by a small, nervous giggle from a woman holding a clip board.

"Who the hell do you think you're talking to?" said Percivale, his stance rigid.

"I know very well who I'm talking to," replied the young man. "Just as I know who your buddy is. He's Montague Pierce-Hasting, something big in the Department of Foreign Affairs and you're Baron William Percivale from somewhere in Scotland, despite this grand home here."

"Then display the courtesy due to your elders and betters and leave us," said Percivale.

"Elders? Certainly. Betters? I doubt it. Certainly not better at chess." The young man was barely suppressing his laughter and enjoyment of the scene.

"There is no possibility that a child in a school uniform is a chess player of the same class as Baron Percivale," said Pierce-Hastings. "It's obviously not even a decent public school, no doubt it's one of those dreadful *grammar* schools. Now, stop this nonsense and get out of here before I have security do it for me."

"Well, My Lord Baron Percivale," said the youth with sarcasm rippling through his tones, "let me take up the challenge that your portly Foreign Affairs pal just threw down. Face me across the chess board and let's see."

"Don't talk nonsense," said Percivale. "I will not lower myself that way. I do not play chess with children. Get out."

The crowd behind this trio had been dead silent apart from the small giggle earlier, but now the silence was broken again.

"Bawk, bawk, bawk," said a soft voice.

"Chicken," said another in response.

Percivale's face tightened, and his lips closed to the thinnest of lines.

"Alright, damn you," he said. "I'm sure you have to be in *school* during the day, so be back here tomorrow at seven in the evening. We'll see who is the better player."

"Indeed we will. And how about we sweeten the match by placing some valuable item as a prize?"

Percivale snorted in contempt. "And just what could a common child like you have that would interest me?"

"How about twelve designs of chess pieces by Pablo Picasso, one of each main piece, and two of pawns, one black one white, each one signed by him and authenticated."

The shock in the Baron's frame was clear. His jaw dropped as he struggled for composure.

"How... how does some peasant like you have something like that?" he whispered.

"That's another story. And while you are obviously not interested in such irrelevancies, my name is Peter Chancellor. So, My Lord, what do you offer to match my proposal?"

Percivale paused, obviously considering something.

"The one and only chess set designed by Fabergé, presented to the Russian Czar," he said finally.

It was Chancellor's turn to look stunned. "The one given to the Imperial Russian War Minister before the revolution?" he said, his eyes wide. "That must be worth a couple of million pounds. I thought it was in the Hermitage in Leningrad. How did you get it?"

"That's another story. Now get the hell out of my house, Chancellor and be back here tomorrow evening."

Chancellor smiled, gave a mock bow and walked away.

There was a small sigh of released breath from the onlookers. They began filing out and the technicians resumed dismantling the cameras and cabling which they had stopped to watch the scene played out before them.

*　*　*

## *16th June, 1964, Percivale Hall, Surrey, UK*

A group of several people entered the room, the same one as had held the match played the day before. Percivale led the group, carrying a small box, accompanied by Montague Pierce-Hasting. Behind them were two muscular young men. Percivale placed the box on the table against one wall, the two young men took stations on either side of the table.

A moment later, Peter Chancellor entered, carrying a briefcase, also accompanied but only by one man. He was still wearing the school blazer and tie. He looked around the room, saw the table by the wall and the two guards and smiled. He and his associate walked to the table, he opened the briefcase and took out a large paper envelope.

Percivale joined him without any greeting from either man.

"Let's see what's at stake, shall we?" said Chancellor pleasantly. He opened the envelope and took out a sheaf of drawings done in pen and ink, each paper enclosed in a plastic cover. He put them on the table.

Percivale stared and slowly extended a hand to pick up one of the drawings of a chess piece. It was a Knight, and the Picasso signature was across one corner of the sheet. A slight tremble shook Percivale's hand as he put the sheet down and picked up one of the white Queen.

"How did you get these?" he asked.

"Not your concern," said Chancellor. "If by some fluke you win this match, then I'll tell you. Now, let's see your offering."

Percivale put down the drawing and opened the box. Inside was a wooden frame enclosing multiple small compartments, each big enough to hold a chess piece. Each compartment was lined with velvet. Percivale took out three pieces, a King, a Castle and a pawn and it was Chancellor's turn to stare, entranced. Each piece was made of gold on a silver centre with black onyx as the base. They were exquisite. Chancellor reached out to take the Queen, but Percivale stopped his hand.

"You don't touch," he said.

"There have been other Fabergé designs made of chess sets," said Chancellor. "But this is unique. It must be what you claimed, the one given to the Russian Czar before the Revolution. It's supposed to be in the Hermitage Museum in Leningrad. I saw it when I visited with a school trip last year. How come you have it?"

"Not your concern," said Percivale with a smirk. He put the chess pieces away and closed the box. "Now, it's time to play chess. I look forward to taking those drawings."

Chancellor didn't respond but moved to the middle of the room, where a chess board had been laid out on a small table. Both men took their seats.

No television cameras, no sound crew, just two men seated across a chess board. Each of them had a second man standing a few metres away. The one behind Chancellor had not given his name nor had he spoken during the sixty-three minutes that the game had lasted so far. The second man behind Percivale was Montague Pierce-Hasting. The two muscular men who had escorted Percivale into the room had left as the players took their seats. There were sixteen pieces left on the board. Percivale was playing White.

Chancellor moved his black Knight and touched the timer. Percivale didn't move a muscle but stared down at the pieces. Much as he had been throughout, his jaw was clenched tightly, and his lips were a thin line. After four minutes, he reached out and moved a Knight, touched the timer and sat back.

Chancellor looked up at him.

"Really?" he said.

Percivale said nothing.

"You see, that's the same sort of carelessness that almost lost you the match against Konrad Richter yesterday," said Chancellor. "But I saw it, he didn't. You've been following the Selznik-Karlov match, right up to the end game, so it's been easy to follow you and prepare the killer move which would have come after nine more moves, but you blew it and now it's mate in seven. Really, My Lord Baron, your belief that you will make Grand Master in the near future is somewhat optimistic."

Percivale stared at the board for several minutes. In an explosion of fury, he threw the board off the table, stood up and walked to the table holding the prizes. He snatched the box containing the Fabergé chess set and walked towards the door.

"My Lord!" shouted Hasting and ran after him, catching him as Percivale flung open the door and pulling him back.

"Get your hands off me!" shouted Percivale, his face red and spit falling from his lips.

"My Lord, you made a bet and wagered a prize. You lost. You cannot renegue like this."

"I can do whatever I bloody well want," shouted Percivale. "You expect me to give my Fabergé set to some damned commoner schoolboy?"

"You made a bet, My Lord. No British gentleman would renegue on a bet."

"And who's going to tell?" snapped Percivale. "Not my men, and nobody would believe that common child over there."

"I will, My Lord," replied Hastings. He took his hand away from Percivale's shoulder. His look of disgust almost radiated from him. "This will spread, My Lord. I tell you now, you are dead in society. No one will recognize you, nobody will speak to you, your seat in the House of Lords will be taken from you. I recommend that you stay out of London, maybe out of Britain."

Percivale looked shaken for a few seconds then turned and walked away.

"Tisk, tisk," said Chancellor.

# Chapter 4

## *20th September, 2025, Coastal NSW, Australia*

"More murders for your attention, Inspector," said the doctor. "But there's something else which I think will blow your mind."

The morgue was a depressing sight. There were two inspection slabs on which lay two bodies that had been cut apart. The chest of each had been cut from neck to waist and opened up almost like butterfly wings. One had a severed arm lying alongside the torso.

"DNA proved what we already knew," said the doctor, pulling back the sheet from one. "The arm of the first body belonged to the body in the grave below it, and I can confirm that cause of death was a knife through the chest sliced upward to the heart."

He turned to the second slab and pulled back the cover.

"Male between thirty and forty, dead about five years, cause of death a severe blow with a blunt instrument to the head, just above the left ear. So far, all conventional "murder by person or persons unknown" with the unsolved mysteries of the black and white coverings and the amateurishly-made helmets."

He turned back to the tables and returned with a small object in each hand.

"There's another strange thing," he said. "As I opened up the chest of each of these, I found additional cuts that were not life-threatening, but on opening them up, I found these."

He opened his right hand. It contained a chess piece of a white knight. "That was in the first body, the one with the helmet which you already suggested was that of a knight chess piece." He opened up the left hand and revealed a black bishop.

"Ah!" said Alex in almost a shout. "I've got an idea about that." He seemed embarrassed at having spoken so loudly. The others looked at him.

"Chess pieces," said the young constable. "Black and white, the two colours of chess pieces, and those cheap helmets, I think they're meant to represent the figures. There are Knights, Bishops, Castles, Queens and Kings as well as pawns. I'd say that wooden horse was in that slot in the first helmet represents a Knight or Rook chess piece, and they're made like horses' heads, but a horse's head would be too complex to make up in that cheap tin. Somebody could be playing a really nasty game, but I've no idea what it could all be about."

"Just as you suggested, Constable, a black Bishop, and what we now see as a White Knight. These were dug into the two bodies." The Medical Examiner looked intrigued.

"Anything special about those pieces?" asked Melanie. "Something unique that might help to identify the owner?"

Rutherford shook his head. "Nothing, Inspector. They're just ordinary commercial pieces made of plastic."

"Well, that was too much to hope for," said Melanie. "But it looks like you have hit on something, Alex. Well done."

"It's just that I'm a chess fan, Ma'am," said Alex. "I wouldn't have thought of that otherwise."

"It could be a useful lead," said Melanie. "But I hope it doesn't mean we'll find more bodies. What are there, thirty-two pieces on the board at the start?"

Alex nodded.

"This whole thing is bizarre," said Rutherford. "Do you know who owns the land?"

"I asked the Council when I first called them to halt digging," said Melanie. "It's a little unusual. This field and some more space around it are managed by an accounting firm in Edinburgh in trust for some organisation. But that's all the Council knows. They don't know the owner, but they bill the trustees for rates and taxes, and they are always paid promptly."

"Curious," said Rutherford. "But that's your problem, mine is to find out what I can about these bodies and the ones you say are coming in. I'd better call for more help."

"Keep me informed," said Melanie and led the way out of the morgue.

*   *   *

Alex drove home in a thoughtful mood. The connection to chess was bothering him but he couldn't identify why. But these thoughts were driven from his mind by the loving greeting he got from his wife as he opened the front door.

"How are you both?" he asked, gently stroking Judith's swollen belly.

"We're fine, but I think Deborah's getting impatient with her lock-down," she replied.

"So are we both," he said and led her back to the living room. "I really do want to meet my daughter.

Now, are you able to cook, or shall I?"

"It's been in the crockpot all day. You can serve."

In warm closeness, they had their meal and after Alex had cleared away the table, they settled down before the television.

But the niggling thoughts returned to Alex, and he lost concentration on the British cop show they were watching. *What the hell was it? Why are there chess pieces in the two bodies they had examined so far? Why the cheap, poorly-fashioned helmets on the corpses in the field...*

"ALEX!"

Judith's sharp call and a slight dig in the ribs returned him from his mental wonderings.

"Sorry, love, something's distracting me about this case."

"I've never seen you go off into La-La land like that," she said. "What brought this on?"

Briefly, he told her of the strange connection to chess pieces in the bodies, and the amateurishly manufactured helmets found so far in the bodies being dug up.

"I would certainly call it all bloody peculiar," she said. "Maybe you're getting nervous about that tournament you're in next month?"

"Could be," he said. "I'll be facing some class players."

"Okay, that's it, time for bed."

**2:00am**

Alex woke with a jolt. He looked at the bedside radio clock, checked that Judith was deeply asleep and carefully got out of bed, put on a dressing gown and went down to the living room. He knew what he needed to see. He located the book on famous chess matches of the past and started looking through the illustrations of board layouts.

At 3:15, he found what he was looking for.

## 23rd September, 2025, Coastal NSW, Australia
## The Midcoast Times

*Strange goings on at the Police pathology laboratories? Reports have been coming in all day that large numbers of official laboratory vehicles have been stationed by the police pathology laboratories. Our reporter queried the senior officer at the station but was told only that a training program is in progress and several pathologists have come for a few days of studies into new techniques in chemical analysis. We are unsure of that, because there does seem to be increased action among the police officers and one person reported some major diggings happening at a field some kilometres from town.*

*Our reporter went to the field in question and saw a number of men in white overalls digging in several different locations.*

*The Council stated that a new pipeline is being dug across that field to increase water supplies to the town and two events are not connected in any way. However, that story does not ring true as a pipeline would only be dug in a single line. The several individual locations indicated more of a search. We will continue to look into this.*

# Chapter 5

## *24ᵗʰ September, 2025, Sydney, Australia*

"Good evening and welcome to another edition of *'In Sydney Tonight.'* I'm your host, Barbara Tellerman. Tonight, we have an extraordinary guest, Peter Chancellor who has become the latest Englishman to earn the title of Chess Grand Master and the first to become world champion. Peter, welcome to Australia and congratulations on the new title!"

"Thank you, Barbara, this is a real pleasure, I've never been here before."

"So what has brought you these shores now?"

"It's an invitation from the Australian Chess Federation to take part in a series of exhibition matches around the country."

"We're not accustomed to seeing Grand Masters from Britain, but I know you are not the first."

"Yes, we do seem more accustomed to hearing Russian names with that title, but Britain has produced a number, many still playing."

"But your feat seems unusual. World Champion! That is unique in Britain."

"Yes, that has thrilled me to the core. It came after I beat Ivan Aliyev last month, the world champion at the time, a title he took from Garry Kasparov the year before."

"So how did all this begin, Peter?"

"My mother was a fine player. She won tournaments all round England and Scotland and achieved some fame. She taught me the game when I was seven and I found I had a knack for it."

"I believe you have quite a story about her?"

"Indeed! What is not well known at all is that she had a wild affair with Pablo Picasso in her late teens. She met him in Barcelona on a summer vacation and it got out of hand. She told me it was just three weeks of utter abandon, then she decided to leave and get home to England to go to University."

"What an extraordinary story! I'm sure she could never forget it! And you said you have something remarkable to show us from that episode."

"Oh yes, I certainly do. Only a handful of people know about this, but Picasso was so enamoured of my mother that he drew her designs for chess pieces, all five of the main pieces, different for black and white, and one each for the pawns, again, slightly different for black and white, so there were twelve drawings, all signed by him."

"Good heavens! And are you going to show us those?"

"Not the originals, they're in a bank vault in Surrey. Very few people have seen them, a couple of friends and the expert who validated the signatures. But a few others have also seen them, and that's something I'm going to tell you about. But I scanned them before I left, and you have the images to show."

"Let's have a look at these unknown Picasso drawings."

Silence reigned in the studio while the images were displayed and transmitted to televisions around Australia.

"That's just the white pieces," said Chancellor. "The black ones are slightly different, but not much."

"That's truly remarkable," said Barbara. "And the people you mentioned are the only ones to have seen these masterpieces?"

Chancellor laughed. "Apart from friends, four other people saw them once, a long time ago and I want to tell you a funny story about that episode that has never been told before."

"Peter, you didn't warn us about that before the broadcast. I suspect this is something that might make headlines. Are you sure this is fit for public display?"

"How right you are! And I'm certain there are a number of people who would not want this story told. Way back in 1964, I was still a schoolboy, aged sixteen and I was able to watch a match between a German Grand Master, Konrad Richter and Baron William Percivale who was right up there, just about ready to reach the same level. Percivale won the match, but only because Richter failed to see a mistake by Percivale that should have let him win. I broke into the admirers and told him the sordid truth that he should have lost by his error. Percivale was furious, so I challenged him to a match the next day. He got all snotty-nosed and declined, so I offered to make it a challenge, winner to take something valuable."

"Good heavens! And you offered the Picasso sketches?"

"I did, and that pushed him over the edge. He offered a chess set designed by Fabergé especially for the Czar of Russia. It was unique and worth possibly a couple of million pounds. The thing is, that was supposed to be in the Hermitage Museum in St Petersburg, then called Leningrad, so either his was a fake or the one in the Hermitage was and somehow they had been exchanged."

"And that match took place?"

"The next day. When I saw the chess set, it was obviously genuine, quite stunning. He was equally gobsmacked by the Picasso sketches. But that makes me wonder if the Russians know theirs is a fake and if not, how will they react when this story is broadcast."

"That's a fascinating question, Peter. And what happened at your match?"

"He made another silly mistake. He'd been following a famous match from decades before, I knew the details, so I just drew him along waiting for a killer move. But I didn't need it. I just said, 'Mate in seven.'"

"And you got the Fabergé set?"

"No, that's the funny part. This British nobleman threw an infantile hissy fit, threw the board over, snatched the Fabergé set and walked out, hotly pursued by his buddy, a senior member of the British Civil Service who told him in no uncertain terms how much he had just dishonoured himself."

"And what happened?"

"Percivale vanished, not to be seen again. The scandal lasted for a few weeks, he was removed from the House of Lords and then it all died down."

"And he was not seen again?"

"No. His wife, Lady Joanna Percivale denied all knowledge of him, and she committed suicide three years later. She was old school aristocracy, and the shame was just too much for her. He might be still alive, he'd be around eighty but nobody knows where he went."

"What happened with the estates and property?"

"No idea. The upper classes arrange their affairs in ways beyond my comprehension."

"And no sign of the Fabergé chess set?"

"Not a sign. The Russian authorities have been quiet on the subject, but I'm sure they'd be embarrassed by the fact that the one they have is a fake. Somehow, Percivale acquired the original and obviously not by legal means."

"Peter, this has been a fascinating evening, I cannot thank you enough. Good luck on the tour of Australia, I hope you see more of the country than just chessboards!"

"Count on it, Barbara! Tomorrow, I'm climbing the Bridge then taking the ferry to Manly, somebody told me it's the most beautiful water trip in the world. Then a concert at the Sydney Opera House."

"Sounds like a good start. To all our viewers, good night from our special guest, newly appointed British Chess Grand Master, and World Champion, Peter Chancellor and from me, Barbara Tellerman."

# Chapter 6

## *26th September, 2025, Coastal NSW, Australia*

Alex knocked on the door of Melanie's office.

"Got a moment Ma'am?"

She looked up and waved him to a chair across from her desk.

"Something up, Alex?

"I think so, but it sounds bit screwy."

"Those are often the best ideas. So what's on your mind?"

He took a sheet of paper out of his inside pocket and laid it out on the desk.

"It's back to what I thought the other day, these bodies are chess pieces. It will be a lot clearer when we've dug out the bodies we've detected so far, but there's something nagging at me." He pointed at the spots marked on the map. "These are the positions of the spots so far identified with a metal object." He pointed at six other spots he had marked with a red circle. "These other ones haven't been identified by Pauline's radar thing, I've put them there myself. There's a pattern to these positions. I think I know what it is. So can I suggest you get the radar machine to check out these spots? I know one or two have been covered without finding anything, but I strongly suspect I know the reason. Can you ask Pauline to look at these locations?"

"Alex, this is weird," said Melanie. "Have you become psychic or something?"

"No, Ma'am, just something nagging at me. Can I ask

you to bear with me for a while? If this turns out to be what I think it is, I'll fill you in totally. If it's just a silly burst of nonsense, I'll go to the dunce's corner and hang my head."

She looked hard at him for a few moments then stood up.

"Alex, you've proved yourself a few times in the past with your hunches. Let's head out to the field and see what the radar lady says."


"You want me to break out of this carefully designed search pattern and do *what?*" Pauline driving the radar device looked furious.

"I know it sounds crazy, but yes, that's what I'm asking," replied Melanie. "Constable Welland has an idea and I've worked with him long enough to trust his hunches. So please, will you check these spots?"

The woman looked with hostility at Alex but took the sheet from him and studied it. "Alright, which one first?"

Alex led the way to a spot a few metres away and scraped a small cross with his heel. The radar operator turned her machine and moved it over, driving it back and forth over the spot and around it. She stopped and stared at the screen on the device.

"There's something there," she said. "Like the others, a tiny echo from something solid, maybe signs of something else, but that could just be a different layer of clay or earth. How did you know?"

"Tell you later," said Alex. "Now, one over here."

Without any remaining hostility, she stuck a flag in the spot, then followed him to another location and repeated the process. After a few passes over the area, she shook her head. "Nothing reflecting," she said. "But there's the same sign of something else, just like the previous spot, again, it could be denser earth, clay, or something not solid."

"Would a body show up like that?" asked Melanie.

The other woman looked thoughtfully at her. "It could."

"Mark it, Alex, then show us the next one."

This time, the radar showed the same small echo of a solid object.

"Okay, Alex, time to explain," said Melanie. "I asked this before, but are you psychic?"

"No Ma'am. But I'm a chess player and a follower of the history of the game. I think that there are thirteen bodies buried here in a very specific pattern."

"Chess? Tell me the whole thing."

"I think those bodies represent the position on the board of thirteen chess pieces before the final move that indicated checkmate in another few moves, at which point, the loser would resign. It was a famous match between Karlov and Selznik and that endgame is a regular feature in chess books. That's why some of the bodies are draped in white, the others black. And those helmets? I think they represent Knights and Bishops. We'll probably find two kings and a white Queen. For some sick reason, somebody wants to represent that match with dead bodies. I cannot possibly imagine why."

"Mark out the remaining spots you've noted, Alex. Let's leave Pauline to complete her search and go and see how Doctor Rutherford is doing with the autopsies.”

* * *

“Report from Pauline,” said Melanie as she and Alex sat in the canteen with a mug of coffee each. She put down the phone. “They’ve dug up two of the points where there was no metal signal, just what she thought was soil variation, but guess what? Bodies. Both in black but no helmets.”

“Pawns,” said Alex. “Ma’am, mind if I go back to searching through Missing Persons?”

“Get to it, Alex. This is getting curiouser and curiouser.”

“It’s worse than the Mad Hatter’s Tea Party,” said Alex and left the canteen.

“I think I have the first one, Ma’am.”

Melanie looked up as Alex appeared at her door and waved him to the seat across from her.

“The description fits the one Doctor Rutherford gave us. Steven John Knight. Height was right, age was right, vanished from Bondi in 2016, so nine years ago, within the estimate that the doctor gave us. The doctor did a good job.”

“Anything of interest in the reports?”

Alex shook his head. “He vanished over the weekend, failed to turn up at the school where he was a teacher on Monday. No clues, no sightings, no known enemies, nothing.”

“Hang on… Knight? His name was Knight?”

"And he wore a helmet representing a horse's head and had a Knight chess piece in his body."

"I have to ask. Was his body in the place where the Knight was in the chess match endgame?"

"As you said, Ma'am."

"This is getting beyond weird, Alex. This is a very sick mind at work."

"Are you thinking what I'm thinking, Ma'am?"

"Damn right. You get on with checking Missing Persons, I'll go and see him."

# Chapter 7

## *27ᵗʰ September, 2025, Coastal NSW, Australia*

"One new grandkid, thirty-three new Alpaca kids," said Jack Savage, placing a slice of apple pie on a plate and handing it to Melanie.

"Amazing production," said Melanie with a smile. "Can I possibly drag you away from all this to help us? This is even sicker than the ninth of the month killings. We need your specialist help."

"That sounds interesting. Tell me what you have." Jack sat forward in his seat, hands together, elbows on his knees.

"We've discovered bodies buried in a field some way away from civilisation. They were buried standing up, they were covered in either black or white gowns and some of them were found with odd little headpieces made of cheap metal, quite amateurish."

"Sounds like chess pieces."

She stared at him. "Stop being so clever, Jack. Yes, that's the current theory."

"How long have they been there?"

"The autopsies so far indicate as long ago as forty years, as recently as five or six."

"And cause of death?"

"So far, stabbed with a hunting knife or head shattered with a blunt object."

Jack sat back in his seat again.

"Try keeping me away! This is within ordinary commute distance, so there's nothing to cause problems. And maybe I'll write another paper on what we find."

"How did you go with the last one?" asked Melanie.

"It went well," Jack replied. "The story of a dominant personality running a writers' group of mostly damaged, submissive personalities was a perfect example of such dysfunctional relationships. The idea that she was able to persuade eleven otherwise normal people each to kill an innocent person and write the event as a short story to be published in a collection was almost beyond belief, but it followed classic patterns of such personalities. My paper was published in the *"Journal of Psychiatry"* and got excellent reviews. So of course I'll come and work with you again."

"That's a relief. I've told you what we know so far, only three bodies autopsied, but possibly ten or eleven more to come. We're digging them out as we speak. And to confirm the chess theory, each body so far examined has had a chess piece like the figure the body was representing dug into the corpse. Alex thinks there will be thirteen, based on some famous chess endgame played some years ago."

"You've got Alex?"

"I had him transferred as soon as I could, once I was posted here. He showed extraordinary intelligence and initiative then and is doing it again now. This whole chess connection wouldn't have been discovered for a long time without his insight."

Savage nodded. "Bright young man, that."

"He is. He got married a year ago, there's a kiddie on the way so we may not get his full attention all the time, but what we get is sure to be invaluable."

"And you still have the same wonder-car! I heard it as you drove up to the house."

"The Gordon-Keeble? For sure. I'm still stunned by the way I got it. Can you imagine a criminal blowing up my first one and then getting an attack of conscience and spending a fortune getting me another?"

"That Allen Miller bloke was a strange one, that's for sure. He was different from the rest of the writers' group, by no means was he a submissive personality. I think he just used the group to hide himself away. Nobody could ever have suspected that he was arguably the world's greatest computer hacker hunted by the FBI for years."

"And when it was time to kill somebody, he did it in the way only he could have without actually taking a life. It was brilliant, breaking into several computer systems and wiping out a person's identity."

"And then later restoring it," said Jack. "It was the same sort of complex personality that made him replace your car after destroying it. You've not heard anything about him since he vanished?"

"Not a peep. He could be anywhere in the world, have any identity, still hacking into computers and stealing millions, anything. Probably the most brilliant person I have ever met, a total criminal but with a conscience."

Melanie's phone rang. Jack nodded his indication to take the call and she lifted it from her handbag.

"Yes, Alex."

"I've found the second missing person, Ma'am."

"Hang on a moment, I'm putting you on speaker. I'm with Jack, I want him to hear this."

"Jack? Good afternoon, nice to see you again."

"Same with you Alex. I'm looking forward to working with you both."

"This one vanished from Kempsey fourteen years ago," said Alex. "Same physical description as the doctor gave. Hold on to your hat, Ma'am. His name is Rudy Bishop."

"For some reason I'm not surprised."

"This is the body wearing a bishop's hat and had a bishop chess piece in his body?" asked Jack.

"That's the one," said Melanie.

"Then there's no way in the world you're keeping me out of this. I produced a great paper from the last case, I reckon there's another one in this. There's a very sick mind involved here."

"Give me a couple of days, I'll clear it with my boss and get you on the payroll."

"Sounds great. There's only one snag, I have to go to England for a few days for a conference at Birmingham University. I'll get stuck into this when I get back."

"No problems, Jack. I should have the paperwork done by the time you get back. But there's no reason why you can't join us for a time before you leave."

"None at all. I'll get there tomorrow morning. I can't wait to get started."

"Good. Can I have another slice of that apple pie?"

# Chapter 8

## *28<sup>th</sup> September, 2025, Coastal NSW, Australia*

"Inspector Carter? Good morning, or should I say good evening? It's about five in the afternoon there, right?"

Melanie studied the face of the fair-haired young man in the monitor, saw the blink of astonishment and ignored it. She smiled.

"Inspector MacIntyre, I assume? Thank you for getting back so quickly, and yes, it's just after six in the afternoon here, so about nine in the morning in Edinburgh?"

"That's correct. It's taken a few days to get the information you wanted, but the judge we asked for the court order seemed interested in the request and gave it immediately."

"Inspector," began Melanie but was interrupted.

"This is much too interesting a case to stay formal," said the detective in Edinburgh. "Would we damage police protocols if you call me Forbes?"

Melanie chuckled, charmed by the pleasant Scottish accent. "Not if you call me Melanie."

"Excellent," said Forbes. "It was fortunate that our two bosses knew each other when they established contact. It made the whole process that much easier."

"Apparently they had met on an Interpol conference in Zurich when they were both Inspectors," said Melanie. "Forbes, I have to tell you that I have two other people in the room." She pointed the camera at Jack and Alex. "On the right is Detective Senior Constable Alex Welland, on the left, our psychiatrist and profiler, Jack Savage. We three had worked together on a case a couple of years ago."

The face in the monitor lit up with a broad smile. "We know all about that case," said Forbes. "Quite bizarre. The idea that a woman could persuade the members of her writing group to kill people and write up the event as a short story has fascinated the detective forces of Britain ever since. Jack, Constable Welland, a great pleasure to meet you both. Jack, I read the paper you produced, it's been circulated round most stations in the UK."

"Glad I could help," said Jack. "I hope you never encounter such a story, but if you do, maybe this will provide some pointers."

"And so to business," said Melanie. "What have you got for us, Forbes?"

"As you know, your Chief Super asked our Chief Super to look into an accounting firm called Maynard Partners here in Edinburgh. We did and found that the head office is in Edinburgh and that office has four partners. They have a Glasgow office with three partners and a similar operation in Aberdeen. I went to visit the head office and asked the partnership about the property in Australia that they hold in trust. They refused to answer any questions, claiming trustee privilege. I did say that the property was the scene of multiple murders, but that changed nothing, total blank wall."

"Sounds suspicious for a start," said Melanie.

"Indeed. That's when we applied for a court order. The meeting with the judge was great! He was fascinated by the story of the bodies in the field, admitted he was a real fan of murder mysteries and granted the court order immediately. And back we went to Maynard Partners."

He paused as if deliberately for dramatic effect and Melanie felt the tension in the room rise a few degrees.

"That field and several other adjacent properties are part of the estate of Baron William Percivale of Ayrshire who disappeared in 1964 amid a major scandal."

Alex shifted in his seat with excitement. "Is or was the Baron a chess player?"

The Scot laughed. "Funny you should mention that, Constable. Yes he was, and a player of considerable reputation, just about to attain Grand Master class. And that's what the scandal is all about."

Swiftly, he related the story of the chess match played against a German Grand Master in 1964, the win resulting from mistakes by both players that was seen on television a few days later, the challenge by Peter Chancellor, a schoolboy of sixteen and the huge row when Percivale lost, threw a major tantrum and walked out without giving up the Fabergé chess set that had been the wager between him and Chancellor.

"And what happened?" asked Melanie.

"He was destroyed," replied Forbes. "He disappeared a few days later, never to be seen or heard of again. Society shunned him, Parliament rescinded his seat in the House of Lords, his wife committed suicide a few years later out of shame. A letter was received later by the Maynard Partnership authorizing them as the trustees."

"Was that letter signed by Baron Percivale?" asked Melanie.

"It was," replied McIntyre. "Which indicates that he was still alive at least up till then."

"And are there any descendants?" asked Jack.

"None known," said Forbes. "The trustees contacted the local council in Australia and have paid rates and taxes ever since."

"Good grief," exclaimed Alex. "I've just remembered! Peter Chancellor is here in Australia. He was on television a few days ago. He's Britain's latest Chess Grand Master and he won the World Championship just a few weeks ago. He's doing a publicity tour of challenge matches around the country. I didn't see the program, but one of the members of my Chess Club did and he told that same story about the match with Percivale. His stake in the bet was a collection of Picasso designs for chess pieces owned by his mother who had been one of Picasso's many mistresses in her youth."

"That certainly confirms the scandal, but we still have some unresolved questions," said Melanie. "We have no idea where Percivale went or if he's still alive. Forbes, do you know how old he would be if he is still alive and kicking?"

"We do. We checked on that, he will turn eighty-three in February of next year."

"And if he's dead, what happens to the title, the estates and everything else?" asked Melanie.

"We looked into that, also," said Forbes. "If he's dead, the estates are returned to the Crown and could be handed over to anyone parliament wished. But if it turns out that there are children by any subsequent marriage, should he have survived and gone into hiding or perhaps with a false identity, the eldest child, male or female would inherit the lot. Of course, that's assuming that such a marriage was legal and had taken place after the death of his first wife. If not, there will be intensive legal questions about the inheritance of both title and estates. Children born from an illegal marriage could not inherit."

"You've done great work, Forbes," said Melanie and watched the detective's face almost melt. "Were you able to identify anyone who could possibly know where Percivale might have gone?"

"Only one," said Forbes, recovering self-control. "We tried to locate his valet, a man called Graham Hunter who had worked for Percivale for only a few months since he inherited from his father. Hunter didn't remain with the estates in Scotland for long, just a few weeks and then left. We have not been able to find him. His tax records show no further employment. We did find Montague Pierce-Hasting, once a senior public servant, considered Percivale's only real friend. He's in his late eighties, retired and in very poor health. He didn't want to talk about the Baron. His disgust was still obvious. He denied any knowledge of where Percivale could have gone and clearly hoped he was dead."

After a few more exchanges of ideas, the group broke up with expressions of mutual admiration.

"Another new convert to worship at your feet," said Jack with a barely concealed smile. "I don't think he'll be able to concentrate much for a few days,"

"Give it up, Jack," said Melanie, ignoring the comment. "Okay, that was all very illuminating, but it doesn't move us forward. We still don't have any idea of who's doing all these killings and why."

"I believe that the whole thing is somehow linked to that story of Percivale's scandal and social destruction," said Jack. "It has all the hallmarks of revenge killing to make a point. Alex, is the layout we've found so far the end game that Percivale was playing against Chancellor?"

"I'll have to do some digging," said Alex. "Being a private match, it may not be recorded, but if it was, that would confirm your theory."

"Maybe we can find Peter Chancellor and get his story," said Melanie. "Who is arranging this tour?"

"The Australian Chess Federation," said Alex. "I'll contact them, see if they can give me his itinerary."

"Good on you," said Melanie. "Let's first review the body count. Alex, take us through what we've got so far."

"This may be it," said Alex. "We've examined every spot where the chess match indicates a body would be and we've found thirteen bodies. Three of the indicated spots were empty with no signs that there had been a body there. If this really is what I believe it is, the end game of the Selznick-Karlov match, then it looks like the layout represents a state in the match several moves before the checkmate would have occurred if allowed to go to the end."

"Do the bodies all correspond to specific pieces?" asked Jack. "And have we identified them all?"

"So far, yes," replied Alex. "We've got two black Bishops and they have been identified by searches through missing persons files as Rudi Bishop of Kempsey and Amelia Bishop of Glenn Innes. Also in black, one Knight, identified as Peter Knight of Bellingen. We have four black pawns but none of them identified so far. On the white side, only two identified bodies, Stephen Knight of Port Macquarie and three pawns, none identified yet. There is also a White Bishop and we identified her as Marie Bishop of Taree."

"You said there are three vacant spots," said Jack.

"Indeed. Neither King is there, and the Black Queen is missing."

"All of the victims within reasonably easy reach of here," said Melanie. "Except for the man from Bondi Beach, that's a good six-hour drive from here."

"So thirteen bodies found, three missing," said Jack. "Which leaves us with some questions. We still have no idea of who has been doing this. Could it be Percivale himself?"

"He's over eighty," said Melanie. "Unlikely, unless he's exceptionally fit and strong."

"Maybe he started the process some years ago and somebody else continued the job," said Alex. "Some of the bodies are thirty or forty years old, according to Doc Rutherford."

"Good point," said Melanie. "So it's really an extra question. Who took on the job? Jack, you said you had one more question?"

"The three unoccupied spots," said Jack. "Could they mean there are three more bodies needed to fill them?"

"It's a horrible thought," said Melanie. "But if that is

the case, given our blank slate now, having one or more murders might be the only way we have of identifying the killers."

"I'll get back to checking that end game layout and going through missing persons," said Jack and rose to his feet.

"Good luck," said Melanie.

## *30th September, 2025, Coastal NSW, Australia*

"This worked well," said Peter Chancellor. He sat comfortably in an armchair in the police station lounge, cradling a mug of coffee. "I was in Sydney for a few days when young Alex here found me and when he told me what it was all about, there was no way I'd miss coming to see you. But I have to say, I don't know how I can help you."

"You may be able to add to the background information we have on Baron Percivale," said Melanie. "You're the only person we know who has all the details of your chess match in 1964."

"And it's amazing how even the smallest detail you noticed might be a help," said Jack.

"But what is it all about?" asked Chancellor. "Alex said you were conducting enquiries into some events, but he wasn't any more informative than that."

"Peter, we're going to give you some information that is not known outside this group, my boss, the senior officer for this region and the pathologist who has been examining a number of bodies. He's had help from other pathologists when the body count expanded, but the others don't know the story."

Chancellor stared at her. "Bodies?" he asked.

Melanie nodded at Alex who took a sheet of paper from a folder and handed it to Chancellor.

"Peter, is this the end game you were playing in your match against Percivale?"

Chancellor gave him a puzzled look but studied the sheet.

"Yes, it is," he said after a few moments. "It's a repeat of the endgame of the Selznik-Karlov match played in Zurich in 1948. I was playing Black, and I didn't think Percivale knew that match because he seemed quite unaware that I was leading him along. At the stage here, he moved a pawn which left his king wide open to my Bishop. I could see mate in seven, said so and that's when he threw the grandaddy of all hissy fits. Now, please, what is this about?"

Alex passed him a second sheet.

"There's a field a few miles away from here. We've found thirteen bodies buried there in a pattern that you will find familiar. Each of the spots marked indicates a body, some dressed in black, some in white with a cheap metal headpiece indicating the chess piece they represented."

Chancellor studied the second sheet with growing agitation.

"Holy shit!" he gasped. "That's the same layout. That's the point at which I declared mate in seven, he lost it and stamped out with the Fabergé chess set. But there are three pieces missing."

"The two Kings and the Black Queen?" said Alex.

"Exactly."

"Which is where my interest lies," said Jack. "From what you saw in his behaviour, is Percivale capable of committing these murders and hiding the bodies in this way?"

"I'm damn sure of it," said Chancellor. "He's certainly vicious enough, but I can't see him actually doing it. If he's still alive, he'd be at least eighty and he didn't look like much of an athlete back then when he was in his mid-twenties. But some sort of act of revenge? Damn sure of it, even if nobody would ever see the bodies."

"That's what we thought," said Melanie. "So Jack is going to take you back to that day and see if you can recall anything that might indicate where Percivale went when he vanished."

"I'd like to put you under light hypnosis, if okay by you," said Jack. "It will probably help."

"Go for it," said Chancellor and placed his coffee mug on the side table next to him.

* * *

### 16<sup>th</sup> *June, 1964, Percivale Hall, Surrey, UK*

Pierce-Hasting returned to the room, his face white, unable to look Peter Chancellor in the eye.

"I am terribly sorry, Mr Chancellor," he said. "The Baron's behaviour was inexcusable, and he will pay dearly for it. By all rights, you should be leaving with the Fabergé set and if I am able to locate it, I will ensure it gets sent to you."

"Not a problem," said Chancellor. "From what I saw of him yesterday, this was not a surprise."

"The valet will get your coat," said the other. "Now if

you will excuse me, I must try and find the Baron and see how things might be repaired."

Chancellor nodded and waited while the young man who had attended Percivale previously approached with the coats of Peter and his associate.

"You really shoved one up the bastard's arse," said the man in low tones. "It was a joy to see!"

Peter stared at him, trying not to laugh.

"You're not impressed by his lordship, I gather?"

The valet sniffed. "That's one way of putting it," he said. "Hey, my name's Graham Hunter, and it's been my misfortune to be the Baron's valet for a few months, ever since he inherited the title."

"Not a fun job, eh?" said Chancellor.

"You have no idea! He's real proof that wealth and nobility don't always come with class. Let me show you out. We'll go through the trophy room, I think you'll find it interesting."

The three men entered a lounge room that could have been the archetypal refuge of a rich man's club. Dark wooden walls were lined with pictures of wealthy men in various robes of societies and one wall had a series of animal heads mounted on plaques. Amid the collection of buffalo, lion and elephant heads, one stood out.

"He's shot all these?" asked Chancellor.

Hunter snorted. "Hardly! They're all imitations, made by special-effects people. I doubt the noble Baron could fire a rifle without falling over."

Chancellor stopped at the last one on the wall.

"A kangaroo?" he asked, trying not to laugh.

Hunter grimaced.

"That one's real, and a bloody great big one," he said. "William was on a tour of the international properties, sent by his father. He was in outback New South Wales and saw the monster, it was well over six feet tall. William foolishly approached it and it attacked him. Those things can rip a man's insides out and William was lucky that his accompanying guardian was able to get his gun up and he fired before it jumped at him."

"Scary experience," said Peter.

"One of the factors influencing his lowly opinion of Australia," said Hunter. "I heard him say to his friend, that Pierce-Hasting twit, that Australia was only good for criminals, silly animals and a place to disappear to if one ever needed to."

"I can't say I like displays like this," said Peter. "I can't imagine his wife appreciating it."

"Hah!" retorted Hunter. "Lady Joanne never comes down to this house. She can't stand the bastard and never leaves the Scottish estate. Theirs was a social contract marriage, arranged for various political alliances. So this room was the Baron's refuge, nobody came here except the cleaners."

As they moved to the end of the room and the door leading out, Peter saw a number of photographs in frames on polished mahogany side-tables. One caught his eye. It showed a pretty brunette with a sweet smile on her lips.

"Her ladyship?" he asked.

"There's not a chance in hell he'd have a picture of Lady Joanne," said Hunter. "He disliked her as much she deplored him. No, that woman is called Felicity, she's the nanny for a couple who work in the maintenance section, and she also helps out with some cleaning and kitchen chores. She looks after the little girl when she gets back from nursery school, sometimes drives her there and collects her afterwards. Sometimes we talk about her downstairs and the general opinion is that she's the Baron's bit of stuff on the side as well as the nanny. The only reason the Baron can display it is because he knows his wife never comes to this part of England, never mind the house and she'll never see it. But I've heard her speak and it was a definite Australian accent."

### 30<sup>th</sup> September, 2025, Coastal NSW, Australia

Jack snapped his fingers and Chancellor stirred slightly. He had not looked as if he was under hypnosis and had seemed fully aware of his surroundings.

"That was interesting," he said. "Was it of any use?"

"I think so," said Melanie. "We're most grateful."

"Good," said Chancellor. "Now then, Alex, got a chess set here?"

"Oh yes," replied Alex, suppressing a grin.

"Good. Set 'em up, let's see what you've got."

Melanie and Jack waited until the two had left the room and Jack stood up and poured two more mugs of coffee at the machine.

"He's here, isn't he?" said Melanie as Jack placed the mug by her.

"Absolutely guaranteed," replied Jack, returning to his seat. "Everything Peter said pointed to Percivale escaping from England and coming here. I'd give decent odds that the young woman, Felicity played a part in that. If he's still alive, he's in Australia."

"Then we have two projects. Alex can get onto tracking her down. If he owned the field with all the bodies, he may well have known her from this region, possibly from his visit here. Or she could be another of the numerous Australians spending a few months in England. There were hundreds of them in the sixties, working menial jobs, sharing apartments with several others in that part of London known as "Kangaroo Valley" because of the numbers."

"Could you contact the local police, see if she could be identified in any way?"

"Possibly," said Melanie, "but it will take a hell of a lot of legwork. Maybe local newspapers have stories about a pretty Australian girl, or immigration records, if we can get permission to get into them."

"Your detective fan in Edinburgh would be delighted to help with getting a court order for that one," said Jack with a straight face. "He'd do anything to earn your smile."

"Can it, Jack," she replied. "But it's worth a try. I'll email him."

"The second one is going to need high-level assistance," said Jack. "If he came to Australia openly, under his own name, he'd have been found out almost immediately. He wasn't, so he didn't."

"The British government would have wanted him hidden and out of the way, I imagine," said Melanie. "He'd have been a terrible embarrassment as a member of the House of Lords, and if he vanished, they'd have been able to remove him easily. But it does seem to be a bit of an overkill for the crime. Could there be some other reasons why they wanted him out of the way?”

“It’s possible. Who was in government in Australia in 1964?” asked Jack. “Wasn’t that Robert Menzies? He’d have been eager to help the British titled nobility in any way he could.”

“So you think Menzies did a deal, let Percivale come here with an assumed name and identity and hide himself away, perhaps with his bit of stuff on the side, as Peter put it?”

“I’d bet the mortgage on it,” said Jack. “If I had one.”

“When Alex recovers from his experience of playing chess with the World Champion, I’ll put him to work,” said Melanie.

“Good,” said Jack. “Email me if anything interesting develops. I’m heading to England tomorrow morning.”

“Have a good trip, Jack.”

## Chapter 9

### *30<sup>th</sup> September, 2025, Coastal NSW, Australia*

"Melanie, how lovely to talk to you again."

Inspector Forbes MacIntyre suddenly looked embarrassed.

"Thank you, Forbes," she replied, seeing his reaction and thoroughly accustomed to it in men of all ages when they met her. For a moment, she wandered sadly if she could ever meet a man who caused the same reaction in her. *It's been too many years, dearest Scott, why did you have to go to Kings Cross that night and get killed?* "My pleasure also. And I need your help again on this Percivale matter."

"Anything I can do, you know that. The whole of the Edinburgh police force is buzzing with this story, and we're concerned about how long we can keep it out of the press."

"We believe that Percivale was having an affair with an Australian girl in the area of his Surrey mansion. All we know is that her first name was Felicity. It's a big ask and I don't know if immigration records were computerised in 1964, but we need to trace her to see if she had any connection with Percivale's departure. We do know that he visited Australia in his youth to examine the estates the family owned, which included the field where we found the bodies. And a witness has reported that he overheard a comment that he considered Australia a place only for criminals and a place to hide if one needed to."

"Good grief," said MacIntyre. "How did you get that?"

"Remember the young man who defeated him in the chess match that caused the scandal? His name is Peter Chancellor, he became World Champion a few weeks ago and he's on a tour of Australia. We saw him on television, traced him and he came to the station. He allowed Jack Savage to put him in a light trance and he recalled that conversation and the connection to this Felicity woman."

"Stroke of luck, eh, Melanie?"

"Bloody oath!" she replied and laughed at his expression.

"Is that the sort of thing you Aussies say?" he said through his own laughter.

"Indeed it is," she replied. "Forbes, can you help?"

"Probably. It will need another court order, but our helpful judge will no doubt come good again. I'll get back to you."

"I'll look forward to it," she said and disconnected the call.

# Chapter 10

### *17th October, 2025, Coastal NSW, Australia*

"Jack, welcome back! How was the time in Britain?"

"Melanie, nice to see you as well, you too, Alex. I have to say, I worked my bum off sitting in libraries and pouring over microfilm screens."

"But by your attitude, it seems you found some interesting stuff?"

"Damn right I did. It's given me a major topic for a new paper. This whole subject of psychopathic traits running in families for generations was an immediate hook for me. But I also had a major stroke of luck. One of the professors at the conference had very strong connections to MI5 and MI6, the British security forces, because he had done a lot of work with them on Middle East terrorism subjects. He fed me a lot of data about the Percivale family."

"This we have to hear, Jack," said Melanie. "But before you tell us, I need to give you my information. Our man in Edinburgh came good."

The other two were clearly interested.

"He got a court order as promised and the Immigration people in London needed no pressure to help. They even put a few young administrative trainees to work. The records were not computerized in the sixties, but they had been microfilmed and these bright young sparks spent nearly two weeks pouring through the files."

"And they found her?" asked Jack, his face revealing some excitement.

Melanie shook her head. "No," she said. "But they did find fifteen possibles. Fifteen women with the first name Felicity, Australian nationals between the ages of twenty and thirty entered the UK between 1962 and 1964. We took that as the last date because Percivale vanished in mid to late-1964 and if this theory is valid, she probably went with him."

"Did they give Australian addresses?" asked Alex.

Melanie looked at him. He seemed to be smiling at some hidden secret.

"They did," she said. "And that may have narrowed the range a bit, but it can't be sure. And the information is sixty years old, so it's most unlikely the addresses will be current. Five of the women came from New South Wales, three each came from Queensland and Victoria and the others from South Australia. We have their family names, so we should be able to trace all of them."

"Bloody useless Pommies," said Alex.

The other two looked at him.

"I suppose you're telling us you found her?" said Jack, not hiding his amusement.

"Bloody oath," said Alex. "She's Felicity Harrison, born in 1944, so she'd have been about twenty when this all blew up. She came from Bellingen, not far from here. She did the usual Australian thing when she was nineteen, went to England, got a work permit, worked as a barmaid, a cleaner, nanny, all the stock-standard stuff that young Aussies did in that time and returned home in September, 1964."

"Good grief, Alex, how did you find that out?" Melanie was staring at him in undisguised admiration.

"Not all that difficult," said Alex. "First thing I did was research local newspapers in the area of Woking in Surrey where the Percivale country property was and still is. I found three of them and called them to ask if they had been operating in the early sixties. Two of them had, so when I explained the situation, they were both eager to help. Rather like the Immigration office, they had microfilmed their back editions. They called in some part-time help and got them looking through the files from 1962 to 1964."

"And they found her?"

Alex opened his folder and took out two sheets of paper, handing them to Melanie. "They emailed me a couple of days ago with copies of the articles. They found two news items about a young Australian woman who had come to England to do the usual young traveller thing and found a job as a nanny, looking after the kiddie of a local couple who served in the Percivale mansion."

Melanie studied the sheets. Each of them showed a grainy picture of a dark young woman with shoulder-length hair and a short article about the Australian girl from Bellingen in New South Wales who had come to England to see the country from which her ancestors had travelled a century earlier. She passed them to Jack.

"Amazing work, Alex," she said. "But without throwing cold water over it, it doesn't prove that she brought Percivale here or even that he's here at all. But it certainly shows how she might have met him."

"Agreed, Ma'am," said Alex. "But I wonder if the same sort of research could be done locally?"

"I'm sure it could. Alex, keep this up. Go to Bellingen when you've had a few days to review all this, check out the local papers, the local council records, maybe the family is still there, perhaps the churches in the area have a record of a marriage between her and some bloke and that may point to Percivale. I'll clear it with the local cops. Meanwhile, we can get help checking immigration records and test our theory that the Menzies government assisted the Poms in letting Percivale come here in a witness protection scheme with a new identity."

She turned to Jack. "Your turn, Jack. Judging by your expression, I'd say you have a lot of good stuff. Everybody fancy some refreshments before we get into it?" Without waiting for an answer, she picked up the phone. "Annie, can you order sandwiches and coffee from the canteen, enough for three? Thanks."

Jack opened a folder and extracted a sheet. "This was my first major find," he said. "I spent ten whole days in Edinburgh in various libraries, making a thorough nuisance of myself with librarians, but they didn't seem to mind. They got as excited as I was by the time we found the critical stuff."

He displayed the sheet in front of him, then passed it to Melanie. She studied it, a photocopy of an ancient document, badly creased, stained by the years and cracked round the edges. The words were incomprehensible, even when legible. She looked across at Jack, the question in her face.

"It's in ancient Scottish Gaelic," he said. "I had to go to the University for help with this, it's actually a dialect of Lowland Gaelic which has died out in the last couple of hundred years, though there are still plenty of modern Gaelic speakers. Anyway, let me give you the rough translation that the University gave me.

"It says that the Laird of the land, whom we can assume to be the first Baron, the one who received his title in 1485 after the Battle of Bosworth Field, built a castle on the site of a previous structure, believed to be a Roman fort. There is a rough map and it covers the area where Percivale's territories were defined and the new structure is in the same spot where the later castle, built in 1848 still exists. But now we get to the interesting bit. The document says that fifteen bodies were found in the ruins of the old fort as construction began. It specifically says that the bodies were not Roman troops, which would have been several hundred years old and just skeletons, but were relatively recent, dressed in contemporary clothing."

"No more than that?" asked Alex.

Jack shook his head. "Nobody would question a nobleman of that status, and of course, there is no evidence that it was the Laird who killed these people. They were just commoners, anyway and death was hardly a surprise in those times."

"So nothing proven there?" said Alex, sounding disappointed.

Jack grinned cheerfully. "Ah, just you wait a while, laddie," he said. "Now I switched my attention to more modern times, still in the same area and I started pouring over microfilm records at the University. Many newspapers of the era survived and were filmed by the University. This is the report from May, 1848."

He handed a sheet to Melanie and Alex.

"Why don't you read it, Alex?" said Melanie.

"Astonishing find in the basement of Castle Percivale now under construction," said Alex, staring hard at the poor-quality printing. "As workers cleared away the last of the ancient castle, built in 1550 by the first of the Percivale line, a number of bodies were found in the basement. Police were called to examine the scene. An announcement was later issued after the doctor had completed an initial survey. Some of the bodies were just skeletons, indicating that they had been there for many years, though the doctor was unable to say just how many. Others were more recent, estimated to have been there for five or six years. None of the bodies has been identified. Baron Donald Percivale who ascended to the Baronetcy in 1816 on the death of his father, Baron Robert Percivale denied any knowledge of these mysteries, saying that the Castle was several hundred years old and numerous people had access, from tradesmen to domestic staff."

Alex looked up. "An interesting coincidence," he said. "Bodies in the Castle. Sounds like an Agatha Christie novel."

"Possibly coincidence, maybe not," said Melanie. "Jack, any more?"

"And so to England," said Jack, extracting more papers from his folder. "Surrey, to be specific. "The stately home of Percivale Hall was built in 1880 by Baron Alisdair who lived from 1830 to 1901 and the son of Baron Donald who built the castle. No bodies that we know of, as nobody has investigated the basement or grounds of the Hall. But some interesting newspaper reports of missing persons. From the completion of the

Hall in 1880 to 1952, eighteen missing persons were reported and never found."

"Who came after Baron Alisdair?" asked Melanie.

"Alisdair's son, Douglas was born in 1860 and gained the title on his father's death in 1901 at the age of forty-one. He lasted until 1924 and his son, Campbell inherited all the goodies at the young age of twenty-one. He's the grandfather of the present Baron, William. William's father, also Andrew was born in 1916 and died in 1958 in a car crash at the age of forty-two when our current suspect became Baron at the age of twenty-two."

"There's just too much ugly stuff going on around this family for it all to be coincidence," said Melanie.

"I agree," said Jack. "This looks for all the world like a family with a pathological streak that has lasted for generations. There have been such cases in the past, but I don't know of one so strong and so long-lasting as this appears to be."

They paused as a canteen worker came in pushing a trolley with a large coffee urn and several plates of sandwiches, and they waited until she had left.

"This is where my friend at the conference supplied me the real lode-stone of information," said Jack. "The first real bastard is the ninth Baron Percivale, Andrew. Remember the Cambridge Five, the bunch of young students who became charmed by the Communist philosophy? He became highly involved with that bunch."

* * *

## *September, 1934, Trinity College, Cambridge University, England*

"I think I know you, don't I?"

The class of young men turned to stare at the object of the lecturer's pointed finger.

"Er.., yes, we were at Eton at one point," said the man. "You were in the Senior Year, I was a junior."

"Ah, that's right. Percivale, isn't it?"

"Yes, it is. We were both in the chess club."

"You were pretty good, as I recall. Didn't you win the Middle School Championship one year?"

"I did."

"Excellent! We'll have to get together some time and play a match. There's a chess club here, I'm sure you know. Anyway, gentlemen, to business. Welcome to your first year of studies at this wonderful Trinity College, one of the most elite and historic colleges at Cambridge. My name is Guy Burgess, I'm a post-graduate student here and I'll be teaching some of the classes together with Professor Armitage."

* * *

"Your father is a Baron, isn't he?" said Burgess as he laid the chess pieces out on the board. "Somewhere in Scotland?"

"That's correct," said Andrew Percivale. He took his seat across from Burgess. Around them there was little sound, just a few murmurs as the chess club set itself up for the afternoon regular meeting.

"How come?" asked Burgess. "Some feat of military brilliance centuries ago?"

"Actually, yes. The first Percivale fought with Henry

Tudor, later Henry the Seventh at the Battle of Bosworth which defeated Richard the Third and ended the Plantagenet dynasty in 1485. The King rewarded him with lands in Scotland and the hereditary title."

Percivale took a pawn of each colour in his two fists, put his hands under the table and switched them around. He held his hands out and Burgess touched one.

"White?" he said. "Okay, I'll start."

Nothing was said for the next forty-five minutes. Then, after a minute of studying the board, Burgess tipped his King on its side to signal surrender.

"Mate in four, well done," he said. "I didn't see that clever Knight's move back there. You're pretty good, Mister Percivale."

"Thank you. That was a better match than I usually get."

"You play a lot, obviously."

"Yes, I've been entering competitions since I was ten. My father taught me and he was a local champion."

"So you'll inherit everything when he passes on, will you? You'll be Baron Percivale?"

Percivale looked uncomfortable. "We don't like to talk about it, but yes, one day I'll be Baron Percivale with the estates in Scotland and a few other places around the world."

"And all the money in the universe, I suppose?"

Percivale shrugged. "I'll get by," he said and stood up. "See you in the class tomorrow."

"Make sure you have the essay done," said Burgess with a smile, and stood up also. "Oh look," he said. "A friend of mine, you two should meet."

They waited while a man approached them from where he had stood up at the completion of a chess game.

"Guy, hello," said the newcomer. "I saw you were playing with this handsome young fellow. Do introduce us."

"Of course," said Burgess. "Anthony, this brilliant young chess player who has just demolished me is Andrew Percivale. Andrew, this is Anthony Blunt who lectures in modern languages."

"Pleased to meet you," said Percivale as they shook hands.

"And I am quite delighted to meet you, young man," said Blunt.

Rather put off by the weak handshake and gushing style of Blunt, Percivale nodded at Burgess. "Let's have tea, the three of us some time," said Burgess, they shook hands and went their ways.

* * *

"Does it ever embarrass you that you have so much while most of the world lives in poverty?" asked Blunt as they sat in the refectory lounge.

Percivale barely looked at him. He found it difficult to tolerate the man and his overt homosexuality. His background had kept him away from such facts of life and his father had always expressed great contempt and disgust at men like this. He knew that such practices were illegal, and he wondered how the men like him at the University avoided dismissal and arrest.

"No it doesn't," he said. "My family has earned its position by services to the country. This is a free country, being poor is just evidence of weakness."

Burgess laughed. "Anthony, my dear boy," he said, "young Percivale, the future Baron knows nothing of our world. But Andrew, you really should think about this. It's fact that the rich keep their wealth by simple oppression of the masses. Who knows what talents, genius, strengths might be uncovered if everybody was allowed to be themselves?"

Percivale felt anger growing. "Oh my God, does this mean you two are communists?"

"Indeed we are, dear boy," said Burgess. "We and several others here believe that communism as implemented in the Soviet Union is the best defence against the horrors of Fascism. It's a shame you missed meeting Donald Maclean, a very strong advocate of Communism. He graduated last year and we are certain he will make his mark on the world."

Percivale rose to his feet. "I consider all of you enemies of my country," he said. "I shall change my subjects so that I don't have to hear your lectures or sit in the same room as you."

He walked out.

* * *

## September, 1934, Trinity College, Cambridge University, England

"Professor Anderson, may I speak with you?"

The tall, slender-built man with scars on his face stopped his slow and painful walk across the quadrangle as Percivale approached him. Leaning on his stick, he looked curiously at the other man.

"And who are you, young man? I don't recognise you as one of my students."

"No sir, I am not. My name is Andrew Percivale. I just started my degree in History. But I would be grateful if I could ask you about a worrying situation I have encountered. I'm worried about who I could trust to talk to about it, but I'm sure a decorated Major and veteran of the War would be secure."

"How curious," said the Major. "Alright, you intrigue me. I have a class ending at four, I'll be free to talk to you then. We could have a coffee in the refectory, or.."

"No sir, I need to talk to you in private."

"My office, then."

"Thank you, sir."

Percivale stood aside and watched the Major limp away, his academic gown swirling in the breeze.

"Alright, young Percivale, what's all this about?"

The major reclined in his armchair, holding a glass of beer. Opposite him, Percivale sat on the front of his seat, hands tight together, elbows on his knees.

"I read your record in the college handbook," said Percivale. "You went through the battles of Marne, the Somme, Passchendaele..."

"Mr Percivale, you did not come here to discuss my war experiences and I have absolutely no desire to talk about them. Now, why are you here?"

Percivale saw a tremor begin in the Major's right hand and the scars on his face became inflamed.

"My apologies, sir. It's just that I need to talk to a genuine British patriot."

"Why?"

"Sir, a few days ago, I met with Guy Burgess and Professor Anthony Blunt."

"Ah," said the Major.

"You know them, of course," said Percivale. "They horrified me. Not only do they seem to be openly homosexual, which is a crime, but they are also firm supporters of the Communist leadership in Russia."

"That we know," said the Major.

"Then why are they permitted to work here? Why are they not removed as criminals and potential traitors?"

"Frankly, that would be my preference, followed by immediate execution. But there are two factors involved. One is that they are very well connected in the corridors of power and considered untouchable. The second is that the very bright minds running our security services consider it better to have them here, easily watched and likely to give away some secrets, like their contacts and the nature of the information they are passing to the Russians."

"So you do have them under observation?"

"Oh yes. And it's almost certain that they know it and take extreme care in contacting their handlers."

"I just never knew anything like this went on," said Percivale.

"It's becoming a very ugly world. Russia's Stalin must be considered a huge danger, as must the disturbing developments in Germany and Italy. If we are not careful, I can see another great war coming."

The major reached out to the side table by his armchair and picked up a notepad and pen. He wrote some details, tore off a page and reached it toward Percivale who stood up and took it.

"I think you should talk to that gentleman in London," Anderson said. "You will learn more interesting things and possibly see some opportunities to help your country. Do not talk about our meeting, under no circumstances tell your new-found acquaintances you have talked to me, in fact, don't tell anyone at all. But go and see that man. I'll call him and let you know you are coming."

"Thank you, sir." Percivale turned to the door.

"And good luck with your studies. History is a wonderful subject, and I strongly suspect the history of the next couple of decades will be even more critical than the past. You are fortunate that you will be able to see it at first hand."

The major drained his glass as Percivale left.

* * *

### 4<sup>th</sup> *October, 1934, London, England*

"Please take a seat, Mr Percivale." The middle-aged, bone-thin man with a florid face and white moustache who had greeted Percivale when a young woman showed him into the office settled back in his chair behind a large desk. "I'm delighted you came to see us. I think we have some interesting possibilities to discuss."

"If a true hero like Major Anderson asked me to do so, I could hardly refuse."

Percivale was feeling over-awed by the morning's experiences. The address in Whitehall was an undistinguished door on a side street away from the magnificence of the main street and it required a large knocker to be employed. It took a minute or two before it received a response and the door was opened.

"Mr Percivale?" said a uniformed army man wearing the three stripes and a star of a Staff Sergeant. The array of ribbons on his chest was extensive. "You brought your passport?"

Without a word, Percivale handed over the very new passport he had received soon after his eighteenth birthday. The Staff Sergeant examined it carefully, checking the picture against the owner and finally opened the door fully, closing it after Percivale had entered.

"This lady will take you to see Mr Faraday," he said, as a young woman in a dark blue dress approached.

After walking through several corridors, none with any open doors, Percivale was stopped at one. The woman tapped on it, received a "Come in" from inside and Percivale was shown in. The woman closed the door behind him.

The man behind the large, oak desk did not get to his feet or offer to shake hands. He gestured to Percivale to take a chair across from the desk and Percivale obeyed without hesitation.

"My name is Faraday," said the man. "So why exactly did you need to express your concerns to Major Anderson?"

"I was absolutely disgusted by my meetings with Burgess and Blunt," said Percivale. "They say openly that they are communists and even worse, they are homosexuals. That's a crime and I don't understand why they are allowed to stay at Cambridge and out of prison."

"Major Anderson may have explained that to you. And they are not the only ones. There was a man called Donald Maclean who was at Trinity College up until the year before. He was close friends with those two."

"They did mention his name as well."

"And he's now working in the Foreign Office as a diplomat." A small smile briefly flickered across Faraday's lips.

"The Foreign Office? But that's dreadful. How do you allow this?"

"As the Major did say, we know about these men and a few more. There's a man called Kim Philby who was at Cambridge a few years earlier. Believe it or not, he works for us here in MI6."

Percivale felt his jaw drop and he could only stare at Faraday who flashed that transient smile again.

"There's a quote by Niccolò Machiavelli that has always been true," he said. "That genius said, "Keep your friends close, keep your enemies closer." That is why we have these people under observation. Not only do we see who they contact, but we can feed them false and misleading data for them to pass on to their handlers in Moscow. It has proved a useful approach."

Percivale felt his breathing ease. "I think I understand," he said. "But it doesn't stop me hating them for all the reasons I've given."

"You are not alone, Mr Percivale. Now, here's why I wanted to see you, because I believe you could be useful to your country and allow you to see some positive results from your hatred of its enemies. Your father, Baron Percivale is a well-connected man. His seat in the House of Lords helps a lot there as well as his general acceptance in the elite social circles of Britain. You benefit from that to a great extent, and you could expand your connections a lot, especially with our assistance."

Percivale nodded. He saw where this was leading.

"Cambridge appears to be a major recruiting ground for the Soviets. So I want you to control your understandable revulsion for Blunt and Burgess, cultivate their society, even indicate that you sympathise with their philosophies. That would let you discover any other people there who they may be cultivating, maybe some of their connections outside the University. When you do, inform Major Anderson and he will pass on the information to me. Can you do that?"

"Gladly," said Percivale. "I think I'd want to kill any of them I find, but I understand why you need them alive and operating."

"Believe me, we all feel the same way, but we are taking the long view. Our experts forecast that Germany will fall under the total control of a man called Adolf Hitler and may well be a threat to world security in the near future. There are also disturbing signs of fascism growing in Italy. If those two unite in common goals, they will be most difficult to defeat. But the Soviets see them as enemies and in the old Arabic phrase, the enemy of my enemy is my friend. We may find we need the Soviets to counter the Fascist threat and suppress our distaste for the communist creed at least for a time."

"I never knew all that," said Percivale. "But now that you've explained it, I understand. I'd like to help you."

"Good. Now Andrew, may I call you Andrew? Now, go back to Cambridge, talk to Major Anderson again and he will guide you along this path. And thank you, we always need men of patriotism, commitment and courage."

Feeling energised, Percivale left the office to meet the same woman who had brought him there. Without a word, he was taken back to the front door, his passport restored to him, and he found his way back to the railway station for the return trip to Cambridge.

* * *

"I must apologise for my behaviour when we last met."

Suppressing his revulsion at the limp fish handshake of Anthony Blunt, Percivale accepted Guy Burgess' invitation to sit down in Blunt's office.

"Please don't apologise, dear boy," said Blunt. "You come from a long line of British aristocrats. It would be natural for you to feel initial hostility to a philosophy that represents the great mass of humanity who would not look all that kindly on your class."

"Thank you for understanding," said Percivale. "But after talking to you, I did some heavy thinking and research into current affairs. I see that Germany is coming under the control of this Adolf Hitler person and all the resentment from the Treaty of Versailles is coming to the surface. Some comments in the press indicate a fear that Germany may start a new war to regain its assets and take revenge against the Allies in the Great War."

"You are correct," said Burgess. "And with the overt

Fascism growing under this appalling Mussolini person, those two may join as allies. We do not believe that Britain and its Empire will have the strength to withstand their combined forces."

"And there's nobody you would trust to help us? What about the United States?" asked Percivale.

An expression like one who had smelled something rancid flickered across Blunt's face.

"The Americans? That country of overgrown children with no thoughts but sex and alcohol and huge cars? No chance. Theirs is a creed of selfishness and nothing else. They would not oppose the Fascists. Indeed, we suspect they might wish to join them instead."

"But Russia will?" Percivale was hearing concepts that had never reached him before. He knew his father had little affection for the USA, seeing them as treasonous rebels and anti-British, but he had not discussed European developments with him. On the few occasions the two men had ever sat and talked, the conversation was usually a long rant by the Baron on how the common people were good for nothing but serving the real masters of the country, the aristocracy and did not merit such luxuries as education or anything above a living wage.

"Russia must," said Blunt. "They fully understand that if the Fascists gain enough power, they will invade Russia for its assets, such as oil and minerals and to limit its powers and threats."

"Then I must support you," said Percivale, feeling a shiver run through himself as he understood that he had just taken a major step that could be dangerous to him.

"Good," said Burgess with a broad smile. "And now we need you to do something that will be greatly helpful." He took a folder from a side table. "We have been talking to two young people who seem enthusiastically in favour of our views, but we are not yet certain of them. We would like you to get to know them, talk to them and sound them out. We need to be certain of them before we give them any real tasks."

He handed the folder to Percivale who opened it and studied the pictures of two young men. They looked ordinary enough, much like every other student at the University.

"I'll see what I can do," he said and left the study, breathing a sigh of relief when he closed the door behind him, so repellent did he find the presence of those two men.

*   *   *

Spotting the two men in the bar was not difficult, nor was it hard to engage them in conversation. After exchanging the usual pleasantries about the courses they were doing, the discussion moved to wider topics.

"Where are you from?" Percivale asked.

"Leeds," said Simon, the shorter, blond-haired boy. "I was at Leeds Grammar School."

"Bradford," said Richard. He was quite tall, very thin and his hair was almost jet-black, over a dark complexion, giving him a Hispanic look that Percivale found most unattractive.

Detecting the north country accents in both of them,

Percivale felt irritated. "And what do your fathers do?" he asked.

"Mine's a teacher at the school," said Simon.

"Mine drives a bus," replied Richard.

Percivale was shocked. "Then how can you afford to come to Cambridge?"

"Scholarships," said Richard. "We both had the highest grades in our school leaving exams and we were awarded places here with funds to cover the costs."

Percivale felt disgusted. Common people should not get places at the best university in the world, places that genuine aristocrats deserved far more richly. And these two were intellectuals, something he despised as pretentious and dangerous.

"How about you?" asked Simon.

"Scotland," said Percivale. "My father's a civil servant."

"Oh, an aristocrat," retorted Simon. "I bet you got a place here without having to compete for it."

"I tell you, when the world becomes a fairer place and people get the rewards they deserve purely on merit, people like you might find yourselves shut out," said Richard.

"So you believe in all that Marxist-Communist crap, then?" said Percivale, sensing the anger rising in him.

"It's the only just way," said Simon. "I look forward to seeing the people here rise up and kick out the parasites with their titles and estates and knighthoods and shit."

Percivale couldn't take any more, stood up and left. He could hardly believe how much he hated these two commoners.

# The Death Gambit

*   *   *

Percivale stood over the body of the dark-haired Richard with an enormous sense of satisfaction and fulfilment. It had been easy to follow the man from a party at another student's house and then creep up behind him in the dark and hammer one severe blow on his head with a cricket bat. He realised that he had enjoyed the process of killing, found it almost orgasmic as he felt the skull crush and the victim collapsed without a sound. Two hours earlier, he had sliced the throat of the blond Simon, using the hunting knife he had been given by his father's gamekeeper when he was five years younger.

He left the scene and returned to his rooms, entering the college with a small crowd of partygoers who were able to pass the gatekeeper without difficulty. Once inside, he scrubbed the knife clean, did the same to his cricket-bat which he then oiled and wiped down. He doubted there would be traces of his work, but also was certain that nobody would suspect the son of the Baron.

As he washed down the knife, he looked at himself in the mirror over the sink. For a moment he was silent and then he laughed with a joy he hadn't felt since childhood. This was the best experience of his whole life.

*   *   *

"I killed them," said Percivale.

Blunt and Burgess stared at him. Blunt spilled his coffee over his lap but seemed unaware of it.

"You... you killed them? Both?" stammered Burgess.

"Both."

"But.. why?"

"They were not what you thought."

"Please explain," said Blunt, regaining his composure. He put the coffee cup and saucer on the side table and went to the sink, soaking a cloth and sponging the coffee stain from his trousers.

"The more I talked to them, the less sincere I found their beliefs," said Percivale. He had spent some time developing and then practicing this line of defence. "They seemed to regard the essential spread of communism as a defence against fascism as more of a joke, they showed no serious commitment to Marxist theories. I have every reason to believe that they would have failed at the first hurdle and run off to the police when asked to do anything the remotest bit difficult."

"Then it's possible you have conducted a successful and most valuable assignment on behalf of world communism," said Burgess. "But that leaves us with a severe problem. The police will have discovered the bodies and will be conducting an intense search for the killer. What happens when they find you? Does that put us at risk?"

"That is not a problem," said Percivale. "I have already contacted my father. His contacts and influence are both extensive. He's a personal friend of the Home Secretary, Sir John Gilmore who is also Scottish, the member for Glasgow and I am assured that no police investigation will touch on me."

"This I can understand," said Burgess. "Much as it helps us in this specific case, it's actually one of the main reasons we need to bring down this entire privileged class structure of Britain. Those two young men will never see justice. I regret that you found this task necessary, Andrew, I trust you do not have to do it again.”

“I hope so, too, Guy. Now, how else may I serve you and the cause?”

“I can understand and even endorse your motivation,” said Major Anderson. “Working class peasants like those two have no right to be at Cambridge but killing them was extreme.”

“I think it helped me cement my position with the communist scum, Burgess and Blunt.”

“Very likely. And it seems the story you told has proved correct. I talked to Faraday and he received instructions from the Home Secretary not to pursue any action that could affect you. The same instructions have gone to the Police authorities in Cambridge. The case will be closed and marked ‘Unsolved.’ Faraday was relieved about that, he believes you show the sort of initiative he needs as an agent.”

“Excellent,” said Percivale.

* * *

### 17th October, 2025, Coastal NSW, Australia

“So Percivale’s father, the previous Baron was a double agent with MI6 and the Soviets?” said Melanie, clearly stunned by the information.

“What is not clear is the extent to which he was assisting either,” said Jack. “His motivations seem very right-wing, but there are some curious attitudes, possibly based on self-interest.”

"Not sure how this affects our case," said Melanie. "It may not, but we have to keep it in mind as things develop. Meanwhile, Alex, time for you to go looking for information over in Bellingen, we'll see if you find anything relevant."

"Yes, Ma'am," said Alex and left the office.

## Chapter 11

### *17th October, 2025, Coastal NSW, Australia*

"I have a suspicion this is going to get seriously complex," said Jack as Alex closed the door. "I think I'm going to get a hell of a paper out of it."

"I hope so," said Melanie. "What's next for you?"

Jack looked thoughtfully at her, as if pondering some tricky subject. "Melanie, while I have you alone, I'm going to be intrusive and ask if we can talk," he said.

Melanie seemed to stiffen up a little and she looked with some irritation at Jack. "What about?" she asked.

"We only talked briefly during our last case," said Jack, settling back in his office chair, trying to signal relaxation to her. "Professionally, I must tell you that I believe you have some emotional issues that are affecting your work performance. I consider it my responsibility to you and to your colleagues to try and identify and perhaps resolve them."

Melanie reacted to the signals and settled back in her seat in the same way as Jack had done, but the reserve in her face did not ease.

"So what do you want to talk about, Jack?"

"Well, I'm a bloke, so I'm really interested in that magnificent car of yours."

"The Gordon-Keeble? Yes, it's incredible, but it's not my first. As you know, Allen Miller blew my first one up as some sort of expression of his superiority at the end of our last case. But then he got an attack of conscience and went to great lengths to find another one and buy it for me."

"I certainly remember the effect the destruction had

on you. I found you in your room, curled up in a tight foetal position, emotionally shattered. It took a lot of professional care to get you back to normal. So tell me how you obtained that car and why that affected you so much."

"Didn't I tell you the first time you rode in it? I thought I did."

"Only the vaguest outline. Give me the full story."

Melanie, looked down at her lap in deep thought.

"Look at me, Jack," she said after a few moments. "I'm not being conceited when I say I'm quite beautiful. I've been told that since I was a toddler. 'Oh Melanie, how beautiful you are!' 'Oh Melanie, you should be a film star, you're so beautiful!' And then my father, 'Oh Melanie, why bother going to University, you're so beautiful you could be a top model and make millions,' blah blah blah. I tell you Jack, it's a bloody curse. I did go to University, I got a first-class honours degree in psychology, but could I get a job? I went to interviews and the women interviewing me refused to believe I wanted to actually do something useful, and the men couldn't stop staring at my boobs or my legs and couldn't believe I had a brain. Interviews were over before they began."

Jack said nothing, but his silence encouraged her to keep going.

"All the men I met, they had the same problem. If I got asked out on a date, it wasn't long before they wanted to get into a wrestling match with me and the idea that I might want to talk about real issues just never entered their little pea brains. Do you know, I never went to a single dance at University because everybody assumed I had some bloke in tow and didn't bother asking me?"

Jack nodded. "I've heard of that happening with some women before."

"I was always surrounded between classes in the coffee lounges at University and at lunch, throngs of blokes and girls, all worshipping at the feet of the Goddess – me. The blokes because they wanted the same thing and the girls because they really wanted to be like me and because they wanted to put up a protective barrier between them and their boyfriends. I may have been popular, but I didn't have any friends. Can you imagine how lonely this was?"

"I can," said Jack.

"Then in the second year of University, I met Scott. He was in the same faculty as I was, he was a nice-looking man, very bright, seemed popular with the girls. But I noticed that if he was in a group and I arrived, he immediately left. If he saw me in a group, he'd avoid it, even though some of the people would call him over. It bothered me. One day, I saw him sitting alone in the student lounge and I went up to him and started talking, raising that very question. He said he was never good at worshipping goddesses and didn't want to be part of the adoring throngs, so he'd always leave. I literally had to ask him to spend time with me and I found him increasingly attractive as time went on. He really did understand my problem, he knew from classes how bright I was and he treated me like a real person. We fell in love and we got engaged. I visited his family and we all got on well. I hadn't realised that the family was hugely rich."

"And the Gordon-Keeble was Scott's?"

"It was. He was a bit of a car nut and he said he'd found pictures of that car in a motoring magazine, did the research and found out what an amazing vehicle it was. There were few of them in existence, they'd gone out of production years before he was born, but he was able to track one down and buy it. It was the pride and joy of his life."

"And what happened?"

"A few weeks after graduation, we'd both got first-class honours and we had planned to get married a couple of months later and we went to a pub in King's Cross. As we left, some hooligan trying to be a big hero with that one-punch thing attacked him, hit him hard and Scott went down, cracked his head on the concrete. I called an ambulance, but Scott was dead on arrival at hospital. I read later that a group of people restrained the thug for the cops. I think he's still in prison."

"And the car?"

"A few weeks later, I discovered that Scott had left me the car in his will, together with a substantial sum for insurance and maintenance. It was all I had left of him and it was the most precious thing in my life."

"So when Miller destroyed it as a gesture, it took away something precious. I can understand your trauma from that."

"It was like losing him all over again."

"And now you've lived with the belief that men will always try and get into your knickers and are worthless, or if you get close to one, he'll die."

"That's about it, Jack. It's crazy, but I can't help it. So I treat men the same way they regard me, of no value except physical. They can provide the occasional essential service.”

“And what do you do about getting that essential service?”

“That’s more than I’m going to tell you, Jack. I’m going to get into my beautiful Gordon-Keeble and go home for the weekend.”

“I hope I’ve helped a little,” said Jack. “I suspect you’ve never told anyone about that, ever. Letting it out may have given some relief. I wish that could indicate that there are more Scotts out there and you’ll be open to a new relationship. Maybe even getting you to talk about it has planted the possibility in your mind.”

“It has helped a little. Thank you, Jack. But you know me from our last case. I’m a super-dominant, I can influence other people, they can’t influence me. Stop trying.”

She got out of her seat, picked up her handbag and walked out of the lounge.

* * *

Her suitcase was already packed and waiting on her bed. She took it back to the car and drove to the airport at Coffs Harbour. She left the car in secure, indoor parking and the commuter flight took her to Sydney Airport where she boarded the flight to Adelaide. In her hotel room, she unpacked, showered and dressed in a close-fitting red minidress that revealed a beautiful cleavage, put on the high heels and studied herself in the mirror.

“Good, time to be the drop-dead gorgeous Melanie,” she said aloud. “Let’s go hunting.”

Feeling the anticipation building up inside her, she left and took a taxi to a club she had researched. On entry, she stood for a second, surveying the scene and sensed the moment's silence that invariably greeted her appearance. The view looked good, she thought, and she took a table near one wall. A waiter appeared almost immediately and she recognised the reaction he showed, the usual stare at her legs and breasts. She ordered a cocktail and waited. It didn't take long.

"If you're alone, may I offer some company?"

She studied the newcomer. Not too tall, nice wide shoulders, a face that showed intelligence. *Not bad, he might do for tonight,* she thought to herself and waved at the seat opposite. He sat down and smiled at her.

"Rob Williams," he said.

"Melanie," she replied.

"No surname?"

"No surname."

A conversation developed along conventional lines, backgrounds, professions and the rest. Melanie remained uncommunicative in her usual style but found herself increasingly attracted to the man's voice and manner. He seemed to be permanently amused at the proceedings and she found that different from the usual eagerness and neediness of her normal prospective partners. After two rounds of drinks, she made it clear that a move to his home was the next order of things.

* * *

She woke as dawn broke and almost got up, ready to leave before the man woke up, as was her regular habit, but something stopped her. He had certainly been very satisfactory sexually, concentrating on her pleasures and needs, uncommon in her experience, and there was something about him that she found unusually appealing.

"Were you planning on leaving?" he asked.

She was startled, not realising he was awake.

"I should," she replied. "I'm hardly dressed for daytime."

"I was thinking we might head up to the Barossa and explore a few wineries," he said, lifting himself on one elbow and looking at her.

*Damn, but he's nice,* she thought and then astonished herself. "How about I go back to my hotel and change and see you back here about lunchtime?" she said.

"How about I run you back to your hotel, instead?"

"No," she said firmly. Some routines could not be broken. He must not know where she was staying and be able to find her identity. "I'll see you back here at noon. Give me the address."

He reached for his wallet, extracted a card and handed it to her.

"I hope I see you soon," he said.

"You will," she replied, continuing to astonish herself.

The day passed in relaxed happiness. She realised she hadn't enjoyed herself in such a youthful manner since her times with Scott. On the return to his home, she allowed herself to have dinner with him at a small restaurant and then by mutual agreement returned to his room for another exciting and highly satisfactory night. She left in the morning, still astonished at her reactions to this man and to breaking her normal rule of a different club and a different pickup each night. She flew home with her mind in turmoil.

## Chapter 12

### *20th October, 2025, Coastal NSW, Australia*

"Hello, Melanie."

Startled, Melanie looked up from the mound of paperwork she was analysing to write her report on the post-mortems being conducted on the bodies dug out of the field. She had sensed the monitor of her computer flicker but hadn't looked at it. Now she did and the shock was immense.

"Allen Miller! My god, Miller, where did you come from? Where are you?"

"You don't need to know either fact," said the face on the monitor. "All you need to know is that I'm here to help you."

"Help me? Miller, you're a murderer, you've stolen millions from governments and corporations around the world, sold state secrets and you're an illegal immigrant, apart from being wanted by the FBI back in the States. Why the hell would you want to help me? And where is this help to be directed?"

"Don't forget that I blew up your beautiful car, too," said Miller, a wide smile on his face. "But I did buy you another one and remember, all the royalties from my best-selling book about our previous adventure went to a series of charities. So I'm not really all that bad a guy."

"I'm well aware of all that, but it hardly makes you a saint. Now, what the hell do you want?"

"This current crime wave has become personal to me," said Miller.

"The details have not been made public. So knowing you, it must be that you broke into the police files and read all about it? I'm not surprised you could do that, nor that you could break in to talk to me, but why? What's personal? None of this has been made public so far."

"One of those bodies, Amelia Bishop," said Miller. "She was my aunt."

"Your aunt? Don't be silly. She'd lived in the area around Glenn Innes all her life, went to school there, she was born there for Christ's sake, she had no trace of any foreign accent... ah, of course."

"Exactly, of course. I created that entire background for her, updated all the necessary computers and I brought her to Australia when things got a bit hot for her in the USA."

"A bit hot? She was as crooked as you?"

"Who do you think taught me my craft? Gloria Carstairs was the greatest con-artist the world has ever seen, but a bit like me, the cops found a tiny mistake in one of her jobs and would have got to her before long. I got her out."

"Gloria Carstairs?"

"My father's sister," said Miller. "I've known her since I was two years old."

"How very sweet," said Melanie with contempt. "Again, how do you plan to help us?"

"For a start, how about I get into the Directory of Births, Marriages and Deaths and see what there is about Felicity Harrison and who she married?"

"You can do that?"

"Don't be silly, Melanie."

"I imagine that's easy for you."

"Couple of days, max. But I tell you what will be harder. You're trying to track down this Percivale turd, especially how did he get out of England without leaving a trace and if he's in Australia, how did he do that and what's his identity now? I'll bet Australia's national product that you're right, he's here in a top-level witness protection program arranged between the British government and Robert Menzies."

"Oh Christ, Miller, how did you know about that? And how did you know about Felicity Harrison? We've only talked about these things. There's nothing in the computer files so far."

"Dear Melanie, you are such a sweet innocent. Computers have microphones, you know."

"You've been listening in on our conversations?"

"Naturally. It's good to see that bright young man, Alex helping you out and that Jack Savage is doing the same. Clever bloke that. Oh, and congratulations on your promotion, too."

Melanie didn't respond. The thought that Miller had been listening in to the discussions was unnerving.

"But like I said," continued Miller, "I want to get whoever killed my auntie. She was the only relative I liked, and I want the bastard who did it."

"I'll talk to the others," said Melanie. "I can't hide the fact that we need the help. This one is complex."

"I'll get back to you," said Miller and the image vanished from the monitor.

# Chapter 13

## *20<sup>th</sup> November, 2025, Coastal NSW, Australia*

"Father Thomas? I'm Alex Welland. We spoke earlier."

"Alex, yes, hello, nice to meet you! You want to look through our registry of marriages for a few years back? Can I ask why?"

"It's a police matter, Father, I didn't want to talk about it on the phone, it's all rather hush-hush."

"How intriguing! Can you tell me more now that you're here?"

"Not much, Father. There may well be a national security issue here."

"Even more intriguing. Now, I did get a letter from your senior officer that you'd be coming, so just to be sure, can you show me your warrant card?"

"Of course."

Alex took out his wallet and presented his identity card. The priest studied it with some intensity and handed it back to him.

"Okay, that all seems legal," he said. "Let's go and have a look at our books." He led the way into the church and into a small office. He took down a thick, leather-bound book and placed it on the table. "The year and the names you are looking for?"

"The year is any time after 1964 and I only have the name of the bride, Felicity Harrison. There is no guarantee that she was married in this church, but this was her home town."

"Alex, this seems wasteful. Wouldn't you have more success with National Registry of Births, Marriages and Deaths?"

"We would, but for two issues," said Alex. "The first is that their files for that period aren't computerized, they're still on microfilm and it would take ages for them to find the record, even if they wanted to. It would take a court order for that request. The second is the thing I mentioned before, the national security issue. The government might not want this record found."

The priest looked disturbed. "Am I breaking the law then by permitting this search?"

"Is it illegal to look back through these records?"

"No, it's not."

"Then you are not breaking the law. Any local historian might make the same request."

The priest looked more relaxed. "Okay then. But how do you know the person is Anglican? Why not Catholic? Or perhaps they were married by a civil celebrant or equivalent?"

"It's almost a certainty that the groom was Anglican," said Alex. "As to the rest, I can't be certain. I will have to check all the Anglican churches in the area, it could take some time."

"And you know the bride came from this town?"

"Yes. We've had several sources of information confirming that. I've also been to the town council, and they found records of the family living here till 1980 when they moved away."

The priest opened the heavy volume and searched back to find the year in question.

"It will be at the earliest, October, 1964," said Alex. "More likely later, however."

The next forty minutes were spent in silence, the only sound coming from the pages being turned. Alex watched, sitting at the priest's left side, reading down the hand-written columns in the registry.

"Ah!" said the priest. "This is it. March 15th, 1966. Felicity Harrison, Spinster of this Parish, aged twenty-one, married Andrew James Macfarlane of Bondi, New South Wales, aged thirty."

Alex let out his breath, not realizing he'd been breathing with difficulty for some time. "Who conducted the marriage?"

"My father," replied the priest.

"And he would have examined birth certificates of both parties?"

"Standard procedure. And my dad was a stickler for doing things by the book."

"Do you have the address for the groom?"

The priest pulled a notepad from a desk drawer and wrote down the details, tore the page off and handed it to Alex.

"This is amazing," said Alex. "Let me tell you a little of what this is about. We have several indications that this Macfarlane bloke is not who he claims, but a fugitive from the United Kingdom. But if he has an apparently legitimate birth certificate, then it's a sure thing that he's in some sort of witness protection program set up by the Australian government."

"Good grief!" The priest looked stunned, staring at Alex with wide eyes.

"So I never told you that and now it's time I headed back home," said Alex. He shook hands with the priest and walked out, found his car and headed back to his home police station.

* * *

"It's a valid address," said Melanie. "I called the local station, they checked the files, but it's an apartment block that got pulled down over twenty years ago for a complete rebuild."

"Any record of an Andrew Macfarlane?" asked Jack.

"Nothing," replied Melanie. "But that only means he didn't commit any crimes."

"And there's no proof that he's the missing Baron Percivale either," said Alex.

"We could use some help there," said Jack. "If it is Percivale as we suspect, he's in some witness protection program arranged at very high level. I don't know how we can break through that."

"I wish we had that Allen Miller bloke," said Alex. "I bet he could find the answers."

Melanie laughed. "I have some information on that subject," she said.

# Chapter 14

## *21st October, 2025, Coastal NSW, Australia*

"Inspector, you have a visitor," said the desk sergeant on the phone. His tone seemed agitated. "He's just walked straight through…"

"Detective Inspector Melanie Carter?"

Melanie put down the phone and looked up, just as Jack and Alex did the same. They saw a dark, lean man in his forties, close-cut hair, bright blue eyes and average height. He wore a dark blue suit, a white shirt and a plain blue tie. Something sent warning flurries up her back.

"Yes," she said, somehow feeling unwilling to show any warmth. "Do you normally just waltz into police stations without officially announcing yourself?"

"And you will be Senior Detective Constable Alex Welland?" continued the newcomer, ignoring her comment and looking at Alex.

"Correct," said Alex, almost radiating hostility at the coldness of the man.

"And before you ask, I am Professor Jack Savage," said Jack, showing the same reaction. "But I'm sure you know that, already."

"Thank you, Professor, I do."

The man walked in and shut the door behind him.

"Gordon Porter, ASIO," he said. He turned his lapel over to reveal a badge

Determined not to show the anxiety running through her, Melanie picked up her coffee mug and took a sip, not taking her eyes off the security agent.

"Really? she said. "This is a small police department in a small country town far from the big city. What are we doing that attracts the attention of the Australian Secret Intelligence Organisation?"

"Endangering national security, Detective Inspector."

"Please explain how," Melanie said.

"Not my task to explain how," replied Porter. "Only to give you the instructions. You will cease all investigations into the Macfarlane family immediately. You will not communicate with them again or risk prosecution by the Federal Government."

"How interesting," said Jack and got to his feet, advancing on the agent who flinched nervously. "Let's have a look at that badge, shall we?"

The man made no further move as Jack turned back his lapel and studied the badge.

"That's a badge, alright," said Jack. "But it's not the official one, it's far too small. Actually, I know that there isn't an official ASIO badge. It's more like the Australian Federal Police badge and any mug can obtain one of those. What else have you got?"

His face expressionless, the man took out a wallet from his breast pocket and opened it to Jack's gaze.

Porter remained still as Jack repeated his examination.

"So, Counter Terrorism Unit, Field Agent Gordon Porter. Yeah, okay, you're ASIO," said Jack and handed back the wallet, returning to his seat.

At last, Porter's rigid stance eased. "Well, thank Christ for that," he said. "You buggers could scare the crap out of me like that."

The atmosphere in the room warmed up several degrees. Melanie smiled and saw Porter's expression change as usually happened when she smiled at a man. She pointed at the last chair in the room against the wall.

"Take a seat," she said and waited until he had pulled it over into the line around her desk. "Now, what the hell's going on?"

"Exactly what I said," replied Porter. "You have to leave the family alone. You will cause the governments of both Australia and the UK considerable embarrassment if you don't."

"Because Baron Percivale is in a witness protection program, one arranged between the governments of the UK and Australia, is that why?" said Melanie.

Porter stared at her. "Christ alive, you know that? How the hell did you find that out?"

"We didn't find it, but it became an increasingly obvious conclusion. It's what we do," said Melanie. "We dig up information and we draw conclusions. We're detectives, right?"

Porter shook his head violently. "That's supposed to be top-secret stuff," he said. "There's no way you could get it. I have to ask how you did it?"

"You're a copper, Gordon," said Jack. "You know how often secrets fall before dedicated, untiring, relentless leg work. Blame young Alex here, he found it by simply grinding away at existing facts and data. We don't have actual proof of this, but the conclusions based on what we found out are pretty damned obvious."

Porter looked sideways at Alex. "You'll go far, young man," he said. "Providing somebody doesn't kill you first."

"I'll take my chances," said Alex.

Porter returned his gaze to Melanie.

"All right, so you probably know the whole story. Neither government wants it known that they've helped a miserable cheat run away from his obligations because he was titled gentry. So that story will be suppressed. Same with the bodies in the field. It is not publicly known that the family owns that field. The identity of the Macfarlanes will remain hidden. The case will be closed."

"And if we keep on working on it?" Melanie felt hostile and frustrated that her case was being shut down for political reasons.

"We know that the Scottish police obtained a court order to force the trustees to reveal the ownership of the property here," said Porter. "They were obligated to inform MI6 when that happened and that was obviously on your initiative. They advised us of the communication. Clever, Inspector Carter, but potentially dangerous. You must not continue."

"Do you sometimes hate what you do?" asked Melanie.

Porter grimaced. "This is not the sort of thing I joined ASIO to do, protecting political heavies from their crimes, but I do realise that letting the story out would cause difficulties for the government and the ultimate end may justify it."

"So we all have to live in a state of confused bewilderment about how or why this whole thing is happening?" said Melanie. "After we've found out so much, we have to pretend to lose interest?"

"Essentially, yes," said Porter. "But I'll break some of the rules and tell you something of what we know about this appalling family. Have you ever wondered about how that Fabergé chess set ended up in the Baron's possession?"

"We have," said Melanie. "If the history is true, it was a gift to the Czar of Russia, passed on to a top military official as a reward for services. But that would indicate some illicit transaction. Do you know something?"

"I do," said Porter. "And it shows something about the ugliness of the family. This has never been revealed."

"Does it have anything to do with the involvement of the ninth Baron Percivale with the Cambridge Five?" asked Jack, a smile on his face hiding the explosive nature of his question. He got the reaction he expected.

Porter stared at him. "Jesus, Harold CHRIST, is there anything you people don't know?" he said, his voice harsh with tension.

"A hell of a lot," said Melanie. "But as we said, dogged, plodding persistence often pays off."

Porter took a breath. "Yes," he said. "It's all about the Cambridge Five, though they weren't known as such until the nineties when the fifth traitor, John Cairncross was uncovered. Let me give you story."

### June, 1962, Percivale Hall, Surrey, England

"I am extremely grateful to have the chance to visit you here, My Lord."

Percivale pulled a face. "Mr Blunt, this all happened

just a few days ago and I can't get used to being a Baron. My name is William, feel free to use that."

"Thank you. As I said when I called you, my name is Anthony Blunt, and I knew your father at Cambridge. My closest friend, Guy Burgess and I were both members of the chess club with Andrew and Guy lectured him in his first year. We were a close group while he was there and maintained contact for a while before events got in the way."

"Odd, he never mentioned either of you," said Percivale. "And frankly, Mr Blunt, my father may have known these people, but I have to assure you, he was not involved in their activities."

"I understand that," said Blunt. "However, may I take this opportunity to offer my condolences on his tragically early death and congratulations on your ascendency to the Baronetcy?"

Percivale nodded. "Thank you," he said. "The old fool was too fond of his fast cars and overly-impressed with his driving skills. I'm just relieved nobody else paid for his foolishness. Now, why did you call and ask to see me?"

"I have an offer to present to you," said Blunt. "How would you like to come to Moscow to play in a series of exhibition chess matches against some of the world's best players? You would be an honoured guest of the Soviet Union."

Percivale looked at him, wide-eyed. "How are you in a position to offer me something like that?"

Blunt smiled. "I received a letter from Guy, sent to me from his home in Moscow via several roundabout routes and we both feel you should have it, given your extraordinary talents you have been showing in chess tournaments. You have obviously inherited more than the title from your late father. He was a brilliant player, beat me easily several times. You would be a huge attraction at the high-profile tournament that is being planned."

"You didn't explain how you can offer me this," said Percivale.

"Well, there I have to open up some major secrets, My Lord Baron. I didn't introduce myself when I called, other than give my name. But I have a rather specialised position in society. I am the Surveyor of the Queen's Pictures to Her Majesty the Queen, Elizabeth the Second and I held the same position for her father, King George the Sixth."

Percivale looked at him with some scepticism. "You are *what?*"

"Essentially, I am the Queen's art curator. As such, I have access to almost all art collections in the world because nobody would refuse me looking at their works. I have visited the Hermitage a few times because I happen to have a rather special relationship with the ruling Communist Party of the Soviet Union. When I was in the Hermitage in Leningrad on a previous visit, I saw in the museum a rather beautiful chess set, apparently made by Fabergé for the Czar some time before the Revolution of 1917."

"That cannot be, Mr Blunt. I have that set in my possession."

"Yes, Baron, you do. But do you know how you came to have that in your possession?"

"My father gave it to me."

"And how did he acquire it?"

"Actually, I have no idea. He said his father had given it to him, but he never told me how he got it."

"Then I can assure you, you do have the original and the one in the Hermitage is a copy."

"How do you know that?"

"Let me tell you, Baron. It's an interesting story."

* * *

### *April, 1917, Moscow, USSR*

"Ambassador Percivale, you do my house great honour."

The heavy-set, elderly Russian rose to his feet from his armchair as Douglas Percivale was shown in by an aide-de-camp in full Russian army uniform.

"The honour is mine, Dmitri Sabelyevich Shuvayev," said Percivale as they shook hands.

"Come, have a seat, let me pour you some of this excellent vodka," said Shuvayev.

Drinks poured and both men settled back in their seats, they lifted their glasses.

*"Za vashe zdarovye,"* said Percivale.

Shuvayev laughed. "You have learned Russian well," he said. "To your health, Ambassador. I knew when we met at the celebrations last week that we would get on well, especially when we discovered a mutual love of chess."

"Worthy celebrations indeed," said Percivale. "Being appointed Minister of War to the Imperial Russian armed forces is a remarkable achievement, especially in this time of war against the German hordes."

"Not an easy task," agreed Shuvayev. "And there are some points we must discuss. So, let me refill your glass and then you will see that I have set up a chess board at the table. These things are best discussed over a game of our great Russian pastime. Bring your glass."

A few minutes later, Percivale sat down at the table and stared at the chess set.

"This is utterly beautiful," he said in a whisper, as he gently touched the King piece.

The Russian stroked his luxuriant white beard. "Indeed it is," he said. "It was commissioned by the Czar from the famed Fabergé as a gift to one of my predecessors, Alexandr Roediger in 1905. But when he fell out of favour, he passed it on to me. I rarely take it out of the storage, but tonight there is a special purpose."

"You honour me, Dmitri," said Percivale. "I have never played with such beautiful pieces. Shall we choose our sides?"

With Percivale playing white, the game started with conventional moves. The next thirty minutes passed in silence, broken only by an occasional grunt of appreciation from the Russian of a move by Percivale. Forty minutes later, Shuvayev tilted his king on its side in surrender.

"You play a serious game, Douglas," he said with a smile. "That needs another drink."

The formalities again concluded, Shuvayev sat back in his seat.

"Now we must talk, Douglas," he said. His tone indicated tension. Percivale sat still.

"We will win this war," the Russian continued. "But this is not the end of the matter. The Czar is not popular, the people are starving and they have suffered greatly from the privations of the winter now coming to an end. We have lost over a million and a half of our soldiers to the Germans so far and almost as many civilians from sickness, starvation and wounds. I hear ideas from many of the ruling classes that the people will not stand for much more. Even more critical, the army may not continue to support us. I do fear that revolution is a possibility, even a probability."

Percivale drank his vodka in one gulp.

"I hear the same from my people, Dmitri," he said. "We are seriously worried about the extent of disruption throughout the Russian Empire if this happens."

"Then this is what I will ask of you, Douglas," said the Russian. "Get my family to safety in England. I cannot leave, I must serve my Czar, my country and prosecute the war to the very end. If revolution comes then, which I believe it will, so be it, I will take my chances. But my family must be safe. Can you do this for me?"

"I believe I can," said Percivale. "I have influence with many people in the corridors of power in London. I have a house in England which could be a safe refuge for them. Get them out of Russia as soon as you can, Dmitri, to a neutral country perhaps in Scandinavia and as soon as the war is over, I will be able to bring them to England. They will receive my hospitality until such time as they can make their own lives."

Shuvayev gestured at the chess set. "This is your fee, Douglas. I hope it will be adequate."

Percivale's eyes widened. "Yes, Dmitri Sabelyevich, I assure you, this is adequate. But I must ask you, can you do this? Is such a gift from the Czar to one of his ministers simply a symbolic loan? Could Roediger give it to you?"

Shuvayev laughed. "You are a true diplomat, Douglas and you understand diplomacy. You are quite right, I do not have legal ownership of this beautiful work of art. But I had a copy made by a fine jeweller in Norway. There is no way the oafish thugs who will take over this country will be able to tell true Fabergé genius, they will be content with the copy when they take over."

"Dmitri, I agree and it would be tragic to let such commoners own this. I will take it back to England with me and display it only to the people who will appreciate it."

"Then let us drink to my family's safety in England and to Russia's survival of the upcoming revolution." Shuvayev refilled their glasses and both men downed the contents in one gulp.

### *June, 1962, Percivale Hall, Surrey, England*

"I had no idea," exclaimed the Baron. "But how do you know all that?"

"Not difficult," said Blunt. "As I said, I have extraordinary levels of contact with the rulers of the Soviet Union. I learnt that the War Minister, Shuvayev was removed from his position after the Revolution and later died in prison. In the process, his captors extracted the story of his connection with your father and how his family was able to escape to England."

"That worries me," said Percivale. "It means they know that the set in the Hermitage is a copy and that I probably have the original. Does this mean I might get a visit from the Russians one day?"

"No, you are safe, My Lord," said Blunt. "Our own security forces, MI6 also know the full story and they keep a careful eye on you at all times."

"I suppose that's a relief," said Percivale, but his face reflected unease. "Though I can't feel comfortable knowing that I'm being watched by MI5. But surely my father didn't have the power to arrange such a thing. The family is nothing special, a Baron is the lowest title on the scale of nobility. How did he do it?"

Blunt repeated his tight smile.

"That's another fascinating story," he said.

### February, 1919, 10 Downing Street, London

"Ambassador Percivale, Prime Minister," said the secretary.

Lloyd George remained seated at his desk as Douglas Percivale was shown into the office. It was well known that there was no liking between the two men and that the Prime Minister had never agreed with Percivale's appointment as Ambassador to Russia. But he had not been in office when the then Prime Minister Asquith had made the appointment. They did not shake hands.

"So, Baron Percivale, what brings you to my office?" He waved at the seat across from his desk and Percivale took it.

"Matters of international importance, Prime Minister."

"International importance, Baron? You no longer have the role of Ambassador, you have no other roles at all, as far I can see, other than your rare appearances in the House of Lords."

"This stems from my time in Russia. Prior to the revolution, I made a commitment to the War Minister, Dmitri Sabelyevich Shuvayev to bring his family to England and offer them sanctuary in my house in Surrey. He was able to get them to Sweden where they now wait for permission to come here. I want you to grant them residency and early citizenship in the United Kingdom."

Lloyd George sat back with a look of contempt.

"Now just why would I do such a thing? The Soviet government would cause difficulties if we openly assist the family of a man they considered to be a Czarist supporter."

"Prime Minister, it is well known that you wanted to offer sanctuary here to the family of Czar Nicholas, but you gave in to pressure from other sources, especially the King. And as a result, the Czar and his family were all brutally murdered by the Communists. Do you want people to see your hypocrisy in refusing sanctuary to another family that had served the Czar loyally?"

"A War Minister is hardly in the same league as the Czar," said Lloyd-George. "Especially one who served for only a short while, one of several during the years since the turn of the century. Nobody in England has heard of this Shuvayev man and nobody could care a damn about him or his family. Baron, you have wasted your time and more critically, mine." He turned to his secretary who had been sitting attentively against the wall, taking notes. "Miles, show the Baron out." He turned his attention back to the papers on his desk.

But Percivale had not stirred. The secretary had risen to his feet and now stood near the Prime Minister's desk. Lloyd George looked up in irritation.

"Still here, Baron?"

"I am not finished, Prime Minister. I suggest you send this young man out of the room for the next few minutes. You do not want him to hear the rest of my information."

Lloyd George stared at him for a full minute and then nodded at the secretary who walked out of the room. "What the hell are you playing at, Percivale?" he said. No title was used.

Percivale took a paper out of his briefcase and slid it across the desk. "I'm not playing, Prime Minister."

Lloyd George looked down at the sheet and his jaws clenched in fury. He read the whole page and looked back at the Baron.

"Who else knows about this?" he asked, his voice harsh.

"Only the woman in question," said Percivale. "Her mother is dead, she is the only survivor. But many people in your hometown of Llanystumdwy in Caernarvonshire know what you got up to in your youth, even if they don't know about this particular incident."

Lloyd George smiled without warmth. "I congratulate you on your pronunciation of my home town," he said. "You must have been practicing."

Percivale said nothing.

The Prime Minister looked down again at the document.

"This is a photograph of the original. Do you actually have that original and if so, where is it?"

"Don't be ridiculous, Prime Minister. Yes, I do have the original, and it's quite secure. You could never find it."

"And is this all you have, Percivale? If you release this to the world, I might certainly suffer some embarrassment, but that will fade in the face of the work this government is doing to recover from the war."

"Quite possibly, Prime Minister. But what if I tell the world about the criminal deal you made with the arms dealer in Derby to sell surplus materials to countries in Eastern Europe? And there is also the matter of the young woman in Aberystwyth when you were a young lawyer. You wouldn't survive that little collection of scandals."

"And do you have similar materials on other people in power?"

"Call it a hobby of mine, Prime Minister. You'd be amazed at the things you hear from all those patriotic British nobles in the House of Lords and how easy it is to collect physical evidence. I could bring this country to its knees if I wanted to."

Lloyd George seemed rigid, his face pale. "Alright, Percivale," he said after a moment of silence. "You win this one. I'll do as you ask. Give the details to my secretary and this family will be granted safe residency in this country."

Percivale reached across and took the paper. "You have my word, Prime Minister, nobody will ever know about this."

"Your word? Is that worth anything from a man who blackmails his Prime Minister?"

"That's your worry," said Percivale and stood up. "Good day to you, sir," he said and walked out.

## *June, 1962, Percivale Hall, Surrey, England*

"Good god!" said Percivale. "My father had blackmail material on the British Prime Minister?"

"Indeed he did and he used it ruthlessly," said Blunt. "We believe that he had a lot more than that as well."

William sat back, with a shock of realisation running through him.

"So that's what all that stuff was," he whispered.

Blunt said nothing.

"Some years ago, I was still a teenager, my dad showed me a pile of papers," continued Percivale. "He said they could make anything I wanted possible if I used the material carefully. He didn't let me look at the material, he didn't think I'd understand it then, but later I should review it."

"And what happened to that material?" Blunt had tensed up and was sitting forward in his seat.

"He said he had put it all in a safety security box in a bank in Switzerland. He gave me the security codes and key, told me to guard them carefully and when I was a few years older, I should go to the bank and have a look at the papers."

"And have you done that yet?"

"No, but now that I've realised what's there, I'll make the trip soon."

Blunt relaxed and sat back. "Indeed you should, My Lord. Meanwhile, back to my original offer. Will you come to Moscow? The contacts you make could help you enormously politically as well as financially."

"How could I refuse?" said William. "We must have a drink to seal this." He pressed a button on his desk and waited. A young man appeared at the door.

"I have a remarkably old and gentle brandy," said Percivale. "I can surely interest you in a nip?"

"You most certainly can, William," said Blunt and Percivale nodded at the servant. A few minutes later, he reappeared with a tray. As he held it for Blunt, he stared hard at him, then moved to Percivale to hold the tray for him.

Half an hour later, Blunt left to return to London.

"May I say something, My Lord?"

Percivale looked up in astonishment. In the months the man had been with him, he had never spoken unless spoken to.

"Er… yes, what is it, er.. Hunter?"

"Forgive the intrusion My Lord, but do you know who that man is?"

"Of course I do, he told me. He's Anthony Blunt, he's the Surveyor of the Queen's Pictures, he was at Trinity College with my father."

"He is also Sir Anthony Blunt, KCVO, knighted in 1956 and a professor in Art History at London University."

"Then he gets higher and higher in my estimation. Now, what is all this about?"

"What you don't know, My Lord is that he is a known agent of the Soviet KGB and has been passing government information to them for years."

"The KGB?"

"The Soviet spying agency," said Hunter.

Percivale stared at him, eyes wide open. "The Soviet... he's a communist?"

"Tried and true, My Lord," said Hunter. "For many years. Together with a few other traitors who were at Trinity College, Cambridge, men like Donald Maclean, Kim Philby and Guy Burgess who was one of your father's lecturers. We believe there are more of them, all in high government positions."

Percivale was having difficulties breathing. "How the hell do you know all this, Hunter?" he gasped.

"It's not difficult, My Lord. The story of the Cambridge group is well known by now. I followed the story out of interest and I recognised Blunt. I doubt he'll remain free for much longer. But given who and what he is, it's certain that the offer of a chess tournament was a bribe, part of the process of recruiting you to their group."

"This is all too much," said Percivale. "But dammit Hunter, if our security forces know all this, why haven't they been arrested and hanged as traitors?"

"I'm sure our people would like to, but I suspect they gain more by leaving them in place and seeing who they deal with, who they make contact with. They can probably also feed them false information to confuse the KGB people. I've heard that is common practice when spies are unearthed."

"Well, I want no more to do with any of this," said Percivale. "Make sure Blunt is never allowed back in this house."

Hunter nodded with a smile. "I'll make certain My Lord. Now, is there anything I can do for you?"

Percivale looked at the floor for a few moments. "In that case," he said, "bring me another brandy."

"Yes, My Lord," said Hunter. "And may I suggest that you do not go to Moscow. You may never return."

### *October, 1962, Geneva, Switzerland*

"Thank you, Baron Percivale, that is all satisfactory," said the tall, slim man in a formal dark suit. "I will unlock the box and then leave you alone and the door will be locked when I leave. You can then use your key to undo the second lock and open the box to remove the contents. When you are ready to leave, please return the box to its compartment, lock your section and ring the buzzer on the desk. I will return, lock the second section and then escort you from the building."

With a small bow, the bank official did as he had indicated, leaving William alone in the room lined with locked security boxes. A few minutes later, William had a metal case on the desk, and he opened it to see the sheaf of papers. Breathing hard, he laid several papers on the desk. Some were obviously originals of varying ages, a few of them yellow from the passage of decades. Others were photographs of originals.

William selected four and studied them.

"Oh my god," he said, his hands starting to tremble. He took two more and the level of shock increased further. Struggling to control his breathing and the trembling of his hands, he selected just four more of the papers, put them in his briefcase and returned the rest to the safety box. Waiting five minutes to restore his composure, he pressed the button on the desk.

## 21st *October, 2025, Coastal NSW, Australia*

"Good grief," said Jack. "He blackmailed Lloyd George?"

"Not a thing we'd like revealed," said Porter. "And there's no doubt he did a lot more over the years. Now you can understand why we have to put a gag on you."

Melanie nodded. "We understand. We're public servants also, we must obey a request from ASIO like this, and we will. Can we contact you if anything changes?"

Porter stood up. "Sometimes we have to do despicable things. I'm glad you understand. Here's my card for when you need it. I'll leave you to it."

"But I must ask," said Melanie. "How do you know all that? A lot of those things happened in private in Percivale's home."

Porter smiled. "We've communicated with MI6 for decades. We had an inside source in the Percivale household for years, ever since we discovered that his father had been involved with the Cambridge mob."

He left with a friendly wave from the others.

"I suppose we have to live with this," said Alex.

"You may have to, I don't," said a voice from the computer on Melanie's desk.

"Oh shit!" said Melanie. "Have you been listening in to all that? I thought I'd turned the computer off."

"Of course I have," said Miller. "And none of it surprised me."

"Then please stay out of it," said Melanie. "You could get us into a whole heap of trouble."

"No worries," said Miller. "What I plan to do could not involve you in any way at all."

The screen went blank.

"Oh bugger!" said Melanie. "That bastard is going to blow up the world."

# Chapter 15

## *6th December, 2025, Coastal NSW, Australia*

"Good morning, Melanie."

Without surprise, Melanie looked at her computer monitor.

"Good morning, Allen. Two calls in a row? Do you have anything of interest for me?"

"I sure do. How about you get your colleagues in here for a chat?"

Sensing Miller's excitement and reacting to it with the thought that he really did have something vital to tell them, Melanie touched her intercom and summoned the other two.

"So you told them I'd introduced myself back into the case?" said Miller.

"You were listening in on the conversation?"

"No, not this time, I just assumed you'd tell them. I was working hard at breaking into a few very high-level security systems."

"I daren't ask," said Melanie and looked up as Jack and Alex entered her office. "Look who's here," she said and turned the monitor round for them to see.

"Holy shit!" said Alex.

"I was wondering when you'd show up again," said Jack.

Melanie moved her chair round to the other side of her desk to join the other two with their view of the monitor. "Allen, you said you had useful information for us," she said.

"I do. But good morning, gentlemen, nice to see you both again."

"Where are you, Miller?" demanded Alex.

Miller smiled in a friendly manner. "Don't be silly, Alex. And my name isn't Miller, not anymore."

"Of course not," said Jack. "So do we understand that the only reason for this altruistic offer of help to us is because one of the victims is a relation of yours?"

"My Auntie Gloria," said Miller. "My favourite relative and my mentor since I was a kid. But no, that's not the only reason. I might have stolen millions from my government and corporations in the USA, but I'm still an American and I have a deep loathing of snotty-nosed British nobility, always have had. If that Percivale creep did kill her, I want him to face the consequences."

"So what have you got?" asked Jack.

"The first piece of information for you is that the woman who got involved with Percivale is Felicity Harrison, she was an Australian from..."

"Bellingen," broke in Alex. "And she married a bloke called Andrew James Macfarlane from Bondi. Yes, we know."

Miller looked startled. "You've found that, have you? I'm impressed. How did you do that?"

"Standard grinding leg work," said Alex. "Real policing. How did you? None of that data was on a computer."

"Actually, it was," said Miller. "Not anywhere you could have found it. So, great work, Alex, but let me take you a long way ahead." He reached to one side and picked up a glass of wine, took a sip and returned the glass to where it had been.

"As you said, Andrew James Macfarlane is Baron Percivale. And that comes from some top-secret files in the computers of your country's spooks. I found the personal letters between the British Prime Minister of the time, Alex Douglas Home and your Prime Minister, Robert Menzies. Douglas Home talked to Menzies explaining that Percivale had got himself into dangerously embarrassing circumstances that would reflect badly on the British Government if the media got hold of it. He needed to disappear completely and asked Menzies' help in hiding Percivale in complete anonymity. Menzies agreed without hesitation and instructed his spooks to set it up. The conversations were followed up by letters confirming the agreement."

"Doesn't surprise me at all," said Jack. "Menzies was the Anglophile to beat all Anglophiles and would have grovelled before the British PM in his eagerness to score brownie points with the Poms."

"So it seems," said Miller with a nod. "Percivale was flown to Australia in an Australian military transport, didn't go through immigration and was given a new identity, passport, a record of his birth in New South Wales and everything he needed to be a perfectly camouflaged Australian citizen."

"Nice to have friends in high places," said Melanie.

"For sure," said Miller.

"How has he managed financially?" asked Alex.

"More high-level help," said Miller. "Menzies' spooks set up a complete and mythical family for him and then a two-million-pound inheritance from the mythical father. The Brits sent the money here hidden in a trade deal and as an inheritance, he only paid taxes on the income from the principle."

"I'm not sure about that," said Jack. "Bear with me as I check something." He took out his phone and tapped in some entries, studying the responses. "Yes, I can't see how that worked. Percivale disappeared in June, 1964. The British Conservative government was voted out in October of that year. The arrangement between Douglas Home and Menzies must have surely taken a lot longer than that to set up and there's no way the Labour Government of Harold Wilson would have gone along with it."

"The letter from Douglas Home to Menzies was dated the twentieth of June and was sent in the diplomatic bag," said Miller. "So Percivale must have contacted his Prime Minister almost immediately after that chess match. Menzies would have initiated the rescue within days and Percivale's flight occurred before the change of government. It seems it was all hidden from the new Prime Minister by the Civil Service Mandarins in Britain. It's well known that a good number of those people are graduates of Eton, Cambridge and Oxford, just as Percivale and Douglas Home were and they looked after one of their own, without bothering to inform that leftie, commie, pinko socialist, Harold Wilson."

"How the upper class live, eh?" said Melanie. "What else have you got?"

"He filed his returns every year until the present," said Miller. "I've had a look at them in the Australian Tax Office computer files."

"So he's still alive?" said Melanie.

"Not only that, but he also has family," said Miller. "Felicity gave birth to a girl called Leah in 1970, a boy called Paul in 1974 and a second son called Andrew four years after that. I can't find any records of any of them getting married, they all go by the family name of Macfarlane."

"You looked at their tax returns too, I suppose?" asked Jack. "So you know where they live."

"Damn right, Jack. And that's the interesting thing." Miller paused and reached down for another sip of wine. "They all live very near each other in a private compound within a few kilometres of where the bodies were hidden."

"So we can easily find them," said Melanie. "And that may solve another problem. Assuming Percivale and maybe his kids committed these murders, how did they dig graves and bury them without being seen or heard? I know that area is remote, not another house other than theirs for a long way, but still, you'd think somebody would have spotted a night-time excavation in process."

"I know the property," said Alex. "It's a sort of compound within a gated area. I haven't had a look at it, just driven past a few times, but I think there are several buildings."

"Have a look at the council records," said Melanie. "There are probably aerial photos too, probably even Google Maps will have a few shots. We have to do a full safety check before fronting up there. Check for registered guns, dogs, heavy machinery, all the usual stuff."

"Will do, Ma'am, "said Alex. "But damn, I can't help but think of something I'd like to see." A half smile flickered on his face.

"What's that?" asked Melanie.

"Getting Peter Chancellor up here and having him accost Percivale. That would be dramatic as hell."

"Hah!" Jack exploded with amusement, but Melanie didn't echo the reaction.

"Alex, that would be disastrous, for God's sake, don't do it! It would warn them off before we get completely informed of everything. Don't do it! We'd get hammered by the authorities."

"No, Ma'am, I won't. But I couldn't help thinking of it."

"I understand, it's a most entertaining idea, but it could kill the investigation."

"Yes, Ma'am, I understand."

"Good. Okay, go and do the safety check and we'll think about when and how we'll visit that compound."

"How are we going to get away with this after the ASIO warning?" said Jack.

"We'll work out some tale," said Melanie.

"I'll see if I can help with my particular expertise," said Miller. "And I'm sending you some of those documents now, particularly the letters between the British and Australian Prime Ministers.

Alex rose to his feet and gave a small wave at Miller's face on the monitor.

"See you, Alex," said Miller and waved back as Alex left the room.

* * *

It took only twenty minutes for Alex to report back.

"Four residential homes and one general purpose building, apparently used as an entertainment or gathering place with full kitchen and bathroom facilities. All the constructions are kit homes, added over the years as the kids grew up."

"A real family compound," said Jack.

"So it seems," said Alex. "We have Andrew James Macfarlane, also known to us at least as Baron William Percivale in house number one. House number two contains Leah Felicity Macfarlane, aged fifty-five. House number three is the residence of Paul James Macfarlane, aged fifty-one and the last one houses Andrew Lachlan Macfarlane, aged forty-seven. There are no dogs registered in any establishment. Each house has a .22 rifle licenced to the owner, each of them has a driving licence, no felonies or offences recorded. The senior Macfarlane and the daughter, Leah each own a Toyota Landcruiser. Each of the brothers has a Toyota Yaris. There is one other vehicle, registered also to Leah, a John Deere backhoe."

"All stock standard equipment for families living with farmable property," said Melanie. "Nothing unusual there."

"What happened to Percivale's wife, Felicity?" asked Jack.

"Nothing known as yet," replied Alex. "But she's not registered as a resident there. Depending on when they divorced or she died, the records could be in the computer files. Maybe you could ask Miller for some assistance, Ma'am?"

"If he appears again, I will. Okay, gentlemen, the property seems to be safe enough, at least on the face of it. Time for us to pay a visit."

"Some day," said Jack as he packed up his briefcase, "I'd love to know just how Miller became this world-beating computer hacker. The motivation and the triggers would make another white paper for publication."

"Lots of luck," said Melanie. "That guy is a locked and chained book."

## Chapter 16

### *April, 1969, Wilmette, Illinois, USA*

"My mom says you're really rich, Aunt Gloria, but she doesn't know how you got that way. She says you must have stolen it."

The attractive young woman with deep red hair and astonishing body laughed.

"Well, Danny, she may be right, but she'll never know for sure."

"My dad says she's jealous. Not just about being rich and living in this great house, but she's not as pretty as you."

"It was always a bit of a problem, Danny. I'm two years older than your mom and I developed well before her, so the boys tended to concentrate on me. You probably don't know what that means, so just say I looked like a full-grown woman while she was still a little girl."

"Mom says you were better at school than she was, too."

"She was right. I've been lucky, I think I was a bit better at school than your mom, but I did work at it."

"So are you really rich, Aunt Gloria?"

She smiled at him. "How old are you now, Danny, nine?"

"Yes, I'll be ten in August."

"Then I think it's time we had a serious talk. You've got to promise we you won't repeat any of this to your parents. Can you do that?"

The little boy nodded, suddenly aware that something critical was happening.

"Danny, you won't know this, but I've been watching you ever since you were four or five. I realised that you liked being here with me rather than at home with your mom and dad, we've always got on well, do you agree?"

Danny nodded.

"And I saw that when you were here, you read books from my shelves, books that were really much too advanced for your age. I began to see that you were really exceptionally bright."

"We don't have any books at our house."

"So I have seen. And no music, either."

Danny shook his head. "They both hate music. Dad says that classical stuff is just for liberals. All that yowling and trumping and mom says the same."

"So that's one thing we have to change. I'll introduce you to some of the world's greatest music when you're here and you can read all the books in the house."

"That'll be great, Aunt Gloria."

"Okay, that's settled. But now we have to talk about the really important stuff. Yes, Danny, I'm rich. I own this beautiful house in one of the wealthiest areas around Chicago and there's a good amount of money in the bank. Do you want to know how I've done this?"

Danny nodded, feeling the excitement building in him. Somehow, he knew his life was about to change.

"I take money from rich people." She laughed at the expression on her nephew's face. "Really, I do. And the strange thing is, many of the people who have given me money don't realise how I did it and nobody has ever gone to the police because they don't want the world to know they've been had by a beautiful woman who is cleverer than they are."

"But how do you do this?"

"I do have one advantage, Danny. Men find me very attractive and sometimes, it doesn't matter how clever and rich they are, they seem to lose it when I pretend I find them attractive as well. Let me tell you about the last one. I rented a cheap apartment down near the South Side, very scruffy, I dressed in cheap clothes and I found one of the most exclusive clubs in town. I stood outside that and when I saw a guy who looked promising, I pretended to cry. It was too easy. He came and asked me what the problem was, I told him I had a need for some surgery, but I didn't have any insurance. It only took a few days, I took him to my cheap apartment, I even let him play around with me a bit and it wasn't long before he gave me fifty thousand bucks in cash. I said I'd get myself organised and see the doctor and I just came right back here. I know he's realised he's been conned, he'll be too embarrassed because he has a wife and two kids, he's a senior partner in some finance house, he won't dare let anyone know."

"Wow, that's amazing! Tell me another one."

"This was one of my favourites. I occasionally go and look at expensive apartments when they have open days. I went to one in downtown Chicago once and I had a bit of a poke around while the agent had the three other potential buyers in another room, and I found a set of keys in a drawer. Later on, I went back, checked the keys were for the apartment and the entry through the security gates to the underground parking area. Then I met a man, very rich, a German banker and he said he was thinking of buying an apartment because he was planning to move to the US with his bank. I'd had some business cards printed showing me as a real estate agent, so I invited him for a showing of this one. He looked around, was very interested and I suggested he could put down a deposit. I pretended to be very attracted to him and he was just putty in my hands. Next day, he gave me a deposit in cash as I suggested he'd get a better deal that way. That was the last he saw of me, of course."

"So do you only do this with rich people, Aunt Gloria?"

"That's my personal rule, Danny. It's supposed to be part of some code of honour that grifters only steal from the rich, but many break that. They don't care if they take the life savings of an old pensioner, but I don't work that way."

"But how do you hide this? Doesn't anybody get suspicious about a woman with all this money? What about taxes?"

"Easy. I've got a legal company as a financial adviser and I pay quite a lot of the money into that, declare it to the IRS and pay genuine taxes. As long as it all seems reasonable, nobody questions it."

"Could you teach me how to do this sort of thing?"

"Hmmm, that's interesting. What might work very well is if you pretend to be my son and we're very poor, needing money for your surgery of some sort. Let me think about it, I have a couple of people I've identified as marks."

### *September, 1970, Wilmette, Illinois, USA*

"I got sixty thousand from that one, Danny. You played that role beautifully, the guy never suspected."

"It was a bit difficult, living in that awful apartment for a few days, but it was a lot of fun watching that fool just melt when he saw you. He really believed that tale about being broke and me needing an operation."

"Like I said, I have this advantage that men find me attractive in a slutty sort of way and I play on that. Now, what do you want to do next?"

"I've been reading up on business in the library, Aunt Gloria. This whole computer thing is becoming an essential part of commerce and I reckon we should look into this. The big corporations, that's where the real money is. I wonder if somebody could use computers to get into it?"

"That's interesting, Danny, a couple of these rich suckers I've been conning have said the same. Tell you what, one of my genuine partners, not a potential sucker, I know he works for one of the computer companies. Let me see if he can suggest something."

## *June, 1976, Wilmette, Illinois, USA*

"It seems I have a real aptitude for this stuff, Gloria. I've learned everything there is to know about operating systems in computers. Your friend says I'm a better programmer than anyone working at his company."

"Pretty cool, young man. Have you found a way yet to make money from it?"

"It's coming. I was able to use a terminal in your friend's office and I actually got into the company's bank account. I pulled out again quickly, so nobody will see the access, I didn't take any money, because that would have been obvious."

"That's amazing, kid. Now what?"

"I need to find some way of hiding the transaction and then some way of moving money to another account. That's going to take work."

"Keep at it, Danny, this has potential."

### *May, 1984, Wilmette, Illinois, USA*

"Gloria, it's time we moved away from this nickel and dime stuff we've been doing, conning rich guys out of a few thousand and move into the big time."

"Better explain yourself there, sonny. We've both got goddammed rich on this nickel and dime stuff over the last few years." Gloria didn't seem offended.

"It's the internet, Gloria. It's finally given me a way to access computers all over the world and I've spent the last five years working out how to get into the files of even the most secure systems and change the data."

"Holy crap, Danny, what can you do?"

"Well, for a start, I opened a bank account for you in England. It's under the name of Amelia Bishop, I've created a rental history in that name for an apartment in Birmingham and now the best bit, I transferred $100,000 into it in pounds sterling, all taken from a couple of big corporations."

"Good grief, Danny, won't they notice that money missing?"

"No chance! I set them as valid payments for various stuff, even updated the inventory records to show the receipt. They won't spot it until they do a stock-take and then they'll just write it off as a book-keeping error."

"I always knew you were a genius, Danny. This may be just in time."

"How's that, Gloria?"

"One of those guys we conned. Remember the Finnish business guy we got to lend me $75,000 to buy him discounted equipment for his firm here? He's reported it to the cops, given them a description. We may be in difficulties."

"Okay, Gloria, we need to move fast. Get your passport, pack a bag and get a plane to London right away before the cops put a travel block on you. Once you get there, go to that address in Birmingham. In a few days, I'll have the bank send you a credit card so you can draw cash out for daily needs. I'll ensure all the utilities are on and set up a payment system."

"I'm going to have to write off this house and my Mercedes, then."

"They're chicken-shit, Gloria. Now, the next thing is a new identity. I'll get all the documents prepared and submitted, you'll have a new passport in a few weeks, and you'll also be getting immigration to Australia."

"Good god, Danny, you can do all that?"

"Like I said, I seem to have an aptitude and I've spent the last few years working on it."

"What about you? What are you going to do?"

"Me? Well, say goodbye to Danny Harper, say hello to Allan Miller. I've got a complete history as an entrepreneur, very rich, I've already been approved as a business immigrant to Australia."

"I'd better go and pack then."

"Damn right, Gloria. See you in Australia."

## Chapter 17

### *7th December, 2025, Coastal NSW, Australia*

The unmarked police car stopped at the gates to the compound.

"I've heard quite a bit about this place down at the station, but this is the first time I've seen it since I was posted here," said Melanie

"What do they say about it?" asked Jack.

"They're mostly curious. The Macfarlanes are considered mysterious, nobody knows them, they're rarely seen in town, they have supplies delivered most of the time."

"One of the cops told me they have a regular serviceman come out from the Toyota dealer to service the vehicles," said Alex. "Same with the John Deere dealership for the backhoe."

"Very mysterious," said Melanie. "Call them, Alex."

Alex wound down the driver's side window and pressed the button on the intercom.

"Who is it?" said the distorted voice from the speaker.

"Detective Inspector Carter, New South Wales Police, to see Andrew Macfarlane."

"He's not here."

"Then we would like to see Miss Leah Macfarlane and the other two residents of this address," said Alex.

"I'm afraid that is not possible," said the voice.

Alex looked across at Melanie and she nodded.

Alex turned back to the intercom. "Tell Baron Percivale that it would be advisable to talk to us."

There was no reply.

"As we thought it would, that's thrown a serious uppercut into the Macfarlane family jaw," said Jack in the back seat. "They'll be having a rather nervous discussion for a while."

There was silence for more than two minutes before the speaker came alive again.

"There's nobody of that name here. Please go away."

"That is Paul or Andrew Macfarlane, is it? Mr Macfarlane, we can either talk now or we can return with a court order. Which is it to be?"

The speaker went silent again. After a minute, sound returned.

"What is all this about?"

"We are making enquiries about a series of murders discovered in a field not far from here," said Alex. "We are talking to all houses in the area."

"We know nothing about that."

"Mr Macfarlane, we have already demonstrated that we have some knowledge about your family that justifies discussion with the police. So, a final word. Open the gate now or we will return with a court order and possibly a stronger presence."

Another moment of silence and the gate began to swing open.

"Thank you," said Alex. "Which house?"

"Number Two," said the voice.

Alex put the car in gear and drove in.

"Well done," said Melanie.

"Thank you, Ma'am," Alex replied.

Number Two was identical to the other three houses, a single-storey home with a covered deck running round all four sides, built of wood with large windows. Solar panels covered the north-facing roofs. They were situated at the points of a square, some fifty metres apart and in the middle of the houses was a smaller structure of the same shape. Alex parked the car as the front door of the house was opened. A middle-aged man stood inside, he was tall, looked very slim-built and his brown hair covered only the back and sides of the head, leaving the rest quite bald.

As the others climbed the three steps onto the deck, the man came out, approached Alex and said, "Inspector Carter? I'm Paul Macfarlane."

Alex avoided the handshake and moved aside. "This is Detective Inspector Carter," he said.

Macfarlane stared at Melanie, his gaze moving from her feet up to her face.

"Er... oh... g'day, Inspector," he said. "I didn't expect..."

"Nobody ever does," said Melanie. "And this is Senior Constable Alex Welland."

"And I'm Jack Savage, psychologist advising the state police," said Jack, rounding out the introductions.

"Come through," said Macfarlane, turning and leading the way into a spacious lounge room. Two people stood there. One was almost a copy of the first Macfarlane, even down to the bald head. The woman was tall, more heavily built than the men with a strong face, a heavy jaw and thick eyebrows that extended over the nose in a single heavy line.

"I'm Leah Macfarlane," she said. "These are my brothers, Paul and Andrew."

Nobody offered to shake hands. The new arrivals announced themselves. No invitation was extended to take seats.

"Is your father joining us?" asked Melanie.

"He's an old, sick man and he's very tired," said Leah.

"Then we may have to see him separately before we go," said Melanie.

"You are a Detective Inspector?" asked Leah. "You don't look like any detective I've ever seen."

"It's been said before," said Melanie. "Let's not waste time with platitudes and pretences. We have done the research and we have established some facts about this family. The first and most crucial fact is that your father is Baron William Percivale of Scotland who left Britain in 1964 after a very public scandal and came to Australia with the secret assistance and agreement of the Prime Ministers of the two countries at the time."

"What absolute bloody nonsense!" The elder brother almost exploded with rage, spit visibly flying from his lips.

"We have the letters between the two PMs making the arrangements," said Melanie. "We have the documents created by the Australian security forces setting up the new identity, the cash transfers from Scotland and then the second most important evidence, the fact that the lands on which this property is set and the field in which a number of bodies were found are all owned by the Percivale estate, rates and taxes paid by an accounting firm in Scotland."

The silence in the room roared like a cyclone.

"Does anyone want to make a comment?" Melanie asked gently.

"We know absolutely nothing about any bodies," Leah finally said. "The field is not ours, nor any of the lands around here, we merely rent the land on which this compound is built."

"You can prove the rental arrangement?" asked Melanie? "Who do you pay those rents to?"

"Directly to the local Council. We were told that the land is owned by a foreign organisation and our rents go to offset the rates and taxes."

"We will of course confirm that with the Council," said Melanie. "Now we would like to talk to your father."

"That's impossible. He's far too ill to see anyone."

"Does he receive medical treatment?"

"A doctor comes here from Coffs Harbour every two weeks to check on him, and a nurse from a local clinic comes once a week."

"I see. You will give me the contact names of these two so we may confirm?"

Leah nodded.

Melanie looked at the two brothers.

"Do either of you have anything to say or does your sister speak for you all the time?"

Neither man showed any signs of having heard her.

"I'm the eldest," said Leah. "I manage all the family affairs, so I speak for the family."

"Then I think we are through here for the moment," said Melanie. "But we will need to speak to all of you again, individually, and also with your father once we have discussed his condition with the doctor. So I will now formally request that all three of you come to the police station in the next few days to be interviewed on a number of subjects. I'll call you when we need to speak to you."

"And what happens if we refuse?' said Leah. She was staring hard at Melanie who felt the force of the personality.

*Oh-oh, a dominant*, she thought. *We met one of those in our previous case and it was a massive battle between her and me. Jack told us all about them. But he said I was a dominant also and I could hold my own against anyone. I'll need to talk to her and let Jack interview the brothers. They seem like weaklings and Jack will break them into small pieces.* "In that case, Ms Macfarlane, I would have no option but to arrest all of you for obstructing the police in the course of their duties. Your call."

Leah said nothing but continued her stare into Melanie's eyes. Melanie felt the pressure, realising how easy it would be to submit and walk away. She drew on her inner resources, stared back, determined that the other woman would wilt. She had no idea how long the battle continued, but Leah suddenly dropped her gaze and looked down into her feet.

"We will come to see you when you call," she said.

Melanie heard a tiny gasp of exhaled tension from all the others, and she turned to leave, sensing a slight weakness in her knees in reaction to the strange battle she had just fought.

In silence, Paul Macfarlane led them out to the front and watched as they got into their car and drove out through the still-open gate.

* * *

"What do you think?" said Melanie.

"Lying through their arses," said Jack. "Your information about the Baron's secret immigration here was well known to all of them, but the fact that you knew it was a massive shock to them. They're frightened."

"Alex, what do you think?"

"I watched the brothers the whole time, Ma'am. They were rigid throughout and they obviously defer to their elder sister. She's another dominant character and she rules them like a tyrant. You forced her back, just like you did with that woman in our last case."

"I agree with that," said Jack. "That battle lasted two minutes. She'll be tough to crack."

"We've done it before, Jack," said Melanie.

"And I'm sure we'll do it again," he said.

The rest of the drive passed in silence, each of them deep in their thoughts.

# Chapter 18

## *14<sup>th</sup> August, 1968, Bondi, NSW, Australia*

"William, I'm sick of all this! I'm bored to fucking tears and I really wonder why I married you."

Baron William Percivale looked down at the furious, tear-stained face of Felicity.

"For a start, you need to remember not to call me William anymore. It took a shitload of political powers to get us here with a clean slate and I don't want anybody starting to ask questions. I'm Andrew Macfarlane and you need to remember that, always."

"Well, I don't give a shit anymore. I thought we would end up living in that lovely house in England, you the Baron, me Lady Felicity, we'd be in London most of the time, having a great life. And you fuck it up with that stupid chess thing."

"Yes, and instead, we have a peaceful life looking over the ocean, nice apartment, enough money so we don't have to work. Most of the world would consider that paradise. So what are you bitching about?"

"I have no life! At least if I was on my own, I could go to work, meet people, go out to dinner, all that sort of stuff. But I can't."

"You know what they said, keep out of social contacts. It's too risky, either of us might drop something, make somebody suspicious and next thing you know the press are all over us, it would be headlines all over the UK and here, our lives would be ruined."

"I suppose so." Felicity wiped her eyes and sat down in an armchair. "But I'm still bored, I've got to do something exciting again. Is this all I can look forward to for the rest of my life? I'm twenty-four and I couldn't even have a decent twenty-first birthday party."

"So what do you suggest?"

"I don't know! It still shits me off that you got screwed by that fucking Pom, Chancellor. He cheated, I'm sure of it. You were almost a Grand Master, he was just a schoolkid. How the hell could he have beaten you fairly? You should have had those Picassos and kicked him out of the house."

"I know, I know, it still hurts like hell. But there's nothing I can do about it now."

"Well, think of something. You were almost a chess Grand Master, you should be able to come up with some way of showing the world you were cheated, maybe signalling that Chancellor shit that you know what he did."

"I think you're right, I should be able to come up with something. Give me some time, I'll tell you when I've got it."

"Can I suggest something? It could be really exciting."

"What's that, love?"

"You need revenge for that debacle with Chancellor. I know how you can have it."

Percivale look startled. "It was a long time ago, Felicity. There doesn't seem much point in revenge now after four years."

"Nonsense, William. I can tell it's been eating at your gut ever since it happened. You need some form of closure."

"What do you suggest?"

"Have you ever killed anyone?"

"What?"

"You heard. I think you need to kill somebody, maybe more than one and somehow link it to that chess match."

"How would I do that?"

"I've no idea but I bet we could think up something."

Percivale looked at the wall in thought. Finally, he looked back at her. "Jesus, but that's an exciting idea," he said. "I never realised, but I have thought about what it would be like to kill somebody. Do you think we could do it without any risk of being found out?"

"Of course we could. The cops are all stupid, they'd never find any links between you and the bodies, and they don't know anything about that chess match, so why would they see any connection?"

"Bodies?"

"Sure, why not? That disaster needs a lot of revenge. If we can do it once, we can do it several times."

"I suppose so, but how would that be revenge against Chancellor? He'd never know I'd done it and he probably would never hear about some murders in Australia when he lives in England."

"That's not the point, sweetie! It would give you the satisfaction and closure for that whole bloody mess. And it would be a lot of fun, anyway."

Percivale began to show some excitement. "Dammit Felicity, you're right, this would be a great thing to do. Let me think about it and see if I can come up with a plan."

* * *

### *28th August, 1968, Bondi, NSW, Australia*

### *11:45am*

"I think I've solved our problem. Come over to the table, I'll show you what I've done."

Felicity looked up from her book, not showing any real interest, but as she recognised the excitement in Percivale's face, she stood up and joined him at the dinner table as he laid out a map.

"This is the area a few kilometres west and north of Coffs Harbour," he said, pointing at a large expanse of open country. His hand circled a large area outlined by a blue marker pen. "That part is actually owned by the Percivale estate. Now here…" he marked out a rectangular shape in the middle of the estate… "is a field that has never been used for anything, it has no building approval and will stay as it is for the foreseeable future. The council has no interest in it."

"That looks expensive," she said. "Who pays the council rates and taxes?"

"When I skipped out of the UK, I arranged for an accounting firm in Edinburgh to be the trustees for the estates. They receive the rents and other income from the properties in Scotland, around the house in Surrey and a few other properties around the world my ancestors acquired, and they pay the taxes and stuff."

"But does that mean they know where we are?" She looked concerned.

"Not exactly. They send me documents to a Post Office box I have in Sydney. They are bound to secrecy, and they know very well that breaking the rules would bring the British spooks down on their heads like a ton of bricks.”

“So what have you done? What's your plan?”

“I've arranged a long-term lease under the Macfarlane name of another area about fifteen miles away, here.” He pointed at an area to the south of the field, still within the estate. “Obviously, nobody can become involved there, it's mine, after all. We'll build a house there, keep completely private and I've already ordered a high fence with secure gates to surround the property. We can buy a kit home, get it installed quickly and move up there before the end of the year.”

“So you are paying money to rent your own property?” Felicity smiled. She sensed something critical was coming.

“It keeps the cover,” he replied. “Now, let me tell you what we're going to do.”

**12:27pm**

“Oh my god,” she said, exhaling with a blast of emotion. “That's incredible! I love it. We need to celebrate. Let's go to bed.”

**1:07pm**

“Oh my god, William, that was fantastic.” Breathing hard, Felicity snuggled up against Percivale's side.

“The best ever,” he agreed, slowly bringing his own breathing under control.

“Maybe nobody will ever know about it, but it will feel good to us, making somebody pay for what that Chancellor shit did to you. They won't find out, will they?”

"Can't see how. The field is a long way from a road or any buildings, there's no chance anyone could be around when we dig the holes. I'll buy a top-quality backhoe and a trailer, we do the burials in the middle of the night, nobody need ever know. Maybe one day, when I'm old, I'll tell the chess authorities about the field, let them see what happened."

"It's brilliant," she said. "William?"

"Yes, love?"

"Can you do that again?"

"Better give me some time, love. You really drove me hard there."

"Okay, but don't take too long."

# Chapter 19

## *12<sup>th</sup> August, 1970, Coastal NSW, Australia*

"William, I think we may have our first!" Felicity pointed at the small car in the lay-by, holding on with her left hand the tiny bundle of their first-born, Leah, born three months earlier.

"Sure looks promising," said Percivale, slowing the Landcruiser and stopping alongside the other car. "Put Leah on the floor and let's see what we can see."

"God, this is exciting," exclaimed Felicity, carefully laying the bundle on the floor, taking the flashlight and then climbing out to join Percivale who had taken a hunting knife and a heavy wrench.

They slowly walked into the trees that were next to the lay-by, illuminating their way with occasional flickers of the light. They didn't have far to go. In a small clearing, the man and woman were making love on a blanket. Felicity directed the flashlight's beam on them and they both shouted with shock.

"What the hell!" exclaimed the man.

Percivale didn't hesitate but walked up to them, bent down and stabbed the man in the ribs just below the heart. The woman screamed in horror and Percivale slammed the wrench onto her head. She subsided without another sound.

"Well done, William," said Felicity, laughing with glee. "That was brilliant."

"Let's get them to the car," said Percivale. With one hand, he dragged the man the few metres to the Landcruiser, opened the back door and lifted him onto the floor which had been covered with tarpaulin for some weeks in preparation for just such an event. Returning to the killing scene, he lifted the slender frame of the woman and carried her to the vehicle, throwing her in on top of the man.

A few moments later, they were back on the road heading to their gated home area.

"It's nearly two," said Percivale. "This should be a good time for the burials."

"My god, we got two to start," said Felicity, cuddling her daughter. "I never thought we'd get so lucky. Where will you put them?"

"They're just pawns," said Percivale. "We'll make them white, so you go and get the gowns while I hook up the trailer."

Placing the baby back on the floor of the vehicle, Felicity ran inside, returning with two white nightgowns that she had bought in a bulk purchase of white and black gowns soon after moving up to their new home a year ago. Percivale pulled up to the shed where he kept the backhoe on its trailer and hooked it onto the towbar. Then he pulled the bodies out, cut away the small amount of clothing on each of them and stood up, staring down at the naked forms. He felt a surge of excitement and joy at what they had done. As Felicity returned, they each dressed one body in the white gowns, needing to cut down the middle of the one for the man to make it fit, returned the bodies to the vehicle and set off again for the thirty-minute drive to the field Percivale had prepared for this moment.

"I marked each spot," he said as they turned into the field. "There are letters painted in whitewash, we're looking for a "P" – ah, there we are."

An hour later, the backhoe had dug two pits side by side, the bodies were lowered into them and the holes filled in and covered over.

"That must be the youngest anybody has ever attended a funeral," said Felicity with a giggle as she picked up Leah and climbed back into her seat. "I'm sorry you weren't dressed appropriately, darling," she continued and kissed the child's head.

Another hour and they were back home, the backhoe on its trailer in the garage.

"We've done our first," said Felicity. "That feels so good. When can we do another one?"

"Not for a long time," replied Percivale. "We need to see when they discover that those two have disappeared and what the cops do. There's not a chance in hell that they can link us to it, but let's just leave it to die down, probably for a couple of years."

"That seems an awful long time," grumbled Felicity.

"Maybe," said Percivale. "They've stopped hanging people, but I don't like the idea of a life term in prison. Let's wait it out and make sure we left no trace."

"Okay, you're right," said Felicity. "Let's go to bed."

## The Mid-Coast Times, August

### 14th *August, 1970*

*Police are baffled by the disappearance of Derek Carpenter and Melissa Derwent of Coffs Harbour. They were last seen on the twelfth at a dinner party at the local club when they left together soon after midnight. Their car was found deserted in a layby on the road to Coffs*

*Harbour and there were signs of occupancy a few yards into the woodland. But there is no trace of either of them. Friends and family fear foul play, but the police will not say anything beyond the fact that investigations are continuing.*

## Chapter 20

### *27th October, 2025, Coastal NSW, Australia 11:00am*

"He's been sitting at the gate since ten," said Paul. "Who the hell is it and what does he want?"

"Don't know, but he's got me spooked," replied Andrew. "Who just arrives, parks by the front and then just sits there for an hour? Why doesn't he use the intercom?"

"Only a madman," said the woman sipping at a mug of tea on the sofa. "I think it's time we talked to him."

"Leah, that's too dangerous," said Paul. "We've no idea who he is or what he wants, and he could be armed."

"And that's why both of you will have him in your sights the whole time and if he gets threatening, you shoot. Get the guns, I'm going out there."

A few moments later, she strode down the path from her house and stopped on the inside of the steel gate. She looked at the man sitting behind the wheel of the car and said nothing. For a few seconds they stared at each other, then the man got out of the car and stood by the door. She saw a middle-sized, slender-built man in his later years, perhaps seventy, she estimated. He saw a tall, heavy-set woman dressed in country tweeds, a strong face with some anger showing.

"Who the hell are you and what you want?" she demanded.

"My name is Peter Chancellor and I want to see Baron Percivale."

The answer shook her badly and she took a step backward.

"You what?" she said, her voice weakened by the shock.

"I said my name is Peter Chancellor and I want to see Baron Percivale."

"There's nobody of that name here. Go on, fuck off or I'll call the police."

"That's the last thing you want to do and you know it. You know who I mean, you know him as Andrew James Macfarlane and I imagine you call him daddy, or something similar. You're his daughter and I assume the two boys are right now looking at me through their rifle sights. But you almost certainly know who he really is. Tell him Peter Chancellor wants to talk to him because Baron Percivale owes him something valuable."

Her face still showing her disturbance, she turned and walked towards one of the houses. Chancellor didn't move but stood silently until she walked back to him.

"You'd better come in," she said and took an electronic controller from the pocket of her jacket. She pointed it at the gate and swung it open enough for Chancellor to return to his car and pass through the gate. She turned and walked back the way she had come, and he followed behind her, keeping the car moving at a crawl. Arriving at the house, he left the car and walked inside as she led the way into a comfortable lounge.

"What the bloody hell do you want?" said the tall, thin, bony man standing by the French window.

Chancellor studied him. He knew Percivale was over eighty, and he looked most unwell. His cheeks were sunken, dark shadows under the eyes made him look even worse. His clothes hung badly on the thin frame.

"You haven't aged well, My Lord Baron Percivale," he said.

"What the hell are you talking about?" snapped the older man. "My name's Macfarlane, Andrew Macfarlane. Now what is all this crap?"

"Your name has certainly been Macfarlane since about 1964, maybe 1965," said Chancellor. "I believe you owe that to the British and Australian secret services and the good offices of the two countries' Prime Ministers of the day. But the last time we met, you were Baron William Percivale, and I wiped the floor with you over a chess board."

"Chancellor? You're that bastard who tried to steal my Fabergé chess set? You cheated, I don't know how, but you cheated. No fucking commoner could beat me at chess. I was very nearly a Grand Master. You were a lousy player then and I bet you still are."

Chancellor laughed. "Let me correct you, My Lord Baron. I became a Grand Master a few years ago and I won the World Championship quite recently."

"You're a liar. Now, get out of my house before I have you shot."

Behind Chancellor, the door opened and the two men entered, both carrying rifles. Chancellor turned and studied them.

"And these are your loyal sons who will carry out the execution, are they?" He turned back to Percivale. "You know why I'm here. I beat you fair and square sixty years ago, you owe me the Fabergé chess set which I suspect you stole from the Russians in some way. Pass it over and I'll leave peacefully."

"No chance, you bastard. Get out of here."

"In that case, I have no recourse but to reveal to the world who you are. It will be easy and interesting. I'm here on a well-publicised chess tour as the new world champion, I've already been on television and talked about our last meeting. It would make a fantastic story for the tabloids and television news channels, not only here but back in Britain too."

Percivale looked even sicker. He was silent for a few moments then appeared to reach a decision. He nodded at Leah.

### 11:54am

"It was necessary," said Leah, seated at the circular dining table in her house. "Chancellor has already bleated out on television about the match he played with Dad and the whole of Australia knows about it. And the cops are sniffing around, they know about it, so they've obviously talked to him as well and now they've traced us. We'll dispose of Chancellor in the usual way, we know the next step. So tonight, some time after midnight, you two take Chancellor's car and get rid of it. It was a rental, so they'll soon know Chancellor was in the region, but not that he was here."

"And when do we deal with Chancellor?" asked Andrew.

"As soon as you get back." Leah's authority over the two brothers was total and obvious.

"It's all a bloody mess," said Paul, looking down at the table like a child being admonished by a parent. "It was all going so well, nobody knew about us, nobody could trace any connection to the field."

"It's that damned woman cop," said Leah. "She may look like a Victoria's Secret model, but I'd say she's pretty well switched on. We may have to deal with her at some point, as well."

"There are still a couple of positions left on the field," said Paul.

"Let's see what happens," said Leah. "Paul, hide Chancellor until after midnight, Andrew get the backhoe ready."

"We're missing something," said Paul. "The world knows about Dad now. If the cops take him away, there's no way in the world he could avoid spilling the whole bloody story. And where would that leave us?"

Leah stared at him for a few seconds, and he dropped his eyes under the pressure. "You're right, little brother," she said. "I think we all know what that means. This will be a busy night."

## Chapter 21

### *28th October, 2025, Coastal NSW, Australia*
### *8:45am*

The Police patrol car stopped on the side of the road and one of the officers walked across to the other side where a steep drop fell some twenty metres onto rocks. A moment later he re-joined his colleague.

"The report was right," he said. "There's a car down there, burned out. Call it in, Dan, it needs scene of crime people to examine that one."

### *10:23am*

"Badly burned, Ma'am." The police officer, clad in overalls, boots and gloves with a helmet held in his hands as he spoke on the radio standing a few metres away from the blackened wreck of the once-white sedan lying on its side, badly bent and broken from the fall onto the rocks. "Nobody in it or around it, so I'd say it was pushed off the road. It's quite cold, so this happened at least two days ago. But the licence plate is readable and it's owned by Avis in Sydney." He read out the plate number.

"Thank you, Steve," said Melanie and disconnected the call. A few moments later, she called the rental car company in Sydney.

### *10:34am*

"It was Peter Chancellor," she said and watched the shock on the faces of Alex and Jack. "So I have to ask you, Alex, did you tell Chancellor that we had identified Percivale?

"No Ma'am, I did not," said Alex. "You made it plain that doing so would endanger the whole case."

Melanie nodded. "I never really thought you did. You would have known what would happen, without any words from me."

"Thank you, Ma'am," replied Alex, obviously relieved.

"Then who the hell did?" said Jack.

"I did," said the voice from the computer monitor on Melanie's desk as a face flickered into sight.

"Miller!" Melanie almost exploded in anger. "What the hell were you playing at? You've caused a hell of a problem."

"I wanted to stir the pot," said Miller. "I want to see those bastards panic and I knew Chancellor couldn't resist going up there and accosting them."

"And in doing so, you've probably killed him," said Melanie, struggling to suppress her anger.

"If so, that's regrettable," said Miller. "But this has pushed them into action, very panic-stricken action, and that means the chances of finding evidence against them improves. 'Bye for now."

The image faded.

"Regrettable!" said Alex in almost a snarl. "What sort of bastard calls the death of an innocent person regrettable?"

"But we have to admit," said Jack. "He's probably right. It certainly looks like they're responsible for this, so I don't think we can expect cool, calm and considered action by the Macfarlanes is all that likely. This latest act may well be what gives them away."

The telephone on Melanie's desk rang and she

picked up the handset. She listened for a few moments, her face expressionless and replaced the phone.

"A patrol car just checked the field," she said. "There are two fresh signs of soil having been dug up."

"Two?" said Alex. "I was expecting Chancellor would be there, but not so soon. So who's the other one?"

"I think I can guess," said Jack.

"Two piles of fresh earth," said Melanie, surveying the field. "Alex, from your map of the chess board as it was, who do you think we'll find there?"

"I'd bet the mortgage that the one over there," he said, pointing at one mound nearest to them, "will be the Black King and the other will be the White King."

"Let's find out," said Melanie and nodded at the two teams of officers with shovels standing by.

It took forty minutes before the first discovery was made.

"A crown alright," said the officer who struck something metallic and had used a trowel to remove the dirt from it. A few minutes later, he spoke again. "A black gown," he said and continued to work at the delicate task of uncovering the face. Twenty minutes later, he stood back and nodded at Melanie. She walked over with Alex and Jack and looked down.

"Peter Chancellor," said Alex, the shock and grief showing in his face. "How could anyone do this? One of the finest minds in the world and somebody has just killed him for some sick reasons of their own."

"I have some ideas about that," said Jack. "These are not healthy minds at work here."

There was a shout from the other side of the field

where the second team was working. Melanie's group walked over and looked down at a similar scene from the first. The crown was the same shape and size as the first and the small patch of cloth around the head was white. It took a few more moments while the face was uncovered.

"Baron William Percivale, I presume," said Melanie. "Also known as Andrew James Macfarlane."

"The White King," said Alex, looking ill. "Jack, what sort of person does this? Is this just revenge for losing a chess match, and why would they kill Percivale now, sixty years after that match?"

"Some people have no concept of relativity," said Jack. "They see any slight as massively offensive. Killing thirteen people because of a lost chess match would seem quite reasonable to such a psychopath."

Melanie began leading them away from the field back to the car. "The cause for worry now is the last body. Alex, confirm for me. You said there should be thirteen chess pieces at that stage of the endgame. We've found twelve bodies corresponding to the pieces. Is it the Black Queen that's missing?"

"Yes, Ma'am," said Alex. "That would be the last piece if this entire theory holds up."

"Time to visit the Macfarlane family again," said Melanie. "And to hell with ASIO. This is a murder case."

**1:19pm**

Nobody was seated. Leah Macfarlane had allowed Melanie's team to enter her house with obvious reluctance and had not called her brothers to join her.

She stood with her back to the fireplace, Melanie directly in front of her, Alex by the door through which they had entered, Jack against the wall, studying Leah intently.

"We would like to speak with your father," said Melanie.

"You can't," said Leah, tension evident in her voice.

"Why not?"

"He's not a well man. He can't cope with busybody cops grilling him whenever they feel like it."

"I'm sorry, Leah, we have to insist."

"Damn you, Carter," said Leah, her voice rising in pitch. "Alright, I'll take you over there." She walked to the door, forcing Alex to move aside and strode out.

"This is interesting," murmured Jack to Melanie as they followed Leah out. "It's either a hell of an act or she really doesn't know her father's dead. Could the brothers have acted independently for once?"

They reached the house occupied by Percivale, Leah pulled out a keychain and opened the front door, walking in without a backward look at the others. There was nobody in the lounge or any of the rooms. The door was closed to one room

"He's probably in bed," said Leah. "He tends to sleep late. Let me see." She knocked on the closed door and called out. "Dad? The cops are here again, they want to talk to you." She opened the door and looked in.

Melanie followed her. The room was empty. The bed looked untouched.

"He must have gone out for a drive very early," said Leah. "He does that sometimes."

"Leah, we need to stop playing games," said Melanie. "We found your father's body this morning in the field with all the other bodies. He was buried in the position that corresponds to the White King's position in the chess match that your father played against Peter Chancellor back in 1964."

Leah seemed frozen. She swallowed twice and then spoke. Her voice was harsh with tension.

"He's dead?"

"He is. You don't seem too upset, Leah."

"You have no idea how I feel," she snapped. "He was my father and a great man. He's a great loss to the world."

"Then may I express my condolences," said Melanie.

"Fuck your condolences. He was my father, not yours and just because I'm not weeping and wailing doesn't mean I'm not upset at his death."

"I understand. There was one more body discovered this morning," said Melanie. "It was Peter Chancellor. "Did you know him?"

"Who the hell is Peter Chancellor?"

"He's the man who beat your father at chess which precipitated the scandal that destroyed him."

"Oh, that bastard. Then he got what he deserved. He was found in the same field?"

"In the position corresponding to the Black King," replied Melanie. "Leah, did you and your brothers have anything to do with these two murders?"

"No, and you will have a hell of a time trying to prove that we did."

"You don't seem surprised that they were murdered, Leah. In fact, you seem to have expected that."

"Why should I be surprised? You found them buried in the field with a number of other bodies laid out in some peculiar pattern, how else would they have ended up there?"

"Fair point," said Melanie. "Where are your brothers?"

"I have no idea," Leah replied. "I'm not their keeper."

"Has Peter Chancellor been here?" asked Melanie.

"No, he has not. Why the hell would he visit here?"

"Maybe to claim the Fabergé chess set he won from your father?"

"I've no idea what you're talking about."

"Leah, when your brothers appear, tell them I want to talk to them. They can come to the station, or I will come here, but if they don't contact us in the next twenty-four hours, I will ask all of you to come to the station for questioning."

"You just told me my father is dead. Do you realise what that means?" Leah glared at Melanie.

"Why don't you tell us?"

"It means I'm the Baroness. I inherit the title and millions of dollars-worth of property here and in the UK. You don't tell me what to do."

"Congratulations on the inheritance," said Melanie. "But you will find that it does not give you exemption from the law. I want to see you and your brothers tomorrow."

"Go fuck yourself," responded Leah.

"Leah, you can either agree to come to my office tomorrow and show up by nine, or I can arrest you now on suspicion of murder. If you do not show up, warrants for the arrest of all three of you will be issued and my officers will be here to take you back in handcuffs. Your call."

Melanie walked out, followed by the other two.

"Lying through her arse," said Jack as they climbed back in the car.

"No doubt," said Melanie. "But I can't see the evidence so far that would persuade the Office of Public Prosecutions to charge any of them."

"She's a powerful character," said Jack. "But nowhere near as dominant as your crazy lady in the last case. You'll break them all down at some point."

"Might be difficult," said Melanie. "If they are still under the protection of the spooks, they may be immune."

"Tackle that problem when we face it," said Jack. "Alex, find us a restaurant. It's nearly noon and we've missed breakfast."

"I know the very place," said Alex and drove out through the gates of the compound.

"But I tell you what," said Jack. "I'd love to know just what material Percivale has on the rich and powerful that he was able to come here and get looked after so well."

"Don't we all," said Melanie. "But we may never find out. Spooks keep these things very close to their chests."

* * *

*2:07pm*

The atmosphere around the table was unpleasant.
"So you're the Baroness now?"

Leah stared at her brother until he dropped his gaze.

"Yes, I am. And all the estate is now in my name."

"This is all wrong. I'm the elder brother, I should be the one inheriting. How come you're getting everything? And why don't Andrew and I know anything about this?"

"Because that's how Dad set it up. It's called Entail Primogenitor and Dad specified that the line would go through his eldest child regardless of sex."

"What, he did that before we were born?"

"Exactly. He did this some years before we were born, while he was still living in Scotland as the Baron."

"So how the hell do you know about this?" Andrew was almost in tears and his voice was croaky.

"The Trustees know all about it. They pay the property taxes on all the lands we have, because Dad gave them a contact to our mother, and it was all arranged. She advised them of the children and Dad's new identity. All I have to do is write to them and everything is transferred to me, including the title."

"And do these blokes know about all three of us?"

Paul was sullen and he stared down at his hands on the table.

"Yes, they do. Mum kept them informed as we were born, so they have all the details."

"And how do they keep up to date after Mum left us?" asked Andrew.

"They write to me at a Post Office Box in Sydney, and I write to them every few months if anything changes."

"You mean all this time we thought we were completely unknown in Australia, some bunch of accountants have known about us the whole time?” Paul's voice had risen a notch in his worry.

“That's correct.” Leah sounded bored and a little irritated. “But why are you in such a panic? Now that he's dead, we can all come out into the open and live normally.”

“So how much is there now?” asked Paul.

“The last report listed properties in Scotland and England, including the family estate in Scotland, worth about five million pounds, the house in Surrey worth a bit more than that, two commercial properties in Sydney, one in Melbourne and quite a bit of farming property here in Australia.”

Both brothers were looking at her with astonishment.

“So how much is the whole thing worth?” asked Andrew.

“Last estimate was a bit over fifty million dollars,” said Leah.

“Jesus Christ!” Paul banged his fist on the table. “Fifty million? Australian dollars?”

“Give or take,” said Leah.

“This is giving me the shits,” said Paul. “All these years, you've known about the whole situation, you haven't bothered to tell us, you keep the whole thing a secret, you just dole out a bit of money now and again when we could have been bloody rich! Who the hell do you think you are?”

“I'm Baroness Percivale and I own the entire Percivale estate, just as our Dad set it up.”

“Presumably there's income from all these properties?” said Andrew.

"Not as much as there could be," Leah said. "The two residential properties in Scotland and England have been closed up since dad left and the incomes from the estates around them are taken up in maintaining them and taxes and stuff and paying the rates on this place. The other Australian properties pay about a half mill a year and that's what we live on. It's not massive wealth but notice that you two have never had to work for a living."

"So what happens if you get hurt or killed?" asked Paul. "Who controls all this stuff then?"

"That's all been taken care of," Leah replied. "My solicitor here has all the details documented and if that happens, the Trustees in Scotland will be informed."

"And if it does, do I then become the Baron and take your place?" asked Paul.

"Exactly."

"Bloody hell!" said Andrew. "But why keep all this under cover? Why not sell some of the Australian properties and get some cash? I'd like a real car instead of that silly little toy you made us buy. I've always wanted a Ferrari, why can't I have one?"

"Same here," said Paul. "I've not done much travel, and now that we can travel again, I'd like to do some. And travel first-class, too. I love those sexy cabins you get in first class airliners. I could spend a year travelling in style, see the USA, Britain, Europe and I want to do a wildlife game park in South Africa."

"And that's why you're not getting that sort of money," Leah said, contempt evident in her voice and face. "You'd just fritter it away like you've done all your lives. Do you know how often the bank has called me to tell me you've overdrawn your accounts by some thousands? It's too bloody often and you've both messed up the cash flow I need to maintain everything."

Neither brother looked at her.

"And anyway, we can't sell the British properties," she continued. "They're owned by the Baron's estates and the Crown does not permit such a sale without government consent. We could possibly get it, but just imagine the publicity if the media found out. They'd go back into that whole chess game that started this crap, we'd have reporters gathering at our front door, following us everywhere we went, it would be a goddammed zoo. Do you want that?"

"No, I suppose not," said Paul in a sulky tone.

"Nor do I," said Leah. "And that's why I'm not going to go public about being a Baroness or owning the properties or anything else. And I want you both to shut up about it."

She stared at each of them hard.

"Do you understand?"

The two men nodded without looking her in the eye, stood up and left to return to their own houses.

## Chapter 22

### *29th October, 2025, Coastal NSW, Australia*

*10:45am*

"Andrew, fancy a coffee in town?

The younger brother looked up from his putting practice on the green they had installed a few years ago.

"Sure, what's up?

"Tell you when we get there," said Paul. "Let's go to that coffee shop on the High Street where that cute waitress works. Couple of things I want to chat about."

"Yeah, okay, just let me change my shoes."

As they left the gates and headed in towards the village, Andrew broke the silence.

"Why not chat in the house?" he asked.

Paul shook his head and put his finger to his lips. Andrew frowned in puzzlement but waited until they had parked near the coffee shop and walked in. They smiled at the waitress and took seats near the back of the shop.

"All a bit bloody mysterious," Andrew said. "What's going on?"

"Something we have to talk about and I'm not sure that bitch hasn't got microphones in our houses and even in the car."

"Holy shit, Paul, you can't be serious!"

"Really? Look at her! She's known all her life about our dad and his story, she's known that she would inherit the title and the money, and she's obviously controlled the money for some years. And she sure as hell is not going to let us get hold of any of it."

They stopped while the waitress approached, exchanged flirtatious pleasantries with her and ordered coffees and some decorative cakes.

"We've done okay with that arrangement," said Andrew. "She kept us out of the problems with Dad."

"No doubt," said Paul. "But I bet she looked after herself pretty well in the meantime. Remember those times she was away two or three weeks at a time? What was she doing? I bet she was travelling somewhere, and I doubt she was going economy."

Andrew looked thoughtful.

"And there's another thing," continued Paul. "Have you ever seen her dating anybody? Even when were a lot younger when she was in her teens and twenties, did you ever see her with a bloke or even talk about one?"

They paused again as the waitress arrived with mugs of coffee and a small tray of cakes. They each took one as the girl walked away.

"Never did," said Andrew, wiping cream from his lips.

"I bet she's gay," said Paul. "And I bet that means she's a man-hater. It's not just careful management that's kept her from letting us have some good things, I bet she's been enjoying making us go without while she got the goodies."

"She's certainly behaved like a hard boss," said Andrew. "It never occurred to me before, but I just thought we didn't have all that much money and after Mum left, she took on the job of being a mother. I never bothered to ask where the money came from."

"And yet she goes to University and gets a degree in accounting," said Paul. "What did we get? Fuck all. Just a state school, no fun trips, no big birthday parties, everything was for her."

"I suppose."

"And then there's the big thing," said Paul. "She made us join in on that insane killing thing. Neither of us ever wanted to kill anybody, but it seems she took over from Mum and Dad and kept filling up that field. I still don't know how she made us do it, but I tell you, if we told her now we didn't want to go on, she'd kill us and put our bodies in that damn field."

"Oh my god, you think so?" Andrew's face had gone pale and the shock was obvious.

"I know so. It's what she threatened when she first told us all about this. You were only ten, so you probably don't remember Frankly, she's as mad as a bloody Islamic terrorist, she just loves killing. Hell, she even made us kill dad and that Chancellor bloke, because it suited her. I don't want to do it again. How about you?"

Andrew just shook his head.

"So here's what I'm thinking," said Paul. He looked around the room, saw there was nobody within a couple of tables, lowered his voice and lifted the menu in front of his mouth. "She said it herself, if she gets offed, I become the Baron and get all the properties and cash. We could start making up for all the restrictions since we were kids."

"Jesus Christ, Paul! You're talking about killing our sister?" Despite the shock, Andrew kept his voice down to a low growl.

"Come on, Andrew, you've never liked the bitch any more than I have. It would be no loss and a hell of a lot to gain. And just think – we could sell some of the properties, cash in a million or two, we could start living. You can have that Ferrari, I can do some high-class travel around the world. What's to lose?"

Nothing more was said while they drove home and separated to enter their own homes.

# Chapter 23

## *3rd November, 2025, Coastal NSW, Australia*

The recording device beeped for a few seconds while Leah stared down at her lap. Across from the interview table, Jack and Melanie watched her carefully, with Melanie well aware that she could be facing a difficult battle of wills. When the beeping stopped, she introduced all three of them to start the recording.

"Leah, you are not under arrest and you have declined legal representation at this time. You have come here voluntarily, and we wish to question you about specific events concerning a number of bodies found in a field twenty-five kilometres from the compound in which you and your family reside. Do you understand?"

Leah looked up and glared at Melanie.

"So I'm not under arrest and I can leave at any time?"

"That is correct," said Melanie.

Leah rose to her feet. "In that case, good morning to you."

"However," said Melanie, "if you choose to leave, I will immediately arrest you on suspicion of involvement in the murders of those bodies found."

Her face furious, Leah sat down again.

"Let's start with what we discussed yesterday," said Melanie. "As we told you, we discovered the bodies of your father and Peter Chancellor in the same field as a number of other bodies which appear to have been killed over a period of some years. What can you tell us about that?"

"Nothing," said Leah, her face tight.

"You indicated yesterday that you knew about Peter Chancellor and his history with your father. Did you ever meet him?"

"No. I would never agree to meet that bastard."

"We found Mr Chancellor's car at the bottom of a cliff not far from your home. And we examined tracks of vehicles outside the gate of your compound and inside, leading up to your house. One recent track matched the tyres found on Chancellor's car, indicating he had been there very recently. Can you comment on that?"

"Tyres are not unique to a vehicle." The scorn in Leah's voice was cutting. "You could find fifty cars with the same tyres in this town alone."

"Maybe, but not one that had been to your compound in the last few days and not one with dirt in the treads that matched the dirt in and around your property. We checked."

That hit Leah hard, Melanie could see. There was no response.

"Let me tell you what we believe happened, Leah. We know from other sources that Chancellor had learnt about the identity of your father and where you all lived. We met him here just a while ago and it was clear he was still angry about the episode of the match he played against your father many years ago and your father's failure to honour his debt."

"You told him? Don't you realise that my father was in a protection program? You broke federal law, I'll report you to the Federal Police."

"No, I didn't. We have no control over the person

who did and we have no idea of how he found out." Melanie didn't bother to mention that her colleagues had already found out those facts. "Let's continue with what we believe happened. Chancellor visited you, demanded his winnings, a Fabergé chess set worth a couple of million and you killed him. You, or one of your brothers took the car to the ravine, forced it over and then came back to the compound. We suspect you killed your father, also, because he had let out the story. Then you took both bodies to the field and buried them."

"Absolute bullshit," snapped Leah. "You have no evidence of any of that fairy tale."

"Let's look at a few other issues," continued Melanie, ignoring Leah's comment. "We have confirmed that the field where all those bodies were buried, including those of Chancellor and your father is owned by the Baron's estates and managed on his behalf by an accounting firm in Scotland."

"Crap," retorted Leah.

"Not so," replied Melanie. "We have had written confirmation from the firm of Maynard and Partners in Edinburgh, listing all the properties owned by the Baron's estates. Of course, if as you claim, you are now the Baroness, all these properties, here and in the UK are now yours."

Leah was silent, seemingly overwhelmed by the amount of information Melanie and her team had unearthed.

"And so to another matter," Melanie continued. "Where's your mother, Leah?"

That arrow hit home, Melanie could see. Leah's eyes

opened wide and her jaw dropped. But it took only a few seconds for her to regain control. Melanie was impressed by the strength shown.

"My mother? I've no idea. She vanished many years when I was just a teenager. One day she was there, next day she'd gone, taken all her clothes, so we assumed she'd had enough of my father and the kids and just buggered off somewhere. Frankly, I couldn't give a flying fuck about her."

"Did you know anything about the bodies in that field?"

"Why the hell should I? My father had nothing to do with that, either."

Melanie sensed that Leah was regaining confidence as it became clear that the police had no serious evidence beyond the ownership of the estates. She began feeling pressure on her mind as Leah began exerting her dominant personality and she started to draw on her own internal resources to counter the force.

"You don't have anything, do you?" said Leah, the volume higher than normal conversational speech. Her eyes drilled into Melanie's. "You know very well that my father had nothing to do with those killings. You know very well that I had nothing to do with the killing of Peter Chancellor, nor did my brothers. It's time that we left."

Melanie found the strength that she had used on several occasions with powerful personalities. She stared back at Leah and the same struggle of wills occurred as had happened the last time they had met.

She felt it ebb back and forth and finally Leah backed down, looking away and staring down at her lap.

"We're done for now," said Melanie. "But now we're going to talk to your brothers and get their version of events."

Alarm showed in Leah's face, her eyes widened again, and she shook her head violently.

"No, you can't," she said loudly. "Those two are weaklings, they're fools, they'll admit to anything if you push them."

"Don't be absurd, Leah," said Melanie. "Even if they did, we couldn't convict them of something without evidence. We'll examine everything they say. But it's interesting that you should claim they're fools and weaklings. Is this how you have dominated them over the years? Is this how you persuaded them to kill Chancellor and destroy his car?"

Leah's face was expressionless, and she didn't reply.

A uniformed policewoman entered the room and stood against one wall. Melanie nodded at her and then turned back to Leah.

"You're going to stay here until Jack and I have finished talking to your brothers. This officer will stay with you, but she won't talk to you, and somebody else will soon come and ask if you need anything, a cup of tea perhaps. If it goes beyond noon, we'll send in some sandwiches for you."

Leah ignored her and Melanie stood up and left the room.

Even as Jack and Melanie walked into the interview room, they could see that the two men were frightened.

The silent officer standing by one wall was totally ignoring them, despite their pleas to know what was going on, the last of which Melanie heard as she closed the door behind her.

Switching on the recorder and waiting for it to be ready while she and Jack stayed silent seemed to frighten the two brothers even more. Their faces were pale, and Melanie could see Andrew's hands trembling.

"Do you know why you are here?" she asked without a preamble.

They both shook their heads.

"Leah said we had to come, but she didn't say why," said Andrew. His voice was harsh with tension.

"Do you always do what Leah tells you?" asked Jack.

"We always have," said Paul. He seemed embarrassed. "She's the oldest and for some reason, she's always had control of the money. Dad gave her the accounts and the chequebooks and all that and anyway, she's been to university, and she always seems to know what's best."

"So you have no idea why we asked you all to come here?" asked Jack

Again, the two brothers shook their heads.

"Have you talked to Leah?" Paul asked.

"We have," replied Jack, "and now we have some questions for you two. First question, and think carefully before you answer. Did you kill Peter Chancellor?"

Both men went rigid, their faces ashen.

*They sure did*, thought Melanie. *If I could have filmed that reaction and shown it in court, no jury in*

*the world would have any doubts. Pity that wouldn't be valid evidence.*

Andrew seemed to be having difficulties breathing and he licked his lips to try and ease a dry mouth.

"No.. no, we didn't. Why would you ask that? It's insane."

"We know that Chancellor called on you at the compound," said Jack. "We've found tyre tracks outside the gate and leading up to Leah's house that match those of his car that was found at the bottom a ravine not far from your home, as well as dirt in the treads that match that inside the grounds. Do you know why he called on you?"

"He was yelling something about a chess match played many years ago and demanding Dad give him a chess set he said he'd won." Andrew had eased his speech difficulties. "I had no idea what he was on about."

"You never knew the story of the match he played against Chancellor back in England, how he lost and how he refused to pay the wager, a Fabergé chess set?"

The mutual head shakes occurred again.

"We knew he'd played a chess match against somebody in England. But we heard that he won and the other bloke called him a cheat and caused a major scandal. A Fabergé chess set? That sounds expensive. I've never heard of that or seen one. What's it all about?" Paul seemed more curious than frightened.

"You never knew your father had such a thing, worth a couple of million pounds?"

"Never," said Andrew. "He never talked about it."

"Hey," said Andrew, looking at his brother. "Remember Dad's safe he had in his bedroom? He never told us what he kept in there. Maybe that's where he had this Fabergé thing?"

Paul shrugged. "No idea," he muttered.

Jack renewed the pressure. "Did Leah tell you to kill Chancellor?"

Andrew and Paul drew in their breaths in panic but said nothing.

"Did she tell you to get rid of the car and then bury the body in that field where we've been digging up a lot of bodies?

The brother's faces were ashen, and they seemed on the verge of tears.

"How about your father?" Jack was remorseless. "Did she tell you to kill him as well, because he was dangerously close to letting out the whole story? And did you all bury the two bodies in that field?"

Melanie and Jack watched in silence as the two men almost fell apart, weeping but saying nothing.

*They did*, thought Melanie. *The bastards let their sister order them to kill Chancellor, get rid of the car and then bury both bodies. Did they kill their father too, or did Leah do that? Did they play a part in any of the other killings? They're guilty as shit, but I've got no hard evidence yet and they probably won't confess on their own initiative. That sister is one dominant woman, alright.*

Jack nodded at her and they walked out of the interview room.

"What a combination, eh?" said Jack. "Two completely submissive ninnies and a massively dominant elder sister. They're guilty as hell, but Leah is the main criminal."

"Trouble is, we've interviewed them without legal representation and despite the weeping and wailing, they haven't actually admitted any crime. I don't have enough evidence to present to the Public Prosecutor."

"True. Just a matter of time, I would say. Let's just keep them a while longer, then release them. They'll do something horrible before too long and then we'll have them. For all the evil, not one of them is all that bright, not even Leah. They'll give themselves away at some point."

"Agreed. I'll let them stew in their obvious panic for a couple of hours then release them. I'd love to hear the conversation with Leah when they meet."

"It would be informative, that's a fact. If we could record it, that would be all the evidence we need, but we can't do that."

"What a pity. Let's go and have a coffee, Jack."

"Let's do that and perhaps we can imagine just how Percivale got two governments to agree to give him witness protection."

"We may never find out, Jack. If that's what happened, I doubt either government would want the world to know about it."

## Chapter 24

*18ᵗʰ June, 1964, 10 Downing Street, London 9:00am*

"Thank you for coming, Sir Richard."

"It sounded urgent, Prime Minister." The Chief of MI6 took a seat across from the Prime Minister's desk.

"It is, Sir Richard. This is going to be difficult for me, but there is a national security risk and I'm going to ask you to help me avoid that and also considerable embarrassment to this government."

The Chief crossed his arms as if to protect himself from attack. "Then it seems to merit my attention, Prime Minister," he said.

"It does. You know Baron William Percivale, the tenth Baron of some muddy patch in Scotland, of course."

A look of scorn flickered across the face of the MI6 Chief.

"Of course. A most contemptible person. We know that he has somehow acquired a library of unfortunate details of many people in power, but we have no evidence that he has used it."

"That is correct, and not only him. His great-grandfather, the seventh Baron Douglas Percivale, the Ambassador to Russia before the Revolution of 1917, blackmailed a previous Prime Minister, David Lloyd George in this very room using information about some youthful indiscretions."

Sir Richard looked startled. "We knew about the reputation of Lloyd George, of course. But I had no idea that any documentation of it existed. It must have been kept very well hidden."

"It certainly was. That story was kept very secure, passed down in an "Eyes Only" document to each Prime Minister since then."

"The family has interested us for decades, Prime Minister. You won't know about this, but the next Baron, the eighth, Campbell was actually a double agent for us, posing as an associate of the Cambridge group of students and academics that were communist agents in the fifties and for some time after."

"That mob with Burgess, Maclean, Philby and Blunt? Bloody traitors, the lot of them."

"Indeed, sir, and we were never entirely sure which way Campbell Percivale's sympathies lay, but he gave us much valuable information about their activities."

"Rotten to the core, the lot of them. But now, our attention must focus on the tenth Baron, William. He has got himself into a massive pit of scandal. Apparently, he renegued on a large bet on a chess match at the Surrey home. Society will be deeply shocked when it comes out and I am deeply concerned that he might unleash some of that secret library he has. It could cause us all serious damage."

"Has he shown any signs of using any of that material?"

"Not so far. However, we tracked him to a bank in Geneva after he had received a visit from Anthony Blunt a few weeks earlier. We can't access what he saw there, but logic suggests that's where the stash of ugly materials is kept."

"You want me to dispose of him, Prime Minister?"

The Prime Minister looked shocked.

"Good god, no. I want you to organise his departure from Britain. I will arrange with the Australian Prime Minister for a new identity with a full Australian history, birth certificate, passport, and all that."

"Will Menzies agree to that?"

"Menzies is the ultimate Anglophile. He loves Britain, he worships the Royal Family, he will do what I tell him. I need you to make the arrangements at this end and keep everything absolutely quiet. Percivale must simply vanish, and it must be done before the general election this year. It's possible that Wilson will win and I don't want him to know about it."

The MI6 Chief rose to his feet.

"Leave it with me, Prime Minister," he said and walked out of the office.

* * *

## 19<sup>th</sup> *June, 1964, 10 Downing Street, London*

### *10:30am*

"Thank you for taking my call so late in the day, Robert," said the British Prime Minister.

"No worries, Alec," said Robert Menzies. "What can I do to serve the Mother Country?"

"We have developed a situation here that could cause considerable embarrassment to the government and to the Crown," said the Prime Minister. He laid out the situation to the Australian Prime Minister. "My worry is that it seems likely that Wilson will win the upcoming general election and lead a typically socialist government that would relish the opportunity to cause the Conservative Party embarrassment. I want this resolved before then.”

“And how can I help?”

“I want this man transferred to Australia with a completely new identity. He will be financially independent, so no burden on you and he must be continually watched by your security forces to ensure he keeps a low profile.

“If only to make sure he does not cause embarrassment to our Queen, I’ll do as you ask, Alec.”

“Thank you, Robert. I’ll initiate the process immediately.”

## 20<sup>th</sup> June, 1964, Percivale Hall, Surrey, UK

Percivale looked up as his valet entered the room. Since the chess match, the Baron had barely stirred out of his room, having his meals served to him there and drinking heavily.

“What do you want?” he snapped. “I didn’t call for you.”

The valet didn’t immediately reply but sat down in the armchair across from the Baron. Percivale’s eyes widened at this casual act.

“Who the hell do you think you are?” he said, his voice raised in anger. “Get out of that seat and bring me a scotch. Remember who you are and what your job is.”

“Baron, shut up and listen,” said the valet. Authority resonated in his voice and Percivale visibly shrank back in his seat. “My name is Graham Hunter, and I may have been your valet for the last few months, but I’m an agent with the British Secret Intelligence Services, something you know as MI6. My job has been to keep an eye on you since you became the tenth Baron."

Percivale stared at him, wide-eyed.

"But.. why?" he said, his voice harsh.

"Well, it could be because your father was associated with a mob of traitors known since their days as students at Cambridge. Or it could because your grandfather was suspected of some illegal arms trading to the wrong people during the Second World War. Or perhaps because your great-grandfather threatened Prime Minister Lloyd George with blackmail in order to get a Russian family to England after the Russian Revolution. Or all the above."

Percivale seemed frozen in his seat.

"But the reality is this, Baron. You've got yourself into a god-awful mess with that chess match debacle. Once it all comes out, you'll be disgraced, you will lose your seat in the Lords, and you will become an embarrassment to the country. We're going to help you avoid all that."

Percivale seemed to show some spark of interest.

"How?"

"Here's what's going to happen," said Hunter. "Later today, you'll leave here and go to a rather specialist private hospital in London. Some minor surgery will be done to your face, nothing painful, nothing major, just enough to change your features in small ways so that you won't look quite like you do now. It's a common thing done for people going into witness protection programs or for our agents going undercover in other countries. Then a few days later, you'll be taken to a military airfield where an Australian air force transport plane will take you to Australia. You'll be given all the documentation needed for a completely new identity as an Australian-born citizen. Bank accounts will be set up for you and a sizeable sum will be transferred to that to allow you to live comfortably. Meanwhile, we will arrange with a professional firm to operate under the strictest secrecy to handle the finances of your estates and keep both properties maintained."

Percivale seemed stunned.

"What about Felicity?" he said.

"Felicity left this morning," said Hunter. "She was put on a Qantas flight to Sydney, and she'll be home in Bellingen in a day or two. You will not contact her for at least three months after you get to Australia, and we'll maintain a close watch on you to make sure of that."

Percivale said nothing. Hunter got to his feet.

"Now, My Lord, please pack what you need for the next few days," he said. "And was that a scotch you ordered? I'll bring it at once."

## *The Times, 27th June, 1964, London, England*

*Great concern has been expressed about the whereabouts of Baron William Percivale who disappeared a few days ago from his family residence in Percivale Hall in Surrey. The Baron was fresh from his famous chess win against one of the finest players of the era, German Konrad Richter and is believed to have accepted a challenge to play another match against one of the onlookers of that match. What happened is unknown, but the Baron vanished soon after and this was only noticed when one of the house staff took him his breakfast in the morning.*

*The family and associates are all deeply worried, but foul play is not suspected.*

## Chapter 25

### *4<sup>th</sup> November, 2025, Coastal NSW, Australia*

### *9:32am*

"The Trustees in Scotland have written to me," said Leah, anxiety spread all over her face. "They want to arrange a teleconference call to update me on significant changes. They've never done this before, I can't imagine what this is about."

"For when? asked Paul.

"This evening at eight o'clock. That's nine in the morning their time. You'd better be here."

Both brothers nodded. "See you back here at eight," said Paul.

### *8:07pm*

"Good morning, Baroness, or should I say good evening. I am Alisdair Craig, Managing Partner. Thank you for meeting with us, and good morning also to your brothers, Andrew and Paul."

"Mr Craig, you said you have important news for us. Could you give it to me?" Leah's voice was harsh with tension.

"Baroness, I regret that I have very bad news. Our computer systems were hacked and a great deal of damage has been done to your accounts."

"What damage?"

The man in Scotland took a deep breath. "For a start, all thirty-one houses in the Percivale estate in Ayrshire have been sold."

"You what? Sold? How the hell could they be sold? Nobody consented to them being put up for sale."

"I know, Baroness. We have top-flight security systems on our computers, but somebody broke through all the firewalls, added the properties to the portfolios of several estate agents in the town and offered them at bargain prices. Offers were entered, contracts completed without anyone in the agents knowing what was going on."

"This is insane. Can't these sales be just nullified?"

"I'm afraid not, Baroness. Everything has been done legally, with every detail completed, the money was received, deeds have been passed to the new owners. They cannot be reversed."

"But what happened to the money? Surely you can recover that?"

"Again no, Baroness. The money was paid into the agents' trust accounts but then transferred out again within seconds with no indication of where the money went. We informed the police, of course, but they are baffled, they have no idea of how any of this could be done. They said it was the most extraordinary feat of hacking they had ever seen."

"And how much is involved?" Leah's face was white and she was gripping her hands together so tightly they were also white. The two brothers' faces reflected the picture.

"Just over ten million pounds, Baroness," replied Craig.

"Ten million… You've lost ten million pounds of my money?"

"And the revenues from those houses. That's not the end of it," said Craig. "There's a lot worse."

"Worse? Good god, what could be worse?"

"Your trust account in our bank was also removed. That contained fifteen million pounds. Baroness, you have been cleaned out."

Leah could do nothing but stare at the monitor.

"Everything has gone?" she stuttered.

"The lands of the estate remain," said Craig. "But there's another problem there."

Leah couldn't speak, she was almost in a catatonic state.

"The lands and the Scottish home, also the Surrey home and lands were integral to the Baronetcy and only owned by the title-holder at the pleasure of the Crown. Because you will be unable to pay the costs of maintaining both properties, the government has decided to revoke that ownership in order to maintain these historic buildings. This was suspiciously fast and we suspect the British security forces had advised the government to do this."

Tears were running down Leah's face and she was struggling to breathe. "What about the Australian properties?"

"The same has happened. Contracts were exchanged on the two commercial properties ten days ago, they were signed and the buyers paid the money immediately. They got them at perhaps seventy percent of the current value. Neither corporation wanted to miss the chance of claiming them. However, one small piece of good news remains."

"Good news? What possible good news could there be after all that?"

"The good news is that the property on which you built your homes and that one field some distance away remain in your possession. At least you will keep your homes."

Leah reached out and disconnected the call before bursting into sobs.

"I don't understand," said Andrew. "Have we lost everything?"

Her face covered with her hands, Leah nodded.

"We're bust," she said and burst into more tears.

## Chapter 26

### *10th November, 2025, Percivale Castle, Ayrshire, Scotland*

"Thank you for coming," said the man in the tweed jacket and black jeans. "My name is Ian McDougall, I'm from the Architectural Heritage Society of Scotland. We know how stressful recent times have been for you, and you are all justifiably anxious about the future. Let me allay some of the fears.

"As you all know, Baron William Percivale died recently and the title passed to his daughter, Leah. However, through processes that nobody can understand and thus cannot correct, all the properties here and in Australia have been sold off, the financial assets stripped, and the family is left penniless.

"This castle remains in the family for certain legal reasons but the British government has determined that the family cannot maintain the upkeep of the building and has exercised its rights to claim ownership. But the first thing to assure you is that all the present staff will be kept on as the new changes take place."

He smiled as a sigh of relief ran through the group assembled in the hall of the castle.

"We in the Society have been assigned responsibility for the management of the castle and have decided that we will convert it into a hotel, resort and golf course with an attached museum of Scottish history. A lot of structural work will be needed, and this will last a year, but if I can repeat my earlier assurances, all of you will be necessary for upkeep and later you will be transferred to the new organisation, which we expect from our market surveys to be highly popular and profitable. And I should tell you that a similar meeting is taking place today at the Surrey mansion of the Percivale family which has also been passed to a private company for redevelopment.

"Thank you for listening, I hope I have eased your fears. Architects and inspectors will be coming here in a few days to start the work. When necessary, accommodation will be arranged for you, and we all hope that the disruption of the next year will be minimised."

* * *

### 10<sup>th</sup> *November, 2025, Percivale Hall, Surrey*

"Good morning, everybody, thank you for coming. I see a lot of anxious faces here, probably expecting bad news about your jobs, so let me tackle that point first. My name is Howard Cormack, I head up a new organisation that we have founded, called Percivale Resort.

"As you all know, Baron William Percivale died recently and the title passed to his daughter, Leah. However, through processes that nobody can understand and thus cannot correct, all the properties here in Britain and in Australia have been sold off, the financial assets stripped, and the family has been left penniless.

"This building was not sold for various reasons but the government has decided that the maintenance and upkeep of the Hall cannot be continued, given the financial crash experienced by the Percivale family. My company was able to buy it, conditional on maintaining it for public use and commercial operations. So the first thing is this, all of you will be transferred to the staff of Percivale Resort at an increase in your present salaries, starting immediately."

He paused as a sigh of relief ran through the ballroom of the building.

"We will convert the building to a high-class hotel, resort and golf course," he continued. "The grounds are perfect for such use, as is the building. Once in operation, all of you will continue to have your jobs, though some retraining may be necessary, and more staff will be required.

"In a few days, this place will be inundated with architects and engineers and remodelling will begin soon after. Naturally, that means some discomfort and disruption, but when needed, accommodation will be found in nearby hotels at the corporation's expense. Your salaries will continue, regardless of whether you are able to work here or not.

"And I should tell you that a similar meeting is taking place today at the Scottish castle of the Percivale family which has also been passed to a private company for redevelopment."

He waved and left amid a rising volume of discussion among the staff of Percivale Hall.

## Chapter 27

### *18ᵗʰ November, 2025, Percivale Castle, Ayrshire, Scotland*

The four men in overalls and safety helmets stared at the massive wooden door. They had descended to the basement an hour ago, cleared away piles of debris and forced open a metal grill gate to find themselves in a small room. They moved in the powerful lamps and then were faced with the door. It looked ancient, solid oak with metal bands across it and one massive handle on the left side.

The foreman tried it and while he could raise it, it didn't turn. Whatever was behind that door was fully protected.

"What sort of key opens a door like that?" asked one of the men behind the foreman.

"A fucking great big one," said the foreman. "This is like some sort of gothic horror story. Have a look around, see if there's any sign of a place where a key could be hidden."

But after an hour of tapping on walls looking for hidden spaces, no results were forthcoming.

"Well, you know what the boss said, open up the whole area," said the foreman. "Mick, get the drill, cut away the area round the hinges."

Two hours later, the door had been freed from the enormous hinges but stayed upright in place. The wood was over twenty centimetres thick, and the door stayed stubbornly where it was.

"Better pull it this way," said the foreman. "No knowing what's on the other side, could be badly damaged if we push it that way. We're here to renovate, not destroy."

He threaded a rope through the gap where the top hinge had been cut away, lowered it until he could grasp it at the bottom hole then pulled it through, tied it to the main stretch and then extended the rope a few metres.

"Okay, let's put some muscle into this," he said, and the four men hauled on the rope. Inch by inch, the right side of the door was pulled away, still staying upright, but after twenty minutes, a space had opened up big enough for a man to step through to the other side.

"Jesus Harold CHRIST!" he said.

* * *

"Twenty-seven bodies," said Detective Inspector Forbes MacIntyre.

"Any indications of ages?" asked Jack. The three of them sat in Melanie's office, looking at MacIntyre's face on the monitor.

"Still being examined," said the Scot. "But the doctor thinks there's nothing more recent than about seventy years, possibly going back perhaps a hundred and fifty. None of the bodies was in a coffin, just wrapped in heavy cloth, a good number of the older ones were just skeletons."

"The stink must have been horrible, surely?" said Melanie.

"Probably," said MacIntyre. "But the bodies were well-wrapped and hidden in a tightly sealed room deep in the basement. The stench of each new body would soon dissipate."

"So the killings probably started soon after the castle rebuilding was finished in 1848," said Alex. "Did every one of the Barons take part?"

"Unknown at this stage," said the Scot.

"I'd put money on it," said Jack. "But remember what I found out when I was in England. At least one of the earlier Barons had killed a few locals at the pushing of his wife. It could go back even further. This looks like the worst case of severe psychopathy running through each generation I have ever read about. Maybe each of them controlled the urge for a few years and then succumbed to it, killed some poor local, hid the body in that hideous room and resumed normal life until the next one."

"There was another interesting find," said MacIntyre. "One of the workers found a small box hidden behind one of the bodies. It wasn't locked, he opened it and found two items, a sheaf of parchments, lots of tight writing, quite indecipherable and very faded, but there was a date that could be made out, looked like August, 1643. We've sent that round to the University, they've got experts in handling stuff like that. The other was a small book, it looked like a diary, but it was very old and the writing was in old Scottish Gaelic, not easily read, even without the fading that had occurred. Luckily, our foreman is a student of Gaelic and he started working on it. He saw the date was 1851 and he slowly read out the first few paragraphs. They seem to back up your theory. Let me read you a little of it."

### *15ᵗʰ June, 1851, Percivale Castle, Ayrshire*

"Dear husband mine, this is a lovely castle you've built, it's got everything we wanted, but what am I supposed to do with my time?" Lady Aisling looked at her husband with the frown that he had learned to dread in the years they had been married.

"My dear, I have no idea," he replied. "I have no knowledge of how ladies of your station occupy their time. I thought your needlework and painting filled your days."

"Well, they don't," she snapped. "You have all your activities, hunting stags, holding the courts to try the criminals on the estates, meeting other Lords to discuss business, but I have nothing."

"What do you suggest?"

"I want to join you in a hunt."

Baron Donald was shocked.

"My dear, that would never do. I know that some women have started riding in fox hunts in England, some are even riding astride, but I think that's disgraceful. It will never be accepted in Scotland."

She sneered. "It's not foxes I want to hunt."

"Not foxes? Surely you don't want to come out stag-hunting? It can be cold and wet and your dresses would hardly allow you to hike over the hills."

"Not stag hunting, either. Just think. What could be the most exciting thing in the world to hunt?"

The Baron looked confused. "I have no idea."

"Really, Donald," she said. "You have no imagination. We can hunt men. Look, you have hundreds of peasants on the estates, they're your property, nobody would miss a few, they'd just think they've gone off to seek a better place. Many do just that."

Instead of shock, the Baron looked intrigued. "My dear, what an exciting idea. You and I could go out after dark, you can wear a man's clothing, I think you will look most fetching that way."

"I'm glad you see it my way," she said.

"Don't I always?"

"If you have any sense, you do," she said and kissed him lightly on the cheek.

"And that's as far as the foreman got," said MacIntyre. "He's going to translate the rest for us and type it up, but I'm sure you can see how this pans out."

"Good grief," said Melanie. "So in this case, it looks like the wife was the one to initiate the killings. Did Baron Donald do any before that, or was she the one that started the process?"

"No idea," said MacIntyre. "But I suspect the parchments will be interesting when we get the translations from the University. Being hidden down in the burial chamber like the diary, it may have something similar."

"One thing puzzles me," said Melanie. "How did they do it? How does one man and perhaps his wife, some of the time quite elderly, kill a full-grown adult, most of them male and carry them into the castle without being seen by anyone, especially the domestic staff?"

"The first part is easy," said MacIntyre. "Look at the family tree. Not one of the Barons was an only child. All of them had at least one sibling, mostly a brother, but a few sisters."

"The pathology extended to the whole goddammed family then," said Jack. "This is getting nastier and nastier."

"As to the second part, how did they avoid being seen, that's a puzzle," said MacIntyre. "We'll keep looking."

"Thanks, Forbes," said Melanie and waved as she cancelled the connection.

### 22*nd* *November, 2025, Percivale Hall, Surrey*

"This is interesting," said the foreman of the working party implementing the architects' designs.

"What is?" asked Howard Cormack, sitting in the lounge room upstairs where he was discussing the progress of the remodelling with the architect.

"There's a bloody great big trapdoor in the floor of the basement."

"Can you open it?"

"Not yet. It's beautifully made, the same wood as the basement floor, hardly noticeable. We only saw it when we moved a wardrobe and found an equally great big padlock."

"Okay, Harry, lose that lock, we'll be right down."

The foreman hauled open the trapdoor and shone his flashlight down into the space.

"HOLY SHIT!" he said.

*   *   *

"Fourteen bodies," said Detective Inspector Charles Grosvenor of the Surrey Police Force in Leatherhead.

"Any estimates of the ages?" asked Melanie.

Grosvenor smiled. It was a pleasant smile, that of a middle-aged, mature man. Melanie estimated his age as over fifty. His head was almost denuded of hair, just a white trim round the side. His face was strong, a man on whom authority and responsibility sat easily.

"The doctor thinks nothing less than sixty or seventy years, perhaps as much as a hundred and fifty, even more. He says he will need to conduct some more hi-tech tests to get accurate data."

Jack looked at his notes. "So probably during the times of Baron Alisdair who built the house in 1880 and up to the last Baron, William who died this year."

Grosvenor nodded. "Though the last only had a few years, from when he gained the title in 1958 through to his departure in 1964."

"Correct," said Jack.

"Inspector, we have sent you all our reports on the investigations into the Percivale family, yes?" said Melanie.

"You have, Inspector Carter. They have been invaluable in clearing up some issues that have existed for decades. We never thought that the Baron would end up in Australia, but between you and me, we have long suspected some high-level involvement. Some of our inquiries have been blocked and not even our Chief Constable was able to get clearance."

"I can't tell you how we know, because our source is itself a major criminal element, but I can confirm your suspicions. Very high-level involvement, indeed."

"We were sure of that. But I'm fascinated by your statement that your source is a major criminal element."

"Maybe one day, I'll be able to explain that to you. But not now. As you know, we are investigating a similar serial killing situation in Australia and the three children of the late Baron are the subjects of our investigations."

The Englishman laughed. "Bodies arranged like a chess match! I thought I'd seen everything, but that beats all."

"It seems this killing spree is linked to the one you have just found and also the one in Scotland at the Percivale Castle. Inspector Forbes MacIntyre has kept you informed on that?"

"He has, except for when he kept blathering on about you, Inspector Carter. Somehow, you made an impression on him and now I can see why!"

Melanie ignored the comment. "One thing that puzzles us is how the Barons, assuming it was the Barons who did all this, got their victims' bodies into the Hall, same with the Castle, without being seen by anyone. So I'd like to ask you a favour."

"Sure. Go ahead."

"Can you bring a few of the household staff together and you and I interview them jointly by videoconference? We may find out how this was done. We'll have Forbes MacIntyre in Edinburgh join in and then all three of us can interview the Castle staff in the same way."

"Sounds like a good idea. I'll clear it with my boss, shouldn't be a problem, and I'll get back to you as soon as I can arrange it. It shouldn't take long, he's fascinated by this case."

"Thank you, Inspector Grosvenor. I'll look forward to hearing from you."

* * *

"Good morning, everybody," said Inspector Grosvenor. "Thank you for coming. Can I reassure you, none of you is suspected of anything, we have asked you here to try and resolve one of the big puzzles we have about the recent horrors at Percivale Hall."

He sat at the head of the conference table and six anxious people sat down the two sides. On the wall at one end of the room, a large monitor displayed a split image.

Grosvenor pointed at the monitor. "The two people on the monitor are Detective Inspector Melanie Carter who is in New South Wales, Australia, the other is Detective Inspector Forbes MacIntyre of the Ayrshire Police who is in Edinburgh for this conference."

He waited while a short buzz of interest ran round the table and faded.

"I can't fill you in on exactly why these officers are here, but it means the inquiries into the murders extend to the Percivale Castle in Ayrshire and to the Percivale family now found to be in Australia."

The small buzz repeated itself.

"Here's our puzzle," the Inspector continued. "The killings in Percivale Hall appear to have occurred probably between sixty and a hundred and fifty years ago, that is since the house was built in 1880 and when the last Baron vanished in 1964. We know that none of you was in service during that period, but I believe a few of you have relatives who were, and you may be able to help. What is puzzling us is how anybody could get a body into the Hall, down to the basement and into that hidden sub-basement without being seen."

There was silence around the table. Then an elderly woman raised her hand.

"I think I may know," she said. "I'm Jenny Russell, I'm the housekeeper at the Hall. My mother worked there also for many years and she was the housekeeper before me, but she was just a maid when the last Baron William was there. She said some of the staff at the time told her of a tradition that used to be there for the previous Baron, Andrew, who was at the Hall a lot. It seems that every two or three years, the Baron would announce that everybody had three days off, they'd be taken down to Brighton on a bus, put up in a bed and breakfast place and then brought back and he would pay for it all. My Mum said she was hoping they'd do that again when William was the last Baron, but it never happened."

Another man raised a hand. "Now that Jenny has mentioned it, I heard about the same tradition. My grandad was the groundskeeper when Baron Andrew was alive and everybody thought that Baron William was a tightwad because they never got that special holiday."

Grosvenor looked round the table. "Anyone else? No? Thank you all, you have been immensely helpful. It looks like you solved our problem. If you would like to go round to our canteen, you'll be able to have tea or coffee and some snacks and then we'll take you back."

When the room had cleared, he looked at the images on the screen.

"Now we know how they did it," he said.

## Chapter 28

### *12th February, 1982, Coastal NSW, Australia*

"Daddy, he's being noisy," said Leah.

Felicity turned round. "Don't worry, darling, he'll be quiet soon. We'll be there in a few minutes."

Leah unbuckled her seat belt and got on her knees to look back at the space behind the rear seat. The man lying there had a bag over his head, his feet were bound and his hands tied behind his back. He was moaning loudly.

"Shut up!" shouted Leah. "You're making too much noise." She continued to stare down at the man but he didn't stop his moans. Leah returned to her seat, buckled her belt. "Stupid man," she said. "I'll be glad when we get there."

Ten minutes later, the Landcruiser pulled into the field and stopped. William took the sheet from the door's side pocket and consulted it.

"Okay, this is the White Knight, he should be just over there." He started the vehicle up and drove a few metres, the huge beams illuminating the field. The dash of whitewash William had painted a few days ago stood out sharply.

"Weren't we lucky to find this bloke," said Felicity. "To think somebody called Knight had been living just round the corner from us in Bondi when we lived there."

"Damn right," said William. He stopped the vehicle and got out, walked to the rear and began unloading the backhoe from the trailer.

Leah jumped out of the back seat. "What happens now, Daddy," she asked.

William walked up, patted her on the head. "This the best part, honey. You're going to love it. Felicity, will you dig the hole this time? You need the practice."

Felicity climbed up into the seat of the machine, started it up and moved to where William pointed at the whitewash. Watched by her husband and daughter, she dug a pit, raised the shovel and backed away before re-joining the other two. William opened the back door of the Landcruiser and hauled out the bound man. He forced him upright and Felicity took a firm hold of the man's arms. He pulled the bag off the man's head to reveal a red-haired, terrified face, firmly gagged.

"It's best when they see what's going to happen," said William to Felicity who was watching intently. He pulled a hunting knife from his belt, waved it at the man who stared in wide eyes, desperately moaning into the gag. Then he plunged it directly into the man's stomach. He fell to the ground, twitching and then subsided.

Leah was jumping up and down and clapping her hands in glee. "Daddy, that was fantastic! When can we do it again?"

"Not for some time," said William. "Maybe your fourteenth birthday and then we can bring the boys along. They'll be six and ten, they should watch as well. Anyway, you can help here. Why don't you cut away all his clothes and throw them in the pit your mum just dug? And cut the gag off, too."

He handed Leah the knife and she ignored the blood all over the handle and began slicing away the jeans and tee-shirt the dead man was wearing. William went back to the car and pulled out a white gown and a helmet made of flexible sheet metal. When Leah had finished removing the man's clothes, he and Felicity manhandled the body and draped the white gown over it, slicing down the back to allow a fit and forcing the arms into the sleeves.

"Okay, the chess piece," said William and extracted a white Knight piece from his pocket. He bent down, sliced open the body on the stomach and inserted the piece in the corpse.

Then they pulled the body to the pit and lowered it feet first, finally pushing the helmet over the head. Felicity climbed back into the seat and scraped the earth back into the pit, leaving a small mound where it had been.

William smiled down at his daughter. "She did really well, eh?" he said to Felicity. "Handled it like a natural."

"She sure did," said Felicity. "Like mother, like daughter."

Thirty minutes later, the backhoe reloaded onto the trailer, the parents and twelve-year old girl were heading home.

### 25*th* *June, 1985, Coastal NSW, Australia*

"Dad, I think it's time I did one," said Leah.

"Are you sure, Honey?" replied William in the driving seat. "It can be pretty messy."

"I'm sure Dad. I've watched you three times, I know I can do it."

"I really don't know, Leah. I think you're still a bit young."

"Oh William, don't be a wuss," said Felicity. "You've seen how well she's handled the last three, no problems cutting the clothes off them and throwing them in the pit. She's nearly sixteen, she's old enough."

"Well, okay, if your mum approves, I can't resist," said William. "How is he doing back there, anyway?"

Leah undid her seat belt and knelt up against the seat back, looking down at the bound man in the luggage space.

"He's quiet," she said, sitting back and fastening the seat belt again. "I'd say Mum hit him pretty hard with the wrench, he's still unconscious."

"Well, he was wriggling too much," said Felicity. "Your dad was having trouble holding him down to get the straps on his wrists, so I had to wallop him pretty hard."

William turned the Landcruiser into the field and the headlights picked out the white marker he had left a day before.

"He's just a pawn this time," he said. "No helmet. Felicity, get the backhoe down and do the hole again. Leah and I will get the chess piece out."

He and Leah hauled out the comatose man from the back of the vehicle as faint groans came from him.

"He's coming to," said Leah. "Goodie! It's much better when they see what's happening and I want him standing up when I do it."

"How do you want to do it, Leah?" asked William.

"A knife, dad," she replied. "In the heart. But I want to cut his clothes off first. I've never seen a naked man before, not alive, anyway and I want to see him like that as I do it."

William laughed. "You're growing up, sweetheart. Okay, get his clothes off now, he should be able to stand up by the time you've finished."

Leah returned to the back of the Landcruiser, extracted the knife from the box in which they kept it and bent down over the bound man. It took her twenty minutes to remove all the clothing and she stared down at the victim.

"Oh wow," she breathed. "That's fantastic."

By this time, the man had recovered consciousness and was moaning loudly into the heavy gag that was tightly bound on his face. Leah could not hide the erotic joy she was hiding, staring fixedly at the man's genitals and touching them with the blade.

For another twenty minutes, this continued as Felicity dug the pit then backed the digger away and joined them. William dragged the man to his feet and held him upright

"That's a fun sight," Felicity said. "We've not done this before. Leah, I like your style. Okay, do it."

Immediately, Leah plunged the knife into the man's rib over the heart. Blood gushed freely down his body, over Leah's hands and onto the grass. William let him collapse and they watched the last of the man's movements.

"Well done," said Felicity. "I couldn't have done it better myself. You're a natural, girlie."

"Got the chess piece, dad?" asked Leah.

William took the white pawn from his pocket and Leah sliced away some of the stomach area and inserted the piece into the body as Felicity returned with the white gown from the car. Another fifteen minutes and the gown was draped on the body and they pushed it into the pit.

"Let's go," said William. "That was well done, both of you. By Christ, one day that Chancellor bastard is going to regret that chess match. When he sees the complete lay-out with all the bodies, he'll know not to mess with Baron Percivale. Leah, a great job. Let's get you home and wash that blood off your hands. Don't get any of it on the seats."

## Chapter 29

### *4th October, 2025, Coastal NSW, Australia*

"I'm delighted we could arrange this conference," said Detective Inspector Charles Grosvenor. "Did I get the time right, Melanie, it's six o'clock there?"

"You got it right, Charles," said Melanie. "Just after six."

"And nine in the morning in Surrey and in Scotland," said Grosvenor. "You blokes in Scotland are awake?"

There was a chuckle from Forbes MacIntyre. "Hell, yes! The cries of the wondering packs of wild haggises roaming the Scottish moors wake us up early."

Concerted laughter rose from Melanie's office where she, Alex and Jack were seated, looking at the monitor showing the faces of the two British detectives.

"So you have some astonishing information from us?" said Melanie when the laughter had died down.

"We really," said Charles. "Forbes and I have been collaborating over recent weeks and we've both had massive clear-ups in our Missing Persons files as a result of finding all these bodies. But we've also been discovering a lot of history about this amazing family of psychopaths, the Percivales."

"We've been comparing notes," said Forbes. "Comparing the body-counts between Percivale Hall and the Ayrshire castle and the dates when the Barons held their titles."

"And then checking against our Missing Persons files," said Charles. "But it's the body counts that will interest you. All the best technology we could apply was directed at the bodies in the Hall and we were able to date all of them. One interesting fact to start with is that none of the bodies dated from the time when William was Baron, between 1958 and when he disappeared in 1964."

"None of them? You mean William didn't kill anybody while he was in the UK?"

"That's how it looks," said Forbes. "We had the same result in the Castle, none of the bodies were dated after 1958 when William became Baron on the death of his father, Andrew in a car crash."

"I may have some additional data on that," said Jack. "But let's leave it until you've given us your finding."

"I'll look forward to that," said Charles. "But to continue. Two of the bodies in the hall dated from the short period of Andrew as Baron. He became Baron in 1955, so he had little time to get into the family business of killing people."

"And none of the bodies in the Castle date from his time, either," said Forbes. "The real killing sprees appear to have started with the father of Andrew, Baron Campbell who held the title between 1924 and his death in 1955. We dated eleven bodies in the Castle from that time."

"And three bodies in the Hall," added Charles.

"But the real horror story is from the previous Baron's time, 1901 to 1924 when Douglas held the title," continued Forbes. "He killed and stored sixteen bodies in his twenty-three years."

"And another six in the Hall," said Charles. "So just about one killing a year. This puts him among Britain's most prolific killers, but he's got a long way to go to match Harold Shipman."

"Yes, I've done a lot of research into Shipman," said Jack. "A doctor who killed as many as 250 people in the same period of time as Baron Douglas."

"Before that, we had Alisdair," said Forbes. "We identified twelve bodies from his time."

"And three in the Hall," added Charles. "It was that one who built the Hall in 1880 and it looks like he didn't spend much time in England, despite his seat in the House of Lords."

Alex looked up from his notes.

"So that makes thirty-nine murders in Scotland and fourteen in England since the start of the twentieth century, fifty-four in all," he said. "How many more are we going to hear about?"

"Before that, we can't date bodies with any accuracy," said Forbes. "But the boffins reckon the remains go back to about 1700 and they total another eighty-three."

"So could this mean the insanity started with the family about then?" asked Melanie."

"Possibly," said Jack. "Or it could mean that a marriage brought this psychopathic characteristic into the family."

"On that subject," said Charles Grosvenor. "We got the translation of that ancient diary back from the history department at the University. It makes fascinating reading. Let me give you just a sample. It was written in 1645 as we already knew and the author is Lady Annas Percivale, wife of Allistor, the fourth Baron. He was one of the longest ruling Barons, winning the title in 1610 at the age of nineteen on the death of his father, and living till 1660, so almost seventy at his death, a long life for that time. But this is what Lady Annas has to say:

*"We made our fifth kill this evening. It is quite easy to select the prey, any number of our serfs and other peasants wander around the country, looking for work or food. This evening, Allistor and I rode to the north of the castle and soon found a young man walking towards the township. Allistor rode over him with the horse and I jumped off and put a knife through his throat. My husband got down and between us, we were able to lift the body onto his saddle and were able to ride back in the dark. If anyone saw us carrying the corpse into the castle, they would not dare to speak because they know we would have them hanged.*

*"This is most exhilarating, but it took a lot of work on my part to get Allistor to join me in this game. I will never tell him that when he is away, I ride out with two trusted servants and I have killed six more in this way. We have buried all of them in the castle basement where a special room with a huge door has been constructed, nobody will ever get in."*

"So the madness goes far back," said Melanie, "and it seems that again, the real motivator is the wife, not the Baron."

"God knows what else we will find as we keep looking at both buildings," said Charles. "Jack, you said you had some comments to make about all this?"

"I do," said Jack. "And they are closely linked to what I just said. Courtesy of Melanie's boss, we were able to get a sealed record of the early years of Felicity MacFarlane, originally Harrison, of Bellingen, New South Wales. The first episode is about a series of shootings of house pets when she was ten. She was never charged with any of these, but the bullets, all .22 calibre were found to come from the same rifle. A couple of years later, her older brother, Brian told the police and submitted his rifle for examination and it was found to be the one used. She was deemed to be too young to be considered a criminal and no more was said. But over the next three years, she was expelled from two schools for un-specified behaviour. My suspicion is that she and William met in Surrey at the hall, immediately recognised kindred spirits in each other and later, when they married in Australia, she triggered the killing need in him."

"So the bodies in the field in your area are his, maybe hers as well and there would have been more bodies buried in Percivale Hall if the chess scandal hadn't forced him out of the country?" said Charles.

"That's my theory," said Jack.

"And have they passed this down to their three kids?" asked Forbes.

"Having met them, I'd put money on the daughter," said Melanie. "She's a highly dominant personality. But the two brothers seem to be weak and totally under her thumb."

"It would not surprise me if we find that Leah has played the role her mother played," said Jack. "What little we saw of William before he was killed and from his history of the chess scandal, he was a weak character also and was easily dominated by the females in the family.”

“And what about Felicity?” asked the British detective. “Has she never been seen again?”

“Not a sign,” said Melanie. “Since she vanished, assumed to have left the family, we’ve not been able to find any trace of her. It remains a mystery.”

“I’d say that was highly suspicious,” said Grosvenor. “Given what we know about this bloodthirsty lot, foul play would not surprise me.”

“Well, they killed their father,” said Jack. “Maybe killing their mother for whatever sick reasons is not impossible to imagine.”

“So we’re all stuck with the same problem,” said Forbes. “William is now dead and there are no murders in the UK we can hang on him. The probable killers are all dead, so although Charles and I have closed a hell of a lot of Missing Persons cases, we can’t close the murder files.”

“And we still don’t have any concrete evidence to charge any of the remaining Percivales in Australia either,” said Melanie. “We just have to keep investigating and hope we come up with something solid soon.”

“We’ll send you the reports of these findings,” said Forbes. “If anything else turns up, we’ll tell you at once.”

“At least, the historians are going to have a blast with all this,” said Alex. “Just look at the unpleasant history of British nobility they can research and publish papers about.”

"This has been invaluable," said Melanie. "I can't thank you both enough."

The two detectives waved, and their faces vanished from the monitor.

# Chapter 30

***12<sup>th</sup> July, 1954, Bellingen, NSW, Australia***

Felicity stared down at the tiny bundle of fur with an expression of contempt.

"I can't see why people get so soppy about cats," she said. "They're useless and stupid. What's so appealing?"

Brian, her brother looked at her with astonishment.

"But she's beautiful," he said. "She's funny, she likes to play. I'm going to call her Mojo. I asked Mum if I could have a kitten for my birthday."

"Then you're both stupid," said Felicity. "Don't expect me to have anything to do with it."

"Okay," said Brian and put the tiny kitten on the floor and rolled a table-tennis ball across the carpet. As expected, Mojo set off in hot pursuit, kicking the ball in all directions. It bounced off the table leg, rolled up to Felicity's foot and the kitten pounced. Felicity kicked it away and screamed, "Get away, you little bastard."

"Felicity, how could you?" shouted Brian and picked up the kitten, cradling it in his arms and stroking it.

"Keep that revolting thing away from me or I'll kill it," replied Felicity and stamped out of the room.

* * *

***15<sup>th</sup> July, 1954, Bellingen, NSW, Australia***

Realising she was alone in the house, Felicity felt a glow of excitement run through her. She walked into her brother's bedroom where he kept the basket the kitten slept in and saw the little animal curled up asleep. The glow became more intense as she picked up the kitten which sat easily in her two hands.

"Now you get it, you little freak," she murmured and moved one hand to circle the kitten's neck. It only took one squeeze and the kitten was lifeless in her hands. She dropped it back into the basket. "That was fun," she said and looked around the room. She had never been in her brother's bedroom before and she spent the next twenty minutes going through his chest of drawers, examining his underwear with interest before moving to the wardrobe. As she moved aside his suit, a couple of jackets and a number of shirts, she discovered something else. The rifle leaned against the back, not chained up in any way. On the floor was a box and when she examined that, she found four smaller boxes containing cartridges. They were labelled as .22 calibre. With a little experimentation, she found out how to open the bolt and insert a cartridge, but with more experimentation, she discovered how to load five cartridges into the magazine.

Carefully, she replaced everything as she had found them. An idea was growing in her mind, but it would need a special day before she could put the idea to work.

* * *

## The Bellingen Times, NSW, Australia

### 5<sup>th</sup> *August, 1954*

*Police are still looking for the person who has shot and killed a number of domestic cats and dogs in the last few days. All have been killed by a .22 calibre rifle at close quarters, indicating the shooter is not an expert shot. Tests of the bullets found in the corpses show that they have all come from a single rifle. Police report that they received a number of phone calls reporting rifle shots on nights when dead animals were found, but on investigation found nobody in the area.*

* * *

"Brian, you're absolutely certain it's your rifle that's been used?"

"Yes, Dad. I haven't used it for weeks, not since the last time you and I went to the range and I cleaned it then. Now it's been used many times, not cleaned and I'm missing a whole box of cartridges."

"Felicity, why did you do this? What horrible motives did you have?"

"What's wrong with you all? I just hate those bloody silly animals. They're useless, they're smelly, I don't know why you all love them so much."

"And she killed Mojo, too, Mum. She's kicked her away when she came too close. Felicity is sick, Mum. I think you should turn her in to the police."

"What do you think, Margot? Do we turn our daughter into the cops and she ends up with a criminal record?

"David, we can't. Just think what it will do to her. She's ten years old, she'd have a criminal record all her life, she won't get to University, her whole future would be ruined. Let's hope this horrible episode is just a phase and she grows out of it."

"Mum, you've got your eyes closed. Felicity is evil, she'll always be evil. I want nothing more to do with her."

"Brian, she's your sister. You have to allow for some things."

"Not this, Mum. She killed my cat, she's killed a lot of other people's pets. I bet she'll start on humans before too long."

"Brian, how could you say that, that's terrible."

"It's true, Mum. Dad, please, turn her in now."

"No Brian, I'll go along with your mother. But make sure you keep your rifle locked up now, same with the cartridges. And Felicity, one more ugly episode like this, I will report you to the police and you can face the consequences. Now go to your room and stay there. You can only come out for meals and to go to school."

* * *

### 19<sup>th</sup> *June, 1962, Surrey, England*

"Felicity, there's a job going at the Mansion House just out of town. I think it would really suit you. It includes a room and meals, so this would be a great way for a young Australian like you to get adjusted to life in England."

"It sounds good. What does it entail?"

"It's rather varied. Much of it is cleaning, it's a big house and there are several domestic staff, so you wouldn't be cleaning the whole place, but you'd be assisting the others. Same with some kitchen work, washing up after meals to help the kitchen staff. And there's one other need. There's a married couple working there, and they have a small child. She goes to nursery school and Belinda, the mother drives her there in the morning and picks her up in the afternoon. But if you can help with the child in the afternoon when she's home, that would be a huge help."

"It sounds like some rich bloke's place. What is it?"

"It's called Percivale Hall, and you're right. It's owned by an actual Baron, William Percivale. He's Scottish and has a castle up in Ayrshire, but he's in the House of Lords much of the time so he lives down here a lot, so the house is always kept in operation. Are you interested?"

"Oh yes, it sounds perfect."

"Good. I'll give them a call and you can go along there as soon as they can see you. Good luck with it!"

## Chapter 31

*20<sup>th</sup> November, 2025, Coastal NSW, Australia*

*3:12pm*

Leah glared with rage at the two brothers and neither could withstand it, dropping their eyes to the tabletop. The furious glare lasted a full minute before Leah broke the silence.

"You're both fucking useless," she said, her tones cold enough to freeze water. "You're no help to me at all. That glamorous tart of a cop walks all over you and all you can do is drool and stare at her tits. That shrink laughs at us, he knows what we've done and all he's looking for is the proof, just like the bitch cop, so he can probably go off and write some sort of academic paper about us."

She paused and stared at each of the brothers in turn but neither could meet her gaze and just stared down at their laps. "Why haven't you shown some initiative, eh? Why does everything have to be left to me? Why can't you show some balls?"

Still no response from the brothers.

Leah slapped the table hard and rose to her feet. "You two had better do something to help. Get rid of one of those two. Not the bitch, she'll have people around her, but that senile old bastard, the shrink, he's old, why don't you two go and teach him not to mess with us?"

She walked out of the room and a moment later, the front door slammed as she returned to her own house.

"I've got an idea," said Paul.

* * *

## 21st November, 2025, Coastal NSW, Australia

### 8:38pm

Paul studied the house through his binoculars.

"Looks like two adults with two kids and the bastard shrink himself," he said.

"They put the kids to bed an hour or so ago," said Andrew. He put his binoculars down. "The quicker we can get this done, the better. This grass is a bit damp."

"We've got to find out which bedroom Savage uses," said Paul. "Then we can get close and shoot him up a bit."

"Looks like we've got to lie here a bit longer," said Andrew. "I'll be glad of a hot shower when we get back."

* * *

### 9:54pm

"Hey, look! Savage has just walked into that room," said Andrew.

Paul raised his binoculars and peered in the direction of the corner room where a light had just come on. "That looks like his," he said. "Yeah, he's starting to unbutton his shirt."

They both watched as Jack drew the curtains and twenty minutes later, the light was turned off.

"Give him half an hour to get to sleep," said Andrew. "Then we'll go over the fence there and get to the house. There's just enough moonlight to see our way."

* * *

**_10:30pm_**

"Glad that fence wasn't electrified," said Andrew, wiping his hands from the mud where he had stumbled as he came down from the fence. He picked up the rifle he had dropped in the fall.

"We'd have seen the warning signs yesterday when we came and looked over the place," said Paul.

"I suppose so," said Andrew. "What's he got in this place, anyway?"

"We saw a few cows. They seemed peaceful enough, not a problem. Leah said they've got a few alpacas, whatever the hell they are. Okay, the house is over there, there's not a light showing. Let's get on with it. Watch out for the cows."

Carefully, they made their way across the paddock, encountering a few cows peacefully eating. As they came across one, it lurched in fright and moved away from them.

"Shit!" whispered Paul. "I hope that doesn't wake up anybody."

"No chance," said Andrew in a similar tone. "It's late, they're all dead to the world."

Another shape moved in front. It was smaller than a cow and in the dim moonlight, it was coloured differently, mainly white.

"What the hell is that?" whispered Paul.

"It must be one of those alpaca things. Looks bloody stupid, can't be dangerous at all. Let's get on with this. That's Savage's bedroom over there."

Something thumped into Andrew's back with a force that knocked him to the ground. He shouted in shock, just as a similar shape attacked Paul. Several more alpacas arrived on the scene and as both men tried to stand up, they were battered to the ground again. Once down, the alpaca began stamping on the men with a fury that would not have been anticipated with the normally gentle look of the animals.

* * *

## 22nd November, 2025, Coastal NSW, Australia

### 6:48am

"They're completely unconscious," said Jack, gently examining one of the fallen bodies. "I've always known alpacas get protective over other animals, but I've never seen anything like this."

"Who the hell are they?" asked Graham, his son.

"No idea," said Jack. "They're faces are covered in blood and badly torn. I hope that ambulance gets here quickly."

"There's a car at the main gate," said Graham. "Assuming it's theirs, the cops will be able to identify them soon. They were carrying rifles, so it was obviously not a social call."

"I suspect the alpacas had the same idea," said Jack and got to his feet as the ambulance siren approached.

* * *

"Broken ribs on both of them, Andrew's left leg is broken in two places, Paul's right arm is almost shattered, it may have to come off," said Alex. "And he has a fractured skull. The docs said they'll have to be kept in an induced coma for days while the surgeons try and repair as much of the damage as possible. There's a fair chance neither will survive."

"I knew alpacas were good protective animals," said Melanie, "but I never realised they could be this aggressive."

"Nor did I," said Jack. "We've raised them from birth, they've lived with the cows from the beginning, they obviously thought of the other livestock as family."

"Leah has gone to the hospital," said Alex. "I was there when she arrived. She seemed more furious than upset, no obvious anxiety about her brothers."

"That is one seriously disturbed woman," said Jack. "All the murderous psychopathy in previous generations of the Percivales seems to be distilled in her."

"I wonder what her mother was like," said Alex.

"It would be interesting," said Jack. "But she disappeared fifteen years ago, nothing heard of her since. It would be interesting to talk to her. She's not a Percivale, so she wouldn't share that psychopathy. But one thing that interest me is that there is no evidence that William killed anybody while he was in the UK and he was there a few years before the chess scandal. I wonder if Felicity was herself a similar psychopath, recognised the signs in William and was the influence that made him a killer after they were married."

"God, what a family," said Melanie. "The two men are out of it for a while, possibly permanently and the chess board in the field has spaces for a couple more bodies. We have to keep a close eye on Leah and we need to go and talk to her. I'll be interested to see her reactions to the damage done to her brothers."

"I asked the doctor to call here when she left the hospital," said Alex.

"Good thinking, young man," said Melanie.

## Chapter 32

### *14th February, 1986, Coastal NSW, Australia*

"Leah, let's you and me have a coffee in my kitchen."

"Sure, Mum, what's it about?"

"I'll tell you when we're settled. Take a seat."

Leah sat at the kitchen table and watched as Felicity slowly pressed the plunger in the coffee pot and poured two mugs of coffee, bringing them over and sitting down across from her daughter.

"I tell you," said Felicity, "the way you killed that bloke a few months ago, that was impressive. I didn't expect you'd be able to do that so soon."

"I don't know Mum, it was easy. It just felt natural and I hope we can do another one soon."

"I think your Dad was a bit surprised. I know I was, but I felt very proud of you."

"That's good to know. Do you think we can do another one soon?"

"Not another chess piece body, no. Your Dad is very careful, doesn't want anyone getting suspicious about seeing the backhoe working at night, so he's keeping them down to two or three years apart unless we find a really good fit, like somebody called Knight or Bishop or something."

"Can't we find somebody called Pawn or Castle?"

"Hah! Very funny, Leah. Pawns aren't important and I've never heard of anyone called Castle. Anyway, your Dad says there wasn't a Castle piece on the board at the time and it has to match the board when he was cheated by that bastard Chancellor."

"I really love the whole thing, Mum. Putting bodies to match the chess board is brilliant, and I really enjoy killing the people."

"Yes, so do I. I discovered how much I enjoyed the process when I was a bit younger than you, I was ten and I borrowed my brother's rifle and shot a few cats and dogs."

"Ooh, you never told me about that! Where was it?"

"When my family lived in Bellingen. I think I knocked off three dogs and a couple of cats and I really enjoyed it. I never could stand animals, I've no idea why people liked having them as pets."

"Nor me, I wish I could have done that. All these kids at school, they all talk about their bloody pets as if they were humans, it's quite sickening."

"You don't say anything about that, do you, Leah?"

"Of course not, Mum. You and Dad really made sure I'd never tell anyone about the chess board and how we're filling it up. I know it's supposed to be wrong, but I've never understood why. What's wrong with killing off useless people?"

"Nothing, dear. But I'm like you, I wish we could fill the chess board quicker. Hey! I've got an idea. Your Dad's going to Sydney for a few days, let's have some fun."

### 16th February, 1986, Coastal NSW, Australia

### 9:12pm

"Okay, this should do," said Felicity. "We're over sixty kilometres from home, a hardly travelled road, it's nice and dark, this lay-by looks perfect." She drove the

Landcruiser to the edge of the lay-by, switched on the emergency flashers and turned off the engine. "Now we wait."

Over forty minutes passed before a car appeared. It slowed down as the driver saw the Landcruiser and it stopped alongside them. The driver wound down the window to reveal a young man in his thirties.

"Trouble?"

Felicity smiled at him from the driver's seat.

"We broke down an hour ago. No idea what's wrong."

"Have you called for roadside assistance?"

Felicity pulled a face. "Would you believe the phone's battery is flat and we can't charge it or use it at all with the car out of action."

At that moment, Leah appeared from the other side of the car. She was deliberately dressed for the part, hoping that a single man would appear. Her skirt was as short as a tennis player's and her white tank top was tight against obviously un-haltered breasts.

The man fell for it. He got out of his car, holding his phone.

"I'll call for you," he said, his eyes fixed firmly on Leah. He bent his head to look at his phone as he started dialling and that moment, Felicity swung a metal bar that she had kept on the car seat. It hit the man's head with a crunch and he collapsed.

"Well done, Mum," said Leah.

"Okay, quick," said Felicity. "Tie his hands and feet and put the gag on him. I'll get rid of the phone." She lobbed the phone as far as she could into the trees by the lay-by, then bent to assist Leah. A few minutes later, the captive was lying in the back of the Landcruiser, and they were back on the road heading home.

***11:20pm***

"You need the practice, so you dig the hole," said Felicity as they dragged the still-unconscious man out of the Landcruiser. As they dropped him on the ground, he began to stir and moan.

"That's good," said Leah. "I want him alive when I do it." She climbed into the driver's seat of the backhoe and began to dig a hole a few hundred metres from the house, at the far corner of the estate.

Thirty minutes later, the hole dug, the captive was fully awake, his eyes wide in fear. Leah approached him, holding the knife she had taken from the car. She waved it in front of the man, and he flinched, the scene fully illuminated by the car's headlights.

Leah laughed, pulled her skirt up to her waist and then her tank-top up over her breasts. "Like what you see?" she said and plunged the knife into the man's chest.

His whole body convulsed and he shook violently. Leah repeated the blow and watched as he slowly went still and stopped breathing. Leah sighed deeply. "That was great," she said.

"Let's get him in the hole," said Felicity and together, they pushed the corpse into the pit. Leah straightened her clothing and climbed back onto the digger and pushed the earth back into the burial pit. She straightened the pile and smoothed it down.

"Good," said Felicity. "You drive it back to the garage, I'll see you back at the house."

* * *

"You're definitely my daughter," said Felicity. She poured two portions of brandy into glasses and handed one to Leah. "I think you deserve a real drink. That was really well done."

"Dad will never know," said Leah. "He doesn't walk around the property."

"I think we're pretty safe," said her mother. "I must say, that was fun. We'll have to do it again some time."

"Not too long," said Leah and sipped at her drink. "Mum, I think it's time I got my own house. Three kids is too much for you and the boys need you more than I do."

"I agree," said Felicity. "I'll talk to your Dad when he gets back, we'll have the builders come and bring another kit house like this one. Another few years, we'll erect two more for the boys. It will be a really nice family compound."

"Sounds great. Mum, I'm worn out, I'm going to bed."

"Nighty night," said Felicity. "I'll do the same."

Both women slept soundly till the morning.

## Chapter 33

### *24ᵗʰ October, 1986, Coastal NSW, Australia*

"Our daughter's growing up, Felicity," said Percivale as Leah walked through the lounge-room.

"I hope that doesn't mean you're thinking sexual thoughts about her." Felicity's tone was cold.

"What the hell do you think I am?" replied Percivale in astonishment.

"I don't know. What are you?"

"Dammit, woman, I merely commented that she's growing up and she looks great. But if you want to know, I do worry about the way she dresses. When I drop her off at school, I see the way the boys all gather round her and it worries me. Can you persuade her to dress in rather less provocative fashion?"

"I'll do no such thing. She's free to dress as she pleases. And if you're getting sexual thoughts about her, I'll cut your balls off."

"Good grief, are you nuts? I'm her father and I don't want her to come to any harm. What the hell's got into you?"

Felicity got to her feet and shook a finger at him. "I think from now on, I don't want you in the same room as Leah unless I'm there as well," she said in a voice louder than usual. Her face was pinched, angry. "Do you understand?"

He stared at her in bewilderment. "What the hell's got into you?" he asked.

She didn't reply and walked out of the room, slamming the door behind her.

"What the fuck was that all about?" he muttered.

Felicity walked up the stairs and walked into Leah's room without bothering to knock. Leah was lying on her bed reading and she looked up at her mother in shock.

"Mum?" she said, a mixture of anger and astonishment. Felicity had always shown some courtesy in dealing with her daughter and this was a new development.

"From now on, young lady, you will never be alone with your father in a room," said Felicity. Her tone was harsh, reflecting her anger. "And you can stop dressing like a tart. Lower those hems, stop showing your tits to the world or I'll lock you in your room and you can miss school."

"What the hell are you talking about, Mum?" Leah sat up on the bed and slipped her legs over the side. "Are you saying I can't talk to my Dad? Why the hell not?"

"You can talk to him when I'm in the room," snapped Felicity. "But not alone. I don't him drooling all over your thighs and tits. Unless I'm there, you stay out and in your room."

"Are you nuts, Mum? You think Dad's got sexual thoughts about me?"

"I can see it. You'll do as I say."

"Like hell I will. You're not stopping me talking to my Dad whenever I want to. What is it, Mum? Are you jealous because Dad thinks I'm pretty? You think he wants to fuck me and not you?"

"You little bitch!" shouted Felicity and advanced on Leah, one hand raised.

Leah stood up, blocked the slap being aimed at her and instead, landed one on Felicity's cheek. Her mother's eyes opened wide in shock, she took a step backward, her hand on her cheek.

"Don't you ever try and hit me again," said Leah. "If you try, I'll beat your fucking brains out. Do you understand?"

For several moments, there was dead silence in the room as the two women stared at each other. Then Felicity marched out, tears streaming down her face.

"Now we know who's the boss," muttered Leah and smiled.

## 27<sup>th</sup> *October, 1986, Coastal NSW, Australia*

Felicity slammed the door behind her as she entered the living room where Leah sat on an armchair reading a magazine. William across from her in the second armchair, reading a chess magazine and sipping on a scotch.

"Leah!" shouted Felicity. "I thought I told you not to be in the room with your father unless I was there as well."

Astonished, both Leah and William looked up.

"Yes, mother, you did," replied Leah. "And I told you that was nonsense, you can't stop me talking to my Dad."

"Look at you," Felicity continued as if Leah hadn't spoken. "Your knickers are showing and half your tits are on display. If this is what you do at school, you can count on being raped by some pervert. Get up and go to your room."

"What the hell is wrong with you?" said William,

staring at Felicity and putting his glass down. "Since when do a father and daughter have to be separated?"

"Ever since you commented that she's looking good," snapped Felicity. "It was clear you were almost drooling over her. You're one sick puppy, William and she's just a tart. You obviously prefer her company to mine and I won't stand for it."

"You're just jealous, Mother," said Leah. "Maybe he does prefer my company, because you've become just a crabby old woman, you're no fun at all."

Felicity screamed and advanced on her daughter, hands raised to strike, but William leapt out of his chair and blocked the swinging hand.

"What the hell is the matter with you?" he demanded.

"I want her to keep away from you," said Felicity, her voice cracking and tears running down her face.

William nodded at Leah. "Best go for now," he said and held onto Felicity's wrist until Leah had left the room.

"I think you're nuts," he said and resumed his seat, picking up his scotch glass and the chess magazine.

Felicity broke into loud tears and ran out of the room.

### 30<sup>th</sup> *October, 1986, Coastal NSW, Australia*

"Tell her to get out of the room," said Felicity as Leah walked into the lounge.

"Can't even tell me to my face, eh, Mother?" Leah's face was full of contempt.

"Tell her!" said Felicity in louder tones.

William sighed. "Leah, please do as she wants," he said. "I hope she'll get over this one day."

"Dad, she's crazy," said Leah, but did as he asked.

* *

### 15*th November, 1986, Coastal NSW, Australia*

Leah drove the backhoe out of the shed where it was usually stored and up to the far corner of the property. Both parents were away, Percivale down in Sydney on business matters of which Leah new nothing, Felicity had gone shopping for the day in Port Macquarie, one of her frequent "Me" days she awarded herself for a day in the malls, lunch at the pancake house and just spending time among crowds. The two women had not spoken to each other since the blow-up of the previous month.

She directed the shovel at a spot a few metres from the small mound of earth, now overgrown with weeds where they had buried the man they had captured and killed fourteen months ago. The excitement and erotic thrill of that experience had never faded and she relived it frequently in her mind. She replayed it again as she dug a pit about two metres deep. As she pulled out the shovel the last time, she saw her mother's car approaching.

"Perfectly on time, Mum," said Leah to herself, leaving the engine idling and staying in her seat.

"What the hell are you doing?" shouted Felicity as she got out of the car. "Who said you could play with that thing?"

"Well, you and Dad both said I needed practice with it, so I thought this would be a good time," said Leah.

"Turn the thing off, for Christ's sake," shouted Leah. "I can't hear myself speak."

"That's okay, Mum," replied Leah with a smile. "I stopped listening to you ever since you told me I couldn't talk to my Dad."

"Is that what this is all about? Jesus, Leah, stop acting like a baby, grow up and put that thing away." Felicity began walking back to her car and Leah judged the timing perfectly. She swung the shovel hard to the left. It smashed into Felicity's head and she collapsed. Leah watched for a few seconds and when she saw Felicity's arm twitch, she raised the shovel and dropped it back on her mother's head. There was no possible sign of life after that.

Leah used the shovel arm to push her mother's body into the pit she had dug, filled it with the earth piled to the side and smoothed over the remains, leaving just a small hillock.

"Looks like I got pretty good with this," said Leah aloud. "Nobody's going to stop me talking to my Dad or telling me what I can wear."

She drove the backhoe to the storage shed, switched off the engine and returned to the car, drove that back to the house and left it with the keys in the ignition. She checked her watch, Percivale had said he'd be back at six. She had two hours.

She went back to her own house and to the writing desk she used for her school work. She took out a writing pad and began composing a letter of farewell from Felicity to her husband. She'd practiced Felicity's handwriting a lot, thinking that one day it would come in useful and now it had.

*"My Dear William,"* she wrote. *"It's been wonderful, but it's time for me to move on. I need more than just these exploits to keep me happy, so I've left to travel. I may be back, but don't expect me. Your loving Felicity."*

Sealing the letter in an envelope, she returned to her parent's house and left it on the dining table. Then she walked into her parents' bedroom, found a suitcase of her mother's and selected a few of her clothes from the wardrobe. She moved to the bathroom, pulled out her mother's toiletries and placed them in the suitcase and then walked back to her own home with a sense of satisfaction of essential work being completed. She hid the suitcase under the bed, knowing her father would never enter the room, then moved back to the lounge. She poured herself a brandy and went back to her bedroom to return to the book she'd been reading. There was plenty of time to get rid of her mother's things.

An hour later, she heard her father's car arrive and she sat back with a sense of anticipation. It didn't take long. Within minutes, he was banging on the front door. She went to it, to see Percivale standing there, looking sombre. He followed her to the lounge room and sat down.

"Your mother's left us," he said.

"Good heavens, Dad, did she say where she's gone and why?"

"Just that she needs to move on. She's taken some of

her clothes and all her toiletries, so I don't expect her back."

"Dad, how do you feel?"

"You know what, Leah, I'm not upset. Maybe this wasn't enough for her. And to be honest, I think it's best for all of us. She was becoming very hard and I really didn't like her much anymore."

"We'll be fine, Dad, I know that. The boys will be upset, they're still very young, but we'll look after them."

"Of course we will. But this brings on something I hadn't planned on for a couple of years."

"What's that, Dad?"

"You and I have to go travelling. There's something I need to show you."

"So where are we going?"

"Switzerland," he said.

## 25$^{th}$ *November, 1987, Geneva, Switzerland*

"It's been twenty-five years since I was here last," said Percivale.

Leah looked around the room lined with security boxes. "It makes me wonder just what's stored here. Bloody millions and millions, I reckon."

"And a hell of a lot of secrets."

"What, like in that box on the table? Are you going to open it, Dad?"

Percivale put his hands on the box which he had unlocked a few moments before, but still hesitated.

"Leah, there's stuff in here that could bring down governments around the world," he said. "It's made the family a lot of money in the last couple of centuries and it's the greatest gift I can give you. I know you'll be sensible, and I couldn't trust the boys the same way."

"I promise I will, Dad."

"When we get home, I'll give you the keys and the security codes for getting in here."

"Okay, Dad."

Percivale opened the box.

# Chapter 34

## *13th March, 1988, Coastal NSW, Australia*

"Paul, Andrew, we need to talk. Can you meet me in the recreation building?"

"What about?" said Paul. He sounded suspicious.

"You'll find out when you get there. Why are you hostile to the idea?"

"Let's just say that every time you call a meeting of us, there's usually some problem and you blame Andrew and me."

"I'm not blaming you, honest. I need your help and it's time you took a bigger part in running this family."

"Okay, see you there in a few minutes."

With coffee and biscuits laid out on the dining table, Leah settled back to wait. She knew this meeting would take a great deal of her authority over her brothers to get the right result. She had only a few minutes.

When the two brothers came in, they looked at the display of coffee and assorted biscuits and stood uncertainly. When Leah had asked them to meet on previous occasions, it had always been for her to lay down some rules of behaviour or to lecture them for some perceived failing. This was unusual.

"What's this about?" Paul still showed some reluctance. Andrew, the younger reflected his elder brother's uncertainty. At ten, he had always lived in the shadow of his siblings and it showed in his low self-confidence. He tended to look to Paul for support.

Leah smiled, something rare in itself and waved at the two seats at the table where she sat at the head.

"Please sit down, boys. I really do need to talk to you and get your help in family affairs."

Still showing reluctance, the two boys took seats on either side of Leah.

"Shall I play mother," she said with a smile and poured coffee from the pot into three mugs. "Help yourselves," she added.

She waited until the first sips of coffee had been made and the first biscuits selected and eaten. She still felt anxious about how this meeting would go.

"What I'm about to tell you must never be repeated outside this room," she said. "This is a matter of international importance."

That got to them, she could see. Andrew was reaching for another biscuit, but stopped and sat back in his chair. Paul put down his coffee mug and stared at her.

"You both know about why Mum and Dad came to Australia back in 1964, don't you?" she said.

"Not really, no," said Paul. "They never talked about it."

"Dad was one of the greatest chess players in the world, actually a Grand Master, the highest rank there is." Leah felt comfortable stretching the truth. "His name wasn't Macfarlane then. Actually, he was a Scottish Baron, the tenth in the line since 1485, the name was Percivale."

"Dad's a Baron?" Paul looked stunned.

"Yes, he is. And he still is legally a Baron with estates and a castle in Scotland. We own another mansion in England and quite a few properties here in Australia."

"Does that mean we're rich?" asked Andrew.

"Yes, we are. That's where our money comes from and why none of us has ever had to go without anything."

"Then why did he leave all that and come to Australia with a different name?" Paul still reflected suspicion.

"That's the real story," said Leah. "Dad played a chess match against some commoner, which of course he won, easily. But that common thug accused Dad of cheating and stealing a valuable chess set. He made a huge thing about it, went to the press, all the sort of stupid things commoners do to get money from real aristocrats."

"And what happened?" asked Paul.

"The trouble was, as I said, Dad's a Baron. He had a seat in the House of Lords and did valuable international work for the Government." Leah continued to stretch the truth. "Actually, all the Barons did. One of them had been the Ambassador to Russia before the first world war. They were very important people."

She paused to consider her next move. She poured herself another mug of coffee and took her time selecting a biscuit from the platter. The brothers remained silent, trying to digest this new and startling information.

"The British government decided that it was best to suppress the whole thing and offered to move dad to Australia with a new identity. He and Mum had already met at the English mansion where she was working and so she returned home to Australia and Dad followed her. They got married a few months later. The government put out a statement that Dad had been given another international post, but it was of great secrecy and nothing could be said about it."

"And he's been here ever since," stated Paul. "And now Mum's run away and left him, so what are we supposed to do?"

"Dad wasn't the sort of man to let this go," said Leah. "In fact, he and Mum were working on a major project to show the world what a cheat and a liar that thug in England was and make everybody look stupid."

She stared hard at each of her brothers in turn, knowing they had never been able to withstand that force.

"So let me say it again, what I'm about to tell you must never be repeated and nothing must be said about it until the project is completed. Understand? Can I trust you both?"

Neither of the boys said anything, but nodded.

"Good. Now, you know that field we occasionally drive past out on the northern country road? It's about a thirty-minute drive. Well, Mum and Dad marked it out as a chess board, not obviously, but with just some pointers as to where chess pieces would be."

She looked at the boys again. They seemed puzzled but attentive.

"Now when Dad won that chess match in England, he was in the end game with thirteen pieces still on the board, some white, some black. What we've been doing for a few years is putting a body in the ground where the chess pieces were in that match."

The brothers stared at her in horror.

"You've been killing people and burying them in that field?" Paul was almost gasping from the shock.

"That's right. And the best thing is they were dressed in white or black and we made them little crowns out of metal to represent the piece. So a Bishop had a Bishop's mitre on his head, a Knight had a little horse's head on a helmet. And even better, we actually slipped the chess piece into their bodies before we buried them."

She sat back and smiled at the boys in satisfaction.

"So what do you think about that?" she said and began chewing on her biscuit.

Paul's face was white.

"But *why?* What's the point?" he stammered.

"When every position is filled, we'll publicise it internationally to show the world that nobody messes with a Percivale. Nobody will know who did this, because we're not Percivales, we're just ordinary people who live in the area."

"But.. but.. *somebody* knows," said Paul, his voice coarse with tension. "The British government, the Australian government, somebody in those will know that Dad is the Baron Percivale."

"No problem," replied Leah, smiling. "It would embarrass the hell out of them if it's discovered that they helped Dad get away, and a hell of a lot more if it's revealed that Mum and Dad did this. And anyway, I happen to know that Dad has a lot of stuff on top people in both countries. They're terrified that it all could come out."

"How do you know that?" asked Paul, shaken to his core by these revelations.

"Remember when Dad and I went overseas for a few days soon after Mum ran away? He took me to where all that stuff is hidden away in a bank vault and I saw some of it. Believe me, nobody would want to see it released."

"Oh Jesus, this is awful," said Paul. "Our parents and my sister are murderers. How are we ever going to get away with all this?"

"I told you," said Leah, showing exasperation. "This will all be tied to the Percivale family, but nobody knows where any of them are and those who do know will do everything they can to keep it secret. We're safe, I promise you."

"Did you kill any of those people?" asked Paul.

"Not at first. Mum and Dad started this around the time I was born. When I was about twelve, they let me come along and help and then later I did kill a couple. Actually, I did a couple just with Mum, just to get experience.

"What do you want from us, Leah?" Paul said sadly.

"Easy," Leah replied. "When Mum and Dad were together, they managed okay, and I just added some strength and help. But Mum's gone now and Dad's not in great health. I need you two to help out on the next few, just the three of us."

"You want us to *kill* people?" Andrew finally broke his silence, having until then watched and listened in mostly incomprehension.

"No, what I need is help with some parts of it. Paul, you're big enough to help carry a new kill into the car and then out to the burial site. You'll be useful keeping them out cold when I've hit them on the head with a club or a wrench. Andrew, you can cut their clothes off when they're safely tied up and then help us shift them into the pit. And Paul, you should learn how to use the backhoe to dig the pit. Dad will be around for a while yet, but another couple of years, he won't be up to it anymore."

"I don't want to do this," said Paul.

"Nor me," echoed Andrew.

Leah switched on her major weapon again, the hard glare into their eyes.

"You *will* do this," she said. "Because if I see you failing to do what I need, I promise you, I'll kill you and put you in one of those chess spots in the field."

The room was silent for a minute while the two boys absorbed what was definitely a sincere threat.

"But what if we tell the police?" said Paul.

"Then the same thing applies, I'll kill you. And then the rest of us will spend the rest of our lives in a maximum-security prison. Which do you prefer, that or continuing to live this affluent life?"

Paul was silent again for a few moments, and then Leah could sense when his resistance broke.

"Okay, we'll do it," he mumbled.

# Chapter 35

## *24th November, 2025, Coastal NSW, Australia*

"Good morning, Melanie," said a voice from the computer monitor.

Melanie looked up from her study of crime reports in the state, not surprised by the interruption. Miller's face was friendly, relaxed.

"Allen," she said. "I was wondering where you had got to. You'd gone silent after the Percivale assets had been looted. That was you, of course?"

"Of course that was me," said Miller, a wide smile on his face. "Any piece of computer hacking that nobody can explain and has got through every security device known to man is almost always my work."

"This was certainly in that category," said Melanie.

"It's even better than anyone thinks," said the face on the screen. "I'd set up a corporation based in Norway and that bought all those houses in Ayrshire. It will continue to receive rentals from them. But then, as you know, the money vanished from the estate agents who seemed to have sold the houses. So I got the money back! Meanwhile, that company in Norway is a legal entity, it employs a few staff, pays taxes and they're paid from the rentals. Bloody brilliant, if you ask me."

"And that was your revenge for the murder of your aunt, I assume?" Despite her professional feelings, Melanie couldn't stop feeling admiration for what Miller had done.

"Correct. That's the worst thing that has ever happened to me and it's bugged me ever since she vanished. Once her body was found and identified and everything pointed to Percivale and his bastards, I decided they'd pay for it."

"They certainly did that," said Melanie. "They still own their compound and the houses on it, but I gather they're in deep trouble paying the rates and taxes to the local council."

"Don't you think it was generous of me leaving them their home?" said Miller, the smile still showing.

"I found it interesting that all the proceeds went to charities," said Melanie.

"Melanie, haven't you realised yet that I'm a warm, kind-hearted man under all this criminal cover?"

"Yeah, sure. I think it's more likely that you didn't want any indications of where you were if you put the money into a personal account anywhere."

"Hah! You may be right! After all, I don't need the money. Anyway, I've decided that the destruction of the Percivale clan is not yet complete."

"What else can you do to them, Allen? They're bankrupt, we're still investigating them for the multiple murders which will earn all of them life sentences. The two brothers are on life support in hospital, even if they recover, they'll be crippled for life. How can it get worse?"

The smile changed into a laugh. "That last bit gave me a good chortle," said Miller. "Attacked by a mob of cute alpacas? Damn, but that has to be the funniest headline you could ever see."

"So far, it's been kept under cover, Allen. We really don't want massive public attention on the family, it will make our case a hell of a lot harder if it's the middle of a massive media circus. Please don't do anything about it."

"Sorry, Melanie, too late."

"Oh shit, Allen, what have you done?"

"I've assembled copies of all the documents about the escape of Percivale from the UK to Australia. All the letters between Menzies and Douglas-Home, the two Prime Ministers, the agreement to put Percivale into a witness protection program, his new identity, his Australian family, everything. It's all in dossiers that will be sent to the media in both countries, including the details of the chess match that set it all off and how Percivale got shunned by British society. This will strip some high-up people quite naked."

She stared at him. "Jesus, Allen, but you really are a malignant prick. How the hell am I going to conduct a serial killing case with all that crap flying everywhere?"

He laughed again. "That's your problem, Melanie. You're a hell of a detective, I'm sure it will work out for you."

"Oh, fuck off, Miller. I've had enough of you."

"Okay," he said. He waved and his face vanished from the screen.

Melanie took a deep breath, consulted her computer file of contacts and located a number in Canberra.


"Detective Inspector Carter? This is an unexpected pleasure." ASIO executive Gordon Porter smiled in genuine pleasure. He had responded to Melanie's Skype call immediately.

"I doubt this will be much of a pleasure, Mr Porter. You may be facing some severe problems soon."

"Please explain."

"Do you know about an American computer hacker, Allen Miller?"

Porter looked surprised. "Hell, yes," he said. "We've had a constant connection with the FBI ever since you uncovered him in your last case. They were furious that they seemed to have missed him by hours after you identified him. Has he been in contact again?"

"He has. Just a few minutes ago, he called me on Skype. I have to tell you that he had been in contact some weeks ago after we'd identified one of the bodies as a woman who had been an aunt of his. His revenge was the stealing of all the family wealth and assets."

"Our technical people had already concluded that was Miller's work," said Porter. "They couldn't think of anyone else with that level of skill, but we didn't know why he'd done it. Now we know."

"And it hasn't stopped there. In a few days, the media in Britain and Australia will receive dossiers containing every detail of the Percivale scandal, including copies of the letters between the two Prime Ministers, the witness protection program, everything."

"Ah."

"Mr Porter, you don't seem upset?"

Porter smiled. "I'm not. On a personal level, I'm quite happy to see the whole shitstorm erupt, I never like to see people of influence sheltered from their crimes. But on a professional level, it's really no longer critical."

"Why not? You seemed pretty sincere about keeping me off the case when you were here. All that stuff about national security, embarrassed governments and all that.”

“That was the official position, Inspector. Since then, we've had meetings with the relevant Minister, some very high-up people in ASIO, talks with MI6, and we've concluded that the situation has changed.”

“How changed?”

“For a start, it's over sixty years ago. In Britain, the Conservative government that made the deal was kicked out by Wilson's Labour government within weeks of the event and no Labour government since would care about embarrassing the Tories, and the Tories have changed a lot since then, anyway. They won't be affected by a sixty-year-old scandal. Much the same here. Menzies has long gone, everybody connected with that era is history. Anyway, the media will be more interested in Percivale's scandal, how they've now lost all their wealth and been reduced to poverty, particularly now that Percivale is dead and his second wife vanished decades ago, quite possibly dead also.”

“So it's not a crisis anymore?”

“Not a crisis, Inspector.”

“So can I resume my investigations into the murders?”

“It looks like you never stopped, Inspector.”

“You knew all the time? Why didn't you stop us?”

“We realised the situation was changing and I really wanted to see what you came up with. You and your team did splendid work.”

Melanie laughed with pleasure.

“Well, thank you, kind sir. So I can keep going?”

"Feel free, with my blessing."

"Thank you, Mr Porter."

Melanie disconnected the call and updated her diary with the day's events.

By six, she'd had her fill. Feeling almost nauseous with fatigue, she picked up her handbag, extracted the car keys and walked out of the police station. She knew that Alex and Jack were still in the building but didn't feel like speaking to them. The Gordon-Keeble stood in a line of police officers' vehicles and as always, she felt the small wave of sadness at the story of how she had acquired it on the death of her fiancé, Scott. She opened the door, slid behind the wheel and as she fastened the seat belt, sensed the hand coming up behind her head.

The aroma of chloroform was familiar but as the soaked rag was clamped over her nose and mouth, she had barely enough time to struggle before she lost consciousness.

# Chapter 36

## *24th November, 2025, Coastal NSW, Australia*

## *9:07pm*

Consciousness slowly returned, accompanied by a thumping headache and pain in her neck and shoulders from having her head slumped over her chest for an indeterminate time. Without moving much, she tested her arms and legs and realised all four limbs were tied to a hard-backed chair. Fighting her panic, she sensed that darkness had not fallen much, so not a lot of time had passed since she had been drugged.

"Waking up, are we?" said a woman's voice from somewhere in front of her.

Raising her head, Melanie looked into the face of Leah, just inches away from her. Her head clearing, she thought she could see a mix of fury and triumph in the other woman.

Leah stood up straight from where she had been bent over to stare into Melanie's eyes and moved to an armchair across from a coffee table. Melanie looked around and realised she was in Leah's house in the compound. Her mouth and throat were dry.

"Its time we had a little chat," said Leah. "I'm sick of the way you and your mates have fucked us around and now you're going to pay for it."

Melanie said nothing, concentrating on recovering her senses and working up moisture to her throat.

"Not saying anything? Well, that's your choice but you'll be begging me for mercy soon, I assure you." Leah crossed her legs and picked up a wine glass from a side table. She took a sip and returned the glass.

Craving for moisture almost overtook Melanie, but she fought it. The headache had eased, but the pain in her neck and shoulders remained. She could barely move and was unable to ease it.

"So let me tell you what's going to happen," said Leah. "When it gets dark, your life comes to an end. I've got a beautifully sharp knife I keep for this purpose, I've knocked off quite a few people who are now buried in that field. You probably noticed, one of the missing pieces is the Black Queen. You're the perfect candidate for that role."

Melanie tried to suppress the shiver of fear that hit her, but sensed it was time to start fighting. Jack had once told her that a personality like Leah's needed an audience, appreciation of their actions and recognition of their dominance. It was time to use that knowledge.

"You really are a very stupid woman, Leah," she said and saw the surprise in the other woman's face.

"Oh? Why's that, bitch?" said Leah.

"The other two will already have found I'm missing and they'll know that this is the only place you could bring me in the time you had. Chloroform doesn't last long and I can see it's daylight. Meanwhile, it will take some hours to get the backhoe out to the field, dig a hole and put me in there. They'll have you in a cell within the hour."

Leah's face eased and she smiled.

"Now who's stupid?" she said. "You think I can't plan this sort of thing? I dug the hole for you a couple of nights ago. Your new home is ready for you when I shove that knife between those lovely boobs of yours. It's a shame my brothers won't be able to help me this time, I could see how they drooled over you every time they saw you."

"And that bothered you, did it?" said Melanie. "I took their attention away from you and you can't stand that."

She felt a small satisfaction at seeing Leah's face show some anger with a twist in her mouth and clenched lips.

"Well, that won't last long. You may look like a Victoria's Secret model now, but you won't in a few hours. I'll have a lot of fun cutting up that beautiful face before I finish you off, and a few days in that pit will make you look like a monster."

Melanie sensed that this was just bravado. She was right about a possible rescue, Jack and Alex would recognise that she was missing fairly soon and that Jack would know that Leah felt most secure in the compound, it had been her only home all her life. But the fear remained that Leah would kill her at any moment. The hatred and rage in the other woman were almost palpable.

"I repeat," said Melanie. "You really are a stupid old woman. You may kill me, but how the hell do you think you'll get away with it? Every police force in the country will be looking for you, you won't be able to get a flight out, every airport and maritime port will be on the lookout. You'll spend the rest of your life in a maximum- security prison."

"Bullshit," said Leah. "We've fooled you dumbfucks for years, haven't we? We've killed lots of people without you finding out and we'd still be unknown if it wasn't for that pipeline. And my Dad got away with that chess match nonsense, got here, he's been undiscovered for sixty years. How clever does that make us and how stupid does that make you?"

Melanie deliberately forced a laugh. "Have you any idea of how your father got to be in Australia? You think he arranged that all on his own? He could never have done it, he's far too dumb. Did he never tell you how the British government was so embarrassed by the behaviour of a member of the House of Lords that they pushed the Australian government to give him witness protection? Don't you know how much effort and money was put into keeping him quiet and unnoticed? And yet we found out where he was, where he lived and all about you three kids?"

She could see that her words had hit home again, but Leah showed fight. Melanie could sense the growing pressure of Leah's almost psychic dominance and she began drawing on her own inner strengths.

"It still remains," said Leah. "I'm a Baroness, I've got millions, I've been planning this for some years. You'll never find me."

"Correction," said Melanie. The battle of dominant wills was heating up. "You *were* a Baroness, you *did* have millions, but now you've got nothing. We know all about the hacker who stole everything and how he did it."

That hit the mark. Leah sat bolt upright in her chair, visibly shaken by what Melanie had said.

"What do you mean, you know about the hacker?"

"His name is Allen Miller," said Melanie. "He's probably the best hacker in the world. He's stolen millions from corporations and governments, he's created multiple personalities for himself and others. He's an American and the FBI have been looking for him for years. We met him on a previous case. Remember how the Trustees of your estate said the British police couldn't understand how all your properties had been sold and the money sent somewhere? That was Allen. He took all your money and gave it to various charities where it will do far more good than supporting you three parasites. We knew what he'd done even before the Trustees told you."

Leah said nothing but her slack jaw and wide-eyed stare told Melanie she was ahead on points. She tried a knock-out blow.

"And you're not a Baroness anymore," she said. "The British cops did some checking. Your parents married some months before his first wife killed herself. You didn't know about a first wife? She committed suicide because of the shame of being married to this cowardly fool. So his second marriage was bigamous. In addition, he married under a false name, so on both counts, your parents' marriage was illegal, and you three siblings are illegitimate. You didn't inherit anything of the estates, not the money, not the title, nothing."

She watched as the fury built up in Leah. She saw the tension grow in her arms and legs, the twisted face indicating massive rage. At the same time, she felt the growing power of Leah's dominant personality, it was even greater than the last time this battle of wills had taken place. She drew even more on her resources, knowing that the climax was coming. Whether it would bring about her death, she tried not to think.

"You're lying," screamed Leah. Her temper had taken over her. "I'm going to kill you now."

She rose to her feet and advanced on Melanie who suppressed her fear and tried to force back the wall of fury coming at her. Leah stopped, still a few paces from Melanie and the two women stared at each other.

This was it, Melanie knew. Digging deeper than she had ever done before, she stared back, exerting her will to stop Leah's attack.

She lost all awareness of the room, her bonds, all the things that had happened in recent months and just fought the living force that was Leah's will power. She had no idea of how long it lasted, but suddenly she sensed a slackening in the power confronting her.

Leah stood silent, her gaze dropping from Melanie and she looked down at her hands.

"It's time to go," she mumbled, looked helplessly around the room and walked out. Moments later, Melanie heard the Landcruiser start up and drive away. She took a deep breath, realised she was sweating and trembling from the experience and prayed for the others to find her.

* * *

**_9:17pm_**

Alex put down the phone and looked at Jack.

"That was the hospital," he said. "Both brothers have died from their injuries. It seems they died within minutes of each other."

"Have they told Leah?" asked Jack.

Alex nodded. "That was their first call. But she's not answering either the home landline or her mobile."

"Is Melanie still here?"

Alex went to the window and looked out. "Her car's still here, but I thought I saw her leave hours ago," he said.

Jack picked up his phone and dialled. A few moments later he put it down. "She's not answering. She can't be in her car."

"Can we try her home number?" said Alex. "Maybe she chose to leave the car behind for an evening."

"Impossible. She'd never leave it outside away from her home. I've got a bad feeling about this," said Jack. "It would not surprise me at all if Leah's gone. It would fit the psychopathic personality, cut off all connection with the past life if there are no more reasons to stay. I strongly suggest that we forget about getting a court order, this is an emergency to save a life. Let's go, and on the way, put out an all points warning to airports, trains, bus stations and ports. She may well be fleeing the country."

"Christ, Jack, do you think she's done something to Melanie?"

"That wouldn't surprise me, either. Revenge seems to be a major characteristic in that personality. This scares me. If she's taking it out on Melanie, there's only one place they could be, the compound. That's been her safe place all her life."

"Oh Christ Jack, the Black Queen. That's the main slot still open at the field. I reckon Leah's picked Melanie for the place."

"That would suit the psychopathy. Let's get going."

Alex picked up the police car keys.

*  *  *

"Didn't even bother closing the gate as she left," said Alex as they approached the compound.

"That fits the pattern," said Jack. "She's totally abandoned this life. Parents dead, brothers dead, all the family wealth gone, her title gone. She can become a completely new person."

"She's taken the car," said Alex. "Unless she's changed licence plates or altered them somehow, she'll be spotted by road cameras somewhere. I'll get onto uniform branch, they can start checking." He took out his phone and began speaking softly.

Jack was silent as Alex drove to Leah's house and parked by the front door.

"Let's take this one together," he said.

Alex made his way to the front door and tried the handle. It opened without difficulty and both men entered. Almost immediately, they saw Melanie tied firmly to a wooden high-backed chair.

"Oh thank god," exclaimed Alex and went to her, starting to tackle the ropes.

"What kept you?" said Melanie. "You missed a really interesting discussion." She got to her feet when Alex undid the final bond, rubbed her wrists and looked at them. "She was going to kill me and put me in the pit in the field. I was supposed to be the Black Queen."

She looked calmly at them, but then her eyes screwed closed, her mouth twisted and she collapsed to the floor, weeping hysterically.

It took an hour before Melanie could calm down. The fear and stress of the confrontation with Leah threatened to overwhelm her and several times, when she seemed to have recovered, she fell into a storm of tears again. The two men stayed with her, saying little, but Jack said that she would benefit just by knowing she was safe and with friends.

But finally, she looked up, smiled and said, "Okay gents, I'm fine now. Let me go and freshen up."

She got up from the armchair where she had been reclining and moved to the bathroom. A short while later, she emerged, looking her usual self.

"Right," she said. "Normal service is resumed. Let's check out this place. I'll look through this house, you two, go and check out the others and let's have a wonder round the outside, too."

She waited until the other two had left and began looking round the house. It looked occupied, as if the resident had walked away and planned to return shortly. Nothing in the lounge room or kitchen suggested abandonment. But in the bathroom, there was no toothbrush in the rack, no toothpaste in the cabinet and no other toiletries anywhere. There were clothes hanging in the bedroom wardrobe, but Melanie could not tell what was missing, if anything. Only the drawers revealed a departure. There were no underclothes in any of them.

Thoughtfully, she strolled around the lounge room, admiring the beautiful wooden floor that was richly stained a golden red. There was an ornate rug in the middle.

"That seems a mistake, to cover up that lovely floor," Melanie said aloud. "Why would anyone do that?"

A thought struck her. She bent down and pulled the rug away. Thin lines, about a metre apart crossed several of the floorboards. Two small holes a few centimetres apart were set in one board, midway between the two lines.

"Interesting," said Melanie and began hunting through the drawers in the lounge room sideboard. It didn't take long to find the handle that fitted those holes. It was neatly engineered with teeth at the bottom and a catch to release them to let the handle be withdrawn.

It took only a moment to insert the handle and lift up the lid of the space under the floorboards. A metal box was revealed, about the size of a computer printer and it had its own handle at the top. Melanie knelt down and lifted the box with little difficulty but saw a lock on one side. The box was sealed. She replaced the lid of the hiding place and went to join the others.

"Nothing," said Jack.

"Same with mine," echoed Alex. "Looks like they're away for a few days, nothing more."

"Much the same," said Melanie. "I can't tell what clothes she's taken, but there are no toiletries and no underwear in the place. She's gone walkabout alright."

"But you found something," said Jack, looking with interest at the box she had carried out with her.

"There was a hidden space under the floor," said Melanie. "It was only by a fluke that I found it. It has to be important. Let's get back to the office and call in a locksmith."

"When we get back, we'll be able to start looking for traces of her on the highways," said Alex. "We might get lucky, unless she's travelling by back roads all the way."

"She should be picked up at some point," said Melanie. "Anyway, let's get our flashlights from the car and have a look at the grounds before we go, just in case there's something else that might have been overlooked. Spread out, let's see what we can see."

Melanie began with searching around the four houses but found nothing. She moved to the nearest fence and walked down that to one corner of the property, then began walking back, a metre or two to the side, but nothing stood out.

Jack had gone to one side and was doing the same, walking up one side, walking back a metre to the side, but seemed to be finding nothing.

Alex had walked to the furthest point, an apex of two sides, some fifty metres from the shed where the backhoe was stored. He stopped, kicked at the small mound and took a deep breath.

"Oye!" he shouted and switched the flashlight on and off to attract attention.

"There's something buried there," said Jack. "Two somethings, in fact. And those mounds look horribly like the ones in the chess burial field. From the weeds growing on them, they've been there some years, so they may date from about the same time."

"Alex, call for some help," said Melanie and waited while Alex took his phone and called the office. "About an hour," he said finally.

"We'll wait," said Melanie. "Alex, bring the car here. It's getting dark, we can put the headlights onto those mounds when the team arrives. But if these are bodies, why aren't they in the chess field? There's something wrong here. And there's another thing bothering me."

The other two looked at her, questions in their eyes.

"Something we've forgotten about," she said. "What happened to the Fabergé chess set?"

"A very good question," said Jack. "I'd call it a safe bet that she's taken it with her."

* * *

"Male, about one-eight-five centimetres, between forty and fifty years old," said Doctor Rutherford. "I'd estimate he's been here about thirty or forty years."

"No black or white gown, no tin helmet," said Melanie. "Does that mean he's not part of the chess revenge story, Jack?"

"Probably," said Jack. "But it's linked. The *modus operandi* is the same as the others, the burial style is the same. I'd say the same person or persons did this, but for some reason, kept it separate from the main story."

"The second one should be out soon," said Alex.

"It will be interesting," said Jack.

"Female, about one sixty centimetres, maybe the same age as the male, been there about the same time," said the doctor. "I'll have a better idea when I've got them on the slab. But there's one major difference. I can't see any sign of violence on the male, so he may have been killed by a knife and there's not enough flesh on the skeleton for me to identify. But the female has been seriously damaged by something heavy. Her ribs and arms are broken and her skull has been almost totally shattered. This is like a collision with a heavy vehicle, but it's worse."

"And again, no gown, no helmet, but this one is fully dressed, whereas the bloke was naked." Jack was thoughtful. "They're linked, probably the same killer, but the clothing is curious. Why is she fully dressed?"

"Let's see what I can find," said the doctor.

* * *

## 25<sup>th</sup> *November, 2025, Coastal NSW, Australia*

"That'll do it," said the thin young man in blue overalls as a small click resounded from the metal case.

"Leave the lid down," said Melanie. "Thank you, see the desk sergeant with your invoice."

"Sure," said the locksmith, looked curiously round the group with one final gaze at Melanie, picked up his toolkit and walked out.

"Let's see what all this is about," said Melanie and opened the case. "A few papers," she said and extracted several sheets. "And some books."

She pulled out a collection of books of varying size, some of them obviously quite ancient, carefully laying them on the table. Each of them took one and carefully opened it.

"Oh hell," said Jack. "This one is really old, almost about to fall apart. I'm not going to look into it much, it needs professional handling. But what I can see is handwriting, quite faint and I can't make out a word of it."

"This one isn't like that," said Alex. "It's fairly old, but I can read the script. It's a diary, the first date is June the third, 1962. Hey! It's Felicity's diary! She's talking about Percivale, says she's just met him and feels a real bond between them."

"This is something similar," said Melanie, gently opening the book she had taken. "Handwritten in a rather florid style, there's a date here, August the twentieth, 1880 and it refers to, I quote, *'My darling but spineless Alisdair is still disappointing me with his refusal to satisfy my need for blood.'* What the hell does that mean? Is this the diary of Baron Alisdair's wife? That would fit the timeline."

"Here's another one, pretty old but readable," said Alex, pulling another book to him. "The date I just found here near the end is February, 1959..." He paused while he stared at the pages, looking almost hypnotised.

"Alex, what is it?" asked Melanie. "You look like a stunned mullet."

"Ma'am, this is incredible," said Alex, looking up at her. "Let me read you this bit.

*'My beloved Andrew was killed in a car crash this morning. The police came this morning to tell me. It seems he was driving down the A34 from a business trip to Birmingham when he was hit by another car that was overtaking him and forced him off the road into thick trees and he was killed instantly. The other car failed to stop and there were no eyewitnesses. The police say they can see what happened by the scrapes on the side of Andrew's Aston Martin and they will be searching for a vehicle with corresponding damage, but they don't hold out much hope. It means that our idiot son, William will become the tenth Baron and I am quite certain he does not have the steel in him to*

*continue the work of Andrew and his predecessors. It took me some years of hard work to persuade Andrew to do the first killing and it was a little while before he truly warmed to the process.'*

There was silence round the table.

"Good god!" Melanie finally broke it. "Does this mean that all the psychopathic barons were actually controlled by their even more psychopathic wives?"

"We'd better see the remaining diaries," said Jack. "I recommend that the ones we can't read should be passed to the university for help in transcribing. Let's pass the others between ourselves and see what we can find out. But to answer your question, it's quite possible that the Barons were the weaker partners. We've seen the signs in several of the previous ones. It looks probable that we'll find that all of them were like this, their weakness was recognised by women who were true psychopaths and dominant personalities, and they led their husbands into the killing sprees which actually satisfied both their needs. I really look forward to getting these diaries read. That could be my next academic paper there."

"It's interesting that with the latest wife, the daughter, Leah has carried on the same psychopathic gene," said Alex.

"Quite right," said Jack. "There's material for several research subjects there."

"Okay, gentlemen, take a couple of diaries each," said Melanie. "I'll do the same and Jack, could you contact the university?"

"Will do," said Jack. "I know the very people for this."

"And let's have a look at these papers," said Melanie. She laid them out, there were only five sheets. "They look like photographs of original articles, none of them looks like a modern photocopy."

She looked at the first one and studied it carefully while Jack too another. The room went quiet for a few moments.

Jack broke the silence.

"Holy shit!" he exclaimed. "This is explosive. It's a letter from a woman in a town in Wales, written to a young solicitor called David Lloyd George. It's dated the fifteenth of July, 1895."

"What, the later to be Prime Minister of Britain?" asked Alex.

"The very same," said Jack. "Listen to this."

*'Dear David,*

*I must tell you the worst has happened. I am pregnant. I discovered this last week. I dare not tell my parents, they will throw me out of the house. You were simply too forceful with me, even though I begged you not to go on. You are a wealthy man and now you are a member of Parliament, I have to ask you for some help. I know that I am not the first to find herself in this situation as a result of your activities. Olwyn, my friend also became pregnant and she died in childbirth last year. I know she never wrote to you. But I must. Please help me.' Carys.*

"There are two other documents photographed with this letter," said Jack. "One is a death certificate for a woman called Olwyn Williams, aged nineteen, died in childbirth on the second of March, 1894. The second is for a woman called Carys Llewelyn, dead by her own hand on the twentieth of September, 1895."

"Oh, good god," whispered Melanie. "That would have destroyed Lloyd George had it ever been revealed."

"Even with his known track record as a womaniser, revelations like that would have been unacceptable in Britain of that time," said Jack. "It was known he had a mistress while married, but the illicit pregnancies and deaths in childbirths were not known."

"Good blackmail material," said Alex, his face sombre.

"So is this," said Melanie. "This is even worse, it's actually treason by the British government. It's a record of a major arms shipment to Finland on the tenth of January, 1940."

"Why is that treason?" asked Alex.

"Because Finland was at war with Russia at that time, had been for a few months," said Jack. "The Second World War had broken out a bit over a year earlier, Russia was theoretically our ally, Finland was theoretically a Nazi ally. It's well known that Churchill hated Stalin even more than he hated Hitler and Britain had supplied weapons and aircraft to Finland well before the war broke out. But supplying arms to the enemy in a time of war was treason by every law that existed. If the Russians got hold of that paper, they could cause huge embarrassment to Britain, even today."

"Could these papers be part of a larger collection, do you think?" asked Melanie.

"I'd call that a safe bet," said Jack. "Men in high stations have always had access to suppressed information and the Percivales were in the House of Lords with all the contacts that would have entailed. There's probably a whole library of sensitive stuff somewhere and if it's all like the ones we've just read, it could cause all sorts of horrible things for the rulers."

"And I've got something," said Alex. "I don't know who these people are, but I assume they were high up in the society of the times. This talks about some men in government during the thirties. Their names are given. They were accused of numerous cases of child abuse, some really ugly stuff. Two of the kids died, they were ten and twelve."

"Yuk," said Melanie. "What happened?"

"Letters here from the Prime Ministers of the time, Ramsay MacDonald and Stanley Baldwin, requesting the police to abandon charging the men and to release them."

"If these few papers represent a cache of documents that the Percivales have accumulated over the years and have hidden away somewhere, they're worse than any Mafia in history," said Melanie.

"The more we learn about the Percivales, the more certain I become that there is such a cache," said Jack. "It would explain the kid gloves with which they have been treated, the police disregarding the multiple disappearances of people over the years and the fact that this latest Baron was allowed to vanish into Australia with a deluxe witness protection program."

The phone on Melanie's desk interrupted further readings.

"The techies have located Leah," said Melanie. "Let's see what they've got."

# Chapter 37

## *25ᵗʰ November, 2025, Coastal NSW, Australia*

"That's her," said Alex. The three of them watched on the computer screen as the Landcruiser moved along the freeway between Newcastle and Sydney. "That was two days ago, a few hours after she left you in the compound and they tracked her to Kingsford Smith Airport. Her car is still there."

"Security says she flew out to Singapore that same day and arrived at Changhi Airport where she went through immigration, left the airport and then vanished," said Melanie. "They've checked all the main hotels but there's no record of her anywhere. She could have gone to somewhere off the tourist track and we'll never see her."

"How about a flight out of Singapore?" asked Jack. "As a non-citizen or resident there, she couldn't just appear at the departure gate with another identity that didn't show her arrival in Singapore."

"Yes, that showed up," replied Melanie. "She boarded a KLM flight to Lisbon a day later, using her original identity and she entered Portugal, still on that identity. But then she vanished. We asked the local police to look out for her but there's no record of a credit card being used, or a hotel in that name, so it seems she must have had some additional, false identity."

"That's a bit weird," said Jack. "How does she vanish like that?"

"She must have a false passport," said Alex. "Before Allan Miller broke them apart, she would have had the money to get a fake identity, open a bank account with substantial cash in there and get a credit card as well."

"That's a real possibility," said Melanie. "We know there are people in Sydney who do that sort of thing for a good price."

"So that's how she arrived in Lisbon, entered legally and then disappeared," said Jack.

"She did, she went through immigration there and then just like Singapore, vanished. There's been nothing since then."

"So is she just running away and starting a new life somewhere or is she heading somewhere in particular? And if so, for what purpose?"

"That's the question," said Melanie. "All we can do is ask Interpol to keep an eye out for her at all transport hubs and request their help in working with immigration officials. We don't want her arrested as we need to know what she's planning. I'd better call Porter for help."

* * *

"Mr Porter, we're tracking Leah MacFarlane. She's left Australia, she seems to have some false identities and she's changing as needed. Currently, she's in Lisbon but we don't know where or where she's going. I need your help."

"That's interesting, Inspector. What can I do for you?"

"We need to know where she's heading and why. Can you use your influence and ensure the security forces wherever she turns up don't arrest her?"

"I think we want the same thing, Inspector. Leave it with me."

"Many thanks, Mr Porter.

* * *

## 4th *December, 2025, Coastal NSW, Australia*

"This came from the German officials at Berlin's Brandenburg airport," said Melanie. "They're not certain, but they think this is Leah. Facial recognition software triggered an alarm."

They studied the picture on the screen intently.

"Red hair, possibly dyed or a wig," said Alex.

"And definitely not her normal style of dress," said Melanie. "That's very low-key, dowdy, not to be noticed clothing. But the real point is her passport. It's in the name of Karen Zehnder, German citizen. She had flown in from Paris five days earlier."

"Is there any record of how she got to Paris?" asked Jack. "How about that name on a flight out of Lisbon?"

Melanie shook her head. "Not that name. Interpol are checking with Lisbon Airport to see if any passenger resembling her boarded a flight. No result so far."

"Is there any other way from Lisbon to Paris?" asked Alex. "How about a train? Is that feasible? Is there a train that does that?"

"Why don't you check it?" said Melanie.

Alex nodded, took out his phone and concentrated. It took only a minute or two.

"There's a daily service," he said. "It's a long ride, about 1500 kilometres, nearly twenty-one hours, leaves about nine in the evening, gets to Paris a bit before six the next evening.”

“Could be,” said Melanie. “Alex, send a query to Interpol, see if anyone with that description did that trip in the right time-frame.”

“Where the hell is she going?” muttered Jack.

“That’s the issue,” said Melanie. “This is getting curiouser and curiouser.”

* * *

### 8<sup>th</sup> *December, 2025, Coastal NSW, Australia*

“Switzerland? My, she’s really moving around,” said Jack.

“The Swiss police recorded her arriving in Geneva, still travelling under her German passport,” said Melanie. “But at the request of Interpol and us, they didn’t arrest her, because everybody wants to know what the hell she’s up to. They tracked her visiting a bank and leaving with a briefcase. Video shows her entering the bank with a new briefcase she had bought in the city, it looked empty, but it appeared full when she left, judging by the way she was carrying it.”

“Documents?” said Alex.

“Count on it,” said Jack. “I’ll bet the farm that briefcase is the cache we’ve thought might exist. She’s just picked up the collection of years of information gathering on top people. Now the question is what does she intend to do with it all?”

“A seriously big question,” said Melanie. “Even the material we’ve seen could cause major problems in some quarters. Where the hell does this mad ride end?”

* * *

### *12th December, 2025, Coastal NSW, Australia*

"So you've lost her, then?" said the voice from the computer.

Without surprise, Melanie looked up. "Good morning, Allen. What unpleasant surprises do you have for me today?"

"Melanie, you sadden me. Isn't it time your realised I have your best interests at heart?"

"I remain unconvinced Allen."

"Okay, so let me tell you some really helpful stuff. I've been working hard to find this awful woman and believe me, it stretched my considerable talents to get the full story. So the first part is simple. Under the name of Enni Hukkinen, a Finnish citizen, she flew into Helsinki three nights ago. Her passport caused no problems. Whoever provided these documents was a real artist. They must have cost a fortune."

"Finland? What the hell is she doing there?"

"That's a fascinating story. Anyway, the Finnish Immigration people were not triggered by any facial recognition software and let her through. I haven't traced any hotel, so it was probably a low-grade place without a computer system. But she did use a credit card in an ATM to access an Australian bank account and it was a different card and account from before. I suggest she's got a whole library of passports and cards. She must have been planning this for years."

"Will you give me the details of her bank accounts? If nothing else, we can block them."

"Melanie, don't be silly. That will alert her to the fact that we're on to her and probably stop what she's doing. I strongly suggest that you all need to know what the full story is, so does ASIO and most likely, MI6 also, if there's an international espionage thing going on that could cause diplomatic problems. Anyway, when all this is wrapped up, I'll clean out her bank accounts."

"I suppose so." Despite her anger and deep wish to get Leah to face justice, Melanie could see the value of Miller's comment.

"But I can tell you where she's going," continued Miller. "On a hunch, I had a look at the systems of a bus travel operation in Helsinki. Your crazy woman is on a bus tour to Saint Petersburg tomorrow."

"Saint Petersburg? Holy shit!"

"That's about what I said. I wondered how she could get a Russian visa so quickly in her Finnish passport, but it seems Finns have easy travel regulations into Russia for vacation purposes. They can get a visa on-line without visiting the Russian consulate. Nobody else can do that."

"So we have to wait until she comes back and maybe then we'll know what she's up to."

"That's if she comes back," said Miller.

"Allen? Why wouldn't she?"

"If somebody alerted the Russians that she was travelling under a false passport, she'd face problems."

"Oh Christ, Allen, what have you done?"

"Like I said Melanie, I haven't finished punishing her for my aunt's murder. A few years in a Russian Gulag might be an interesting closure."

Miller's face disappeared from the screen.

## Chapter 38

### *13ᵗʰ December, 2025, Vyborg, Russian Karelia Peninsula*

The bus stopped outside a large building complex on the fringes of the town through which they had just passed. The tour guide spoke into her announcement system but spoke only in Finnish. The door opened and a tall, thin man in military uniform entered, followed by a young woman, also in uniform. He spoke briefly, Leah assumed in Russian, but she heard the word "Passport" and extracted hers from her handbag. The military pair advanced slowly down the bus checking the passports of the fifteen other passengers and finally got to Leah. She handed over the document, trying to stifle the anxiety that was racing though her body and look unconcerned like any other tourist.

The man studied the passport carefully, reading every page before handing it to his colleague. She repeated the process studying the pages intently, giving special attention to the photograph and comparing it to Leah's face as Leah's anxiety climbed to a sense of panic.

What was wrong? Was there something in her passport that was causing a query?

The Russian continued to stare at Leah until the woman handed him the passport, then he spoke and Leah felt her blood run cold.

"Miss Macfarlane, you will come with us," he said in English.

*Oh my god, they know who I am*, thought Leah, icy fear sweeping through her.

Under the curious gaze of the other passengers, Leah was escorted off the bus.

The room was bare of all but the desk at which Leah sat on a hard, wooden seat across from the two people who had arrested her. The table had a recording device, but it had not been switched on. There were no windows. Leah tried to look for a camera but could see nothing.

"So why are you entering the Russian Federation under false pretences, Miss Macfarlane?"

Leah took a deep breath. After all, she was where she had intended to be for purposes that had been in her mind for a decade. It was time to let it all out.

"I knew I'd be unable to leave Australia and travel here under my own name," she said. "But I have a good reason to be here, and I'd like to discuss it with you."

"We'll come to that in a moment," said the officer. His English was near perfect, no trace of any accent was detectible. The woman next him had a constant gaze on Leah's face but showed no emotion. Leah assumed that she spoke equally excellent English. "Why would it have been so impossible for you to travel here under your own name?"

"Because I was suspected of having been part of a series of killings and the burial of bodies in a field near my property. It was my parents who had committed these murders, I had nothing to do with any of them."

"So why did the police suspect you?"

"Because both my parents are gone. My father is dead and we think it was by somebody seeking revenge for one of the bodies buried in that field. My mother disappeared many years ago, we have no idea what happened to her."

"I see. So it will no doubt be a surprise to you that two bodies were recently dug up from your property, one male, one female and the female's DNA showed that it was your mother."

Leah sat back in her seat, almost feeling a hard blow to her body. Her breathing faltered and she felt her skin crawl.

"How.. how do you know that?" she stammered.

The officer smiled a cold smile. "We are not without resources, Miss Macfarlane. Now let us turn to the question of why you are here."

Leah took a deep breath and struggled for composure. This was the whole point of her travels.

"To return property to the Russian authorities that had been stolen many years ago."

The woman reached down to a briefcase by her feet and placed the chess set on the table.

"This perhaps?" said the man. "The Fabergé chess set presented to Czar Nicholas the Second in 1916 and given as a reward to one of our greatest Generals?"

Leah felt herself get calmer. "Yes, that," she replied. "You may not have realised it before, but the one you have in the Hermitage is a fake."

"We have known that for years, Miss Macfarlane and we know how it came to be in your father's possession. It was given by the Czar, Nicholas the Second to one of our most successful generals and military commanders for his services to Russia during the war. He had made a copy for possible future use and he gave it to your ancestor, the seventh Baron in return for his services in getting the general's family to safety in England."

"Then you'll be happy to have it back?" said Leah, finally summoning up a smile.

"Most," replied the officer. "However, there is the matter that it is property stolen from the Russian government and that is a criminal matter. No doubt you were expecting some financial reward?"

"Actually, the chess set is the lesser of the gifts I am bringing to you."

"The lesser?" The Russian allowed some interest to show.

"I think that you have allowed yourself to be misled by the obvious beauty and value of the chess set," said Leah. She smiled a small, cold smile. "You clearly have not examined the remains of my luggage."

"Just clothing and a briefcase with personal documents," said the Russian.

"Those documents could just be the greatest weapon over the Western world your country could have."

The Russian nodded at his colleague, and she left, returning a few minutes later with Leah's briefcase. The agent took out a sheaf of papers and spread some of them on the desk, reading through in silence. After ten minutes, he looked up.

"I see your point," he said. "Several Western countries would regard these as nuclear."

"I was hoping you would see your way to compensating me."

"Of course you were. You are financially ruined, you have lost all your properties and cash apart from the $47,000 you have in two bank accounts in Sydney held under different names. You no longer have the title of Baroness, you have nothing."

Leah felt the breath escape her lungs for a second time.

"So as of now, what we have on you, Miss Macfarlane, is your criminal involvement in the stealing of Russian Government property, your illegal entry under an assumed identity into the Russian Federation and the fact that Britain and Australia have both issued calls for your arrest for multiple murders. We can also add incitement to murder, in the way you persuaded your brothers to attack the home of Mr Jack Savage, a psychologist working with the police investigating you. You may also be guilty of homicide in that situation, because both your brothers died as a result of the injuries sustained in that attack. But you may be relieved to know that we shall make no mention of these documents. We shall take possession of them, however."

"My brothers are dead?" Leah tried to feel some emotion but couldn't.

"They are. I am going to hold you in custody while I consult my superiors in Moscow as to the next step."

The two Russians stood up, but Leah felt unable to do the same until pulled to her feet by the Russian woman. She felt numb and hardly felt the woman's hand on her arm as she was led out of the room, down a corridor and into a small cell. The door closed behind her and Leah collapsed onto the narrow, hard bed against one wall.

She had no idea how long she remained there. Darkness had fallen when the cell door was opened, and the Russian officer stood there.

"Miss Macfarlane, come with me," he said.

Standing on wobbly legs, Leah got to her feet and walked out of the cell as the man stood aside. A short distance away stood the young woman and behind her, two soldiers stood by the wall. The Russian walked off down the corridor closely followed by the young woman who had taken Leah's arm again. The two soldiers followed.

Leah felt mounting dread. This was not what she had expected would happen. She had expected a welcome, thanks for the return of the chess set and an offer of compensation commensurate with the value of the set as well as considerable reward for the explosive documents.

The Russian stopped. "Please go ahead, Miss Macfarlane," he said. "When you get to the end, there will be a door, that will be your new home for a while."

Leah began to walk on down the corridor.

She never heard or felt the bullet strike her at the back of her head and she was dead before she hit the floor.

The Russian officers walked away without a word. The two soldiers picked up the body and carried it away.

## Chapter 39

### *14ᵗʰ December, 2025, Coastal NSW, Australia*

"All that remains now is to identify the remaining bodies in the field," said Melanie. She stared down at the documents on her desk. "This has been a horrible exercise. But I suppose Jack, you have a new publication coming out?"

"I do, but it's a horror story. The whole family for generations back appears to be comprised of psychopathic killers but I rate Leah as the worst. Heaven knows what her total of murders would have been had we not interrupted her."

"The case is closed," said Melanie. "But in a most unsatisfying way. We didn't get to prove the guilt of any of them, we made no arrests, we didn't get to see them tried, sentenced and put away for life."

She closed the folder on her desk and put it away. "The Percivale saga is over. Who's for a drink? I'm buying."

"That's good enough for me," said Alex.

"And me," said Jack.

"Let's go," said Melanie.

After getting home, Melanie changed out of her usual business attire of a loose-fitting pantsuit, poured a glass of wine and sat down before the television. But she found herself unable to concentrate on the drama and sensed her mind wandering. When she realised what was bothering her, she was badly shaken. It took half an hour of thinking, trying to clear her mind before she came to a decision. She reached for her handbag, extracted the small card and picked up the phone.

"Hello, Rob," she said. "It's Melanie. I wonder if you feel like getting together this weekend."

www.ingramcontent.com/pod-product-compliance
Lightning Source LLC
Chambersburg PA
CBHW070115120726
47909CB00002B/611